I0645048

A Grievous Sin

A. C. Mason

A Wings ePress, Inc.
Mystery Novel

Wings ePress, Inc.

Edited by: Jeanne Smith
Copy Edited by: Joan C. Powell
Executive Editor: Jeanne Smith
Cover Artist: Trisha FitzGerald-Jung

All rights reserved

Names, characters and incidents depicted in this book are products of the author's imagination or are used fictitiously. Any resemblance to actual events, locales, organizations, or persons, living or dead, is entirely coincidental and beyond the intent of the author or the publisher.

No part of this book may be reproduced or transmitted in any form or by any means, electronic or mechanical, including photocopying, recording, or by any information storage and retrieval system, without permission in writing from the publisher.

Wings ePress Books
www.wingsepress.com

Copyright © 2018 by Arlene C. Messa
ISBN-13: 978-1-61309-635-2
ISBN-10: 1-61309-635-6

Published In the United States Of America

Wings ePress Inc.
3000 N. Rock Road
Newton, KS 67114

What They Are Saying About
A Grievous Sin

"A. C. Mason knows South Louisiana, both its pretty and its gritty side. She spins them together to create gripping mysteries you will enjoy reading."

—Lynn Shurr, author of *A Taste of Bayou Water*, *Blessings and Curses*, and *The Courville Rose*

"Settle back and lose yourself to a good mystery set against the backdrop of a small bayou town in Louisiana. Susan Foret is off on another adventure that begins when she stumbles upon a murdered victim close to where her husband was previously killed. As she uncovers a criminal ring involved in smuggling drugs, ancient artifacts and the trafficking in illegal aliens, she soon finds herself a target. Will her tenacity and uncanny insight into those responsible be enough to save her?"

—Sylvia Rochester
Author of eleven published novels of various genres Her latest release is *Deceptive Assassin*

Dedication

In memory of the "real" Katy the cat (2000-2017).
Wiley and I miss you.

* * *

Alas, a grievous sin have we determined to commit, in that for greed of sovereignty and pleasure, we are prepared to slay our brothers.

—Bhagavad Gita

One

Allemand Parish, Louisiana

Wednesday July 22

Sunlight glistened on the water. Large cypress trees laden with Spanish moss lined the banks. Two egrets waded in a secluded cove among a patch of water hyacinths.

A picturesque sight. In stark contrast, beyond the sunlit bayou lay the darkness and danger of the swamp. I knew full well the mystique of Louisiana swamps—full of life, yet often deadly.

My heart raced in time with the boat engine. The thought of viewing the spot where Jim had been shot made my stomach flip. My hands tightened on the flower pot I held in my lap. I intended to plant these gerbera daisies on the site.

Exactly one year ago today my husband was killed—murdered by people he thought were friends and brother police officers.

I glanced at my neighbor Rachel Marchand as she expertly negotiated the bayou's curve. I'm glad she drove because I would have probably crashed into the bank.

Friends, including Rachel, had all urged me not to go to this isolated place. They warned me that the stress of revisiting the place where he was shot and left for dead would be too much trauma. Maybe they were right, but it's too late now.

I needed to come. Why? I didn't truly know the reason. I felt compelled to bring flowers to plant on the spot and to say a prayer. Perhaps I hoped to contact his spirit or something ridiculous like that.

Rachel slowed the motor to an idle and steered toward the bank. After cutting the engine, she turned to me and was quiet for a long moment. "Susan, are you sure you're ready for this?"

I nodded, hardly able to speak because my throat kept constricting. I placed the flower pot on the bank and caught hold of a low tree branch to keep us from drifting out into the bayou.

Rachel, quite fit for a woman sixty-five, jumped onshore and tied a rope to the branch to secure our boat.

My legs wobbled as I stood, trying to balance in the swaying craft. Rachel grabbed my hand and helped me onto the bank. I retrieved the flower pot and surveyed my surroundings. The area appeared pretty much the same as I remembered from my visit last year.

Beyond the cypress trees, wide-leafed palmetto, tall grass, and other swamp plants swayed slightly in a meager breeze. However, much of the vegetation past there seemed trampled as if a herd of animals had run rampant through it. Packs of feral pigs have been reported out here from time to time.

One thing for sure, the humidity and mosquitoes were still here. In the swamp, mosquitoes swarmed day and night. I swatted the buzzing pests away. A foul odor hung in the air.

My eyes met Rachel's anxious gaze. "Dead fish?" Sometimes lack of oxygen in the water caused huge numbers of fish to die.

"I sure hope it's only a fish kill." She wiped perspiration from her forehead with her hand.

"Me, too." The sinking feeling in my stomach told me the odor wasn't dead fish.

The farther we walked, the stronger the smell. A pile of what appeared to be discarded clothing could be seen near some bushes ahead. Rachel and I both stopped short and exchanged a knowing look.

I knew immediately without even looking closer. Inside those clothes was a decomposing human body.

Why do I keep discovering dead bodies? Am I jinxed? I swallowed hard. What in the world ever possessed me to return to this place? Last year I promised myself never to come back again. But here I was looking at another dead person.

We knew better than to disturb a crime scene. I didn't know if I wanted to get a closer look anyway. Yet my curiosity almost got the best of me. With a great deal of restraint I stood frozen to the spot.

From what I could see, the deceased person appeared to be a woman with long black hair or else a small male who wore his hair long.

Rachel seemed to be having the same problem. Despite our age difference, she and I think alike. She wanted to see if she could identify this person as much as I did.

She pulled her phone from her pocket and started to make a call. "No service. We'll have to get back in the boat and ride until I can connect with the sheriff's office."

As soon as we walked back to the boat, she made another attempt to get a signal on her phone and was successful.

"I'll call Danny first," she said, referring to her husband, formerly the Allemand Parish sheriff, now retired. "If he doesn't answer, I'll go through nine-one-one."

Despite the smell, I was glad we didn't have to leave. The victim had been out here alone for at least several days. I thought it cruel to desert the person now.

Irrational perhaps, but times in the past when I discovered a dead body, rational thinking went out the window. Without a doubt this death was murder. I kept thinking of all the possible scenarios.

Maybe he or she died alone because no one discovered the scene in time. Maybe this person died immediately. I didn't want to think about suicide, although this place had been the location of one, and of Jim's shooting which was staged to look like suicide.

Rachel and I waited on shore next to our boat for the sheriff's flotilla to arrive. We didn't have to wait long. About fifteen minutes after her call to Danny, sounds of racing boat motors filled the air. Flashing lights appeared in the distance.

Despite the heat I felt a chill flow up my spine. I knew I was about to jump off the proverbial cliff into a real life murder case, much different from the fictional murders I write about in my mystery novels...and much more dangerous.

Two

Several members of the sheriff's office, including the newly elected sheriff Brad Theriot and Danny, Rachel's husband, hopped off the two patrol vessels and headed toward me and Rachel.

Danny reached us first, followed by the sheriff and four other men.

He exhaled loudly. "I knew I shouldn't have let you two come up here by yourselves."

Rachel stood with her hands on her hips, looking up at him. "Nothing would have changed if you had been here with us. There would still be a dead body over there."

Brad Theriot gave me an amused look. I guess he intended to lighten the scene by focusing on the sight of a five foot three woman like Rachel giving a six foot four man what for. I didn't feel amused. That's one of many reasons why I could never make it as a cop. Finding something humorous at a murder scene might be the way a police officer could cope with seeing a body. I wouldn't be able to think of anything but the person and imagine how horrible their last moments had been.

Seeing my distress, Brad's expression quickly turned serious. "Did you get close enough to the body to identify the victim?"

I shook my head. "We didn't want to disturb any evidence."

He nodded to me and Rachel. "You two, stay here. Danny, let's go see what we've got."

The two men strode toward the crime scene. The others trailed along after them.

"I don't know about you, but I want to see if this person is someone I know," Rachel said, focusing her gaze toward the location.

"Me too," I agreed. "I believe the body is that of a woman." I pointed toward the scene. "See the long black hair?"

"I noticed something shiny, like jewelry." Rachel shrugged. "Of course, men do wear jewelry and wear their hair long."

The roar of a boat engine again cut through the air. Another vessel belonging to the sheriff's flotilla pulled up. I recognized Dr. Devall, the parish coroner, on the deck, preparing to debark.

Dr. Devall and two morgue attendants hopped off the boat and walked slowly toward the body as if they all wore lead shoes that impeded their movement.

I couldn't blame them. Even people like coroner's office personnel and police officers who see death often get tired of witnessing the inhumanity of humans to their fellow man...or in this case woman. Yes, I was convinced this victim was female.

Tired of standing, I sat on the ground in the shade of a Chinese tallow tree, which intermittently favored me with a breeze. After a few minutes Rachel joined me.

"I guess we'll be here for a while," she said, keeping her focus on the deputies.

"Maybe not. Dr. Devall might not be able to tell anything before an autopsy since there's probably a lot of decomposition."

For fifteen minutes the coroner was hidden by a ring of men surrounding the body. Guess they didn't want us weak women to see anything that would cause fainting. I'm being facetious, of course. Curiosity has been my downfall, but I wanted to know the identity of the victim. I had the awful feeling I knew her.

Finally, the coroner's assistants placed her in a black body bag, zipped it up, and transferred her to a hand-carried stretcher. The terrain was too rough for the usual gurney on wheels. The coroner trudged along behind them.

When they neared the boat, I rose and strode over to them. Rachel followed me. "Dr. Devall, have you identified her yet?"

"Sadly there wasn't any identification on her," he replied.

"Can we take a look? We may know her."

The coroner grudgingly agreed. "Unzip the bag part way," he ordered one of the assistants.

The man lowered the stretcher to the ground and knelt beside it. He moved the zipper on the bag enough for me and Rachel to see her head and neck. The sight was not pretty. I almost wished I hadn't asked.

My assumption had been on target. The deceased person was a woman with long black hair. Her face had been disfigured somewhat from lying in the open for what may have been several days. I recognized the Native American style turquoise necklace she wore.

I grabbed Rachel's arm. "I know who she is...Celina Baum."

"Oh, my God! Miriam's daughter."

~ * ~

"Why the hell did you have to shoot her?" He clenched his jaw in an attempt to restrain himself. He would have put the idiot's lights out if this conversation were in person and not over the phone.

"She saw me. I couldn't take the chance since she knows me. I thought she might be after the package."

"Not my problem. You shouldn't have gotten involved with her. Now because of your screw-up, the emeralds have disappeared. You better find a way to get them back."

"How am I supposed to accomplish that? I don't even know where to look for the carrier."

"That's what you signed up to do. Find him. You better hope you locate him before he gets picked up by the cops." He narrowed his eyes even though his associate couldn't see his angry look over the phone. That feeling would come through in his words. "I have a suggestion. Start with the man you saw kneeling next to her body. Find him."

Three

Cypress Lake, Louisiana

Thursday July 23

I had that familiar sinking feeling in my stomach as I watched the news story on Channel 7's morning show…the murder of Celina Baum in Allemand Parish. Why I continued to watch confounded me. I had seen the story last night. Not to mention, the real thing.

Seeing the video caused a replay of yesterday in my mind and several other times when I discovered a body. The victim was always someone I knew. Heck, this time I even knew Remi Granger, the television reporter who did the story.

Here she was again, updating the story live in the TV studio:

"Yesterday we reported that the body of a woman was discovered by two fishermen in a wooded area off Bayou Jean Baptiste. The victim has now been identified by the Allemand Parish Sheriff's Office in Cypress Lake as twenty-six year old Celina Baum of Foretville. At present there are no suspects or motive for the murder. Anyone with information about this incident is asked to contact the Sheriff's Office…"

Remi's voice trailed off in my head as I turned my thoughts to the latest victim in my pantheon of murder victim encounters.

Celina Ramirez Baum volunteered on a regular basis at a food pantry and mission established by several local churches. I also showed up over there occasionally to help wherever I could...mostly paperwork.

She spoke fluent Spanish and afforded a great service to those from Mexico and Central America who didn't speak English.

Since my husband was killed, I've kept busy with my writing and doing volunteer work. Even with raising eight-year-old twins, days and nights sometimes seem to drag by.

The pot of gerbera daisies I intended to plant yesterday sat on the kitchen counter. That was a stupid idea anyway. I'll take them to the mausoleum tomorrow.

A knock at the kitchen door interrupted my thoughts. I saw Rachel through the window and invited her inside with a wave. "It's open."

"Susan, you need to go back to keeping your doors locked," she admonished as she walked in.

I smiled. "Yes, Mother." Rachel and Danny were both in their mid-sixties—old enough to be my parents. We had been close friends since Jim and I moved to Cypress Lake from New Orleans.

Rachel returned my smile, but her expression quickly turned serious as she glanced at the television. "Do you have any idea what she could have been doing out in the middle of nowhere?"

"Not a clue. I wouldn't want to be in Miriam Baum's position right now. She must be beside herself."

Rachel nodded. "Miriam adopted Celina and her sister as toddlers, so even though they're not her natural children, her pain is certainly deep. As you know, Miriam isn't my favorite person, but I wouldn't wish the loss of a child on my worst enemy."

"I didn't really know Celina very well. I'd spoken to her at the pantry on occasion. She was very devoted to the cause of helping these people. From what I've heard, she practically lived there."

Rachel eyed me cautiously. "Do you know if all immigrants who receive aid at the pantry are in this country legally?"

"I don't know for sure, since I don't personally accept them into the fold, so to speak. However, I suspect most are not. Priests and other church people don't really question the paperwork of these individuals. Besides, not every person who comes to the pantry is an immigrant. There are a number of families in the parish who can't make it on what they earn."

"True," she said. "So, what is your job over there?"

"Basically, ordering and accepting supplies and donations. I go over there two or three days a week. Every once in a while, someone from one of the Caribbean islands where a lot of French is spoken shows up, I'm asked to talk to them if no one else is available." I shrugged. "My French isn't so great but it serves the purpose in a pinch. There are other people who speak French a whole lot better than I do. Of course they aren't always present at the time."

"I don't imagine a French speaker arrives very often," Rachel said. "Most people coming into the country are Hispanic, right?"

"The majority of them are." An occasion when I was called upon to speak my limited French came to mind. "A few months ago, a man and his wife arrived who spoke no English. It turns out they were from the island of Martinique. At least that's what their paperwork indicated."

"Do you know what happened to them?"

"No, but I can probably find out." Her questions certainly were curious. "Why are you asking me all these questions?"

"There's a rumor going around that the spot where Celina Baum's body was found is a drop off place for illegals being transported into the country. Another rumor claimed some of the newer arrivals are Haitians."

"That doesn't surprise me at all. There have been drug smuggling operations going on in Allemand Parish, so why not human trafficking?" My stomach clenched, reminding me that Jim's murder had happened when he tried to stop a drug operation. I changed the subject...sort of.

"Remi did a great job of reporting the murder." I referred to Danny's granddaughter, Remi Granger who worked for Channel 7. "Thank goodness she didn't mention our names. We were identified as two fishermen."

"She reminds me a lot of you."

My hand went to my chest in a reflex action. "Me? How so?"

"She's drawn to those crime scenes like bugs to a light bulb. She recently mentioned she'd like to get into writing crime stories."

"Well, she certainly can get a lot of ideas working out of New Orleans." I feigned a worried look. "Hmm...more competition for my mysteries."

"I doubt that. Real life crimes and the actual scene intrigue her too much."

"There're always plenty of readers of true crime. She could go that route." I looked at Rachel with more than a little suspicion. "What's the real reason you want to find out about the couple from Martinique?"

"Curiosity." She made a weak attempt to sound matter-of-fact. I caught on immediately.

"Don't tell me you want to take up my penchant for solving murders."

Her smile seemed rather sad. "I suppose Miriam's connection reminded me of when I set out to prove my brother didn't murder Ellis, Miriam's husband."

"I remember you telling me about that. Miriam and your brother Jay were having an affair at the time. You met Danny when he was a detective with the sheriff's office. It was almost the same situation as my meeting Jim for the first time. It's amazing how similar many events in our lives were."

"Those events are probably the reason we clicked, despite our age difference."

My thoughts strayed back for a moment to an April many years ago when my brother became the prime suspect in the murder of his wife. Jim was a homicide detective with NOPD at the time. We met during his investigation.

"Tomorrow I'm going to the food pantry," I said. "I'll see what I can find out about the Martinique couple, although I doubt they have any connection to Celina's murder. How about some coffee? I'm going to have a second cup."

She agreed, following me into the kitchen. I rinsed out my blue mug, grabbed another cup from the cabinet, and filled both mugs. I brought them to the table, eyeing my neighbor with concern.

Something else other than Celina's murder was bothering Rachel. "Okay, what else is on your mind beside Miriam?"

"It's ridiculous how you knew that." She absentmindedly stirred her coffee.

"Come on, out with it."

She shook her head. "Danny is about to drive me nuts. I should have expected he would go stir-crazy after he retired."

"I suspected as much after overhearing a conversation between him and Brad at the last get together we had at your place."

She frowned. "What did he say?"

I shrugged. "Basically, retirement wasn't all it was cracked up to be."

"He's talking about signing on as a reserve deputy."

I arched my brows. "Would that be so bad?"

"Maybe, maybe not," she said. "But I can't see him not getting totally involved in a case. And Brad…"

"And Brad would likely pull him into a case, namely Celina's murder."

"Yes, I worried about Danny so much during the last few years he was in office. Cypress Lake and Allemand Parish had always been quiet and peaceful."

"Until the area started growing by leaps and bounds."

After Rachel left, I couldn't help thinking of another reason the parish became violent. Murder seemed to follow me around. That same eerie feeling I had yesterday about becoming embroiled in another murder case grew a lot stronger.

For the rest of the day one question kept filtering through my thoughts: What reason did Celina have to be out in the middle of nowhere at night? Her passion for aiding all immigrants might have led her to go to extremes and start smuggling them into the country herself. I nixed that idea. Celina was too good-hearted. She probably thought she could rescue a few.

The house felt empty without Matthew and Caroline. My brother Steven and his wife Megan had taken my twins to Gulf Shores, Alabama where Steven owned a condo on the beach.

I was invited to go along, but declined. I needed to work on my latest work-in-progress, a story about a murder in an antebellum plantation home. However, I couldn't seem to concentrate on writing and did a lot of pacing up and down for the rest of the afternoon. All I could think about was Celina Baum and imagine what her last moments must have been like.

Four

Friday July 24

Brad Theriot sat in his vehicle for a while mulling over his encounter yesterday with a reporter from a television station in New Orleans. When he returned from the crime scene, Ray Travis had more or less ambushed him at his office asking questions he couldn't answer. Where the hell did that damn reporter get word about a human smuggling operation? That was confidential information between him and ICE.

No doubt in his mind, Celina Baum's death had something to do with the transport of illegals into the country. All he could do now was hope neither Remi Granger nor any other news people ever got wind of the situation before those responsible were caught.

He had to admit he'd rather have Remi know about it than Ray Travis. She might be trusted to keep the story quiet. He also wouldn't mind getting to know her better on a personal level. She was an attractive woman.

Big green eyes that could see right through a person...Gorgeous blond hair...*Whoa, man, let's not get carried away. My ICE contact and I have a murder to solve and human traffickers to catch. Besides that, Remi is Danny's granddaughter.*

He exited his unit and strode over to a picnic table located in a nearby park where Jack Holden, an agent for Immigration and Customs Enforcement, was waiting for him.

"What's the latest," Holden asked.

"I thought once we got our victim positively identified, we'd get a better idea about whether she's part of the smuggling ring, or if she happened to be in the wrong place at the wrong time. However, that's not exactly the case."

Holden nodded. "Any observations or gut feelings?"

"She could have a connection due to her job at the food pantry. There are a lot of illegals coming there for help. We don't deal with them for you guys unless they commit a crime or traffic offense."

"That's more than some places do," Holden grumbled.

"So I've heard. By the way, the coroner says Celina was killed either late Saturday the eighteenth or early the next morning." Brad gave the ICE agent a worried look. "One of the media in town yesterday asked if Celina could be part of the human smuggling operation. He also mentioned the Gallaghers. If the reporter was anyone other than Ray Travis, I wouldn't be concerned."

Holden jerked his head up. "How the hell do they get wind of everything we want to keep quiet? This is why I don't want to make too many appearances in town."

"Tell me about it. Our victim has to be involved in some capacity. Why else would she be out in the middle of nowhere?"

Holden's disgusted expression mirrored Brad's feelings. "Could she have been killed elsewhere and dumped?"

Brad shook his head. "Blood evidence at the scene indicated she was shot right where she lay. There's indication of a lot of foot traffic out there. My guess is that's a drop off spot."

The ICE agent appeared to consider Brad's statement. "Could be. Did this Travis fellow stick around after you made your comments?"

"Yeah, but I ordered Ronnie Hart to make sure the reporters kept their distance from our crime scene. It would be just like the frickin' media to hire a boat and travel out there. We kept the original call off line so reporters wouldn't hear the call on their scanners."

"Hart is your chief deputy?"

"Right, he'll make damn sure Travis or any other media types won't get any info we don't want them to have."

Holden frowned. "How many reporters were in town? I wouldn't have thought New Orleans viewers would be interested in a murder out here."

"One other reporter," Brad said. "Remi Granger from Channel Seven. She didn't mention the subject and Travis was out of her earshot when he asked me. As far as I know, she doesn't read lips."

"I've seen her a few times on TV. She's a beauty. You know her well enough to know she can't read lips?" Holden chuckled. "Or maybe you'd like to know her well."

Brad silently cringed. *Am I that obvious?* "Like you said, she is a beauty." *Back to business.* "You asked why New Orleans viewers would be interested in a murder down the bayou. For one thing, New Orleans channels are all the folks in this area can pick up."

"I should've known. Guess I've been away too long. New Orleans and the Biloxi station were all we could pick up on the coast." Which coast he referred to was evident by his drawl.

Brad smiled. "You sure didn't lose that accent by being up North for years. You from Mississippi?"

"Yeah, I'm from Miss'ssippi. I held on to my accent. It's part of my charm." He shrugged. "Besides, it comes in handy sometimes like when I need to get info from a woman." Without looking at Brad he added, "This case may require my charm. You never know."

Holden's a pretty decent guy for a Fed. A little full of himself, maybe. That said, he wasn't sure about the ICE agent's method of gathering information from women. However, he suspected Holden's technique was a necessary evil for undercover work. He never had the opportunity to go undercover. Not in this sorry place. Live and learn. If the case goes well, his reward could be a ticket out of this backwoods parish. His brother Dave who had moved to Houston made a lot more money working for that big department.

"There is another reason for the interest in this area," Brad said. "Ever since we had two high profile murders at Mardi Gras a few years ago, and the murder of the former police chief Jim Foret last year, the area media jumps on everything related to Allemand Parish."

"Yeah, I heard all about those cases," Holden said. "I tried to keep up with crime on the home front. South Louisiana and the Miss'ssippi Gulf Coast is my old stomping ground."

"I should mention another possible problem. One of the people who discovered this body is Susan Foret. Since she knew Celina, she might stick her nose where it doesn't belong."

"She's Jim Foret's widow, right? I heard she practically solved the whole case singlehandedly."

"Well, I wouldn't go that far, but she deserves credit for her part in finding all the sorry SOBs who were involved in Jim's murder. The federal trials for those guys are coming up soon. Problem was with Susan, and still may be, she ended up getting into a bunch of trouble."

"Then she could be a big problem for our investigation. If our subjects know we're looking at them, they'll move their operation elsewhere. I'll be tracking them again for another ten years."

"I want those scumbag traffickers out of my parish as much as you. We'll have to make damn sure there aren't any leaks. Danny might be able to keep Susan in line."

Five

The atmosphere at the food pantry reflected the mood of everyone there…sorrow mixed with a little bit of fear. Questions swirled about the reason Celina happened to be at such a desolate spot. Was she aiding illegal immigrants? Was she dealing drugs? No one wanted to believe either of those scenarios.

In light of the fact I'd heard about the possibility of traffickers smuggling illegal immigrants, my theory settled on a more likely situation. One of the traffickers in the group shot her because they mistook her for a federal agent. However, my theory didn't explain her presence in the swamp. So I kept my opinion to myself.

I returned my attention to the order forms and receipts stacked up in front of me on the desk. Just as I started checking figures, Sandy Dugas, coordinator of the volunteers, waltzed into the office.

"You wouldn't happen to know the scoop on Celina's murder, would you?"

Surprised, no, shocked, I squeaked out the question. "Why would you ask me such a thing?" Had word leaked out that Rachel and I discovered her body?

She grimaced. "I'm sorry. That was extremely callous of me. All the volunteers are doing nothing but gossiping and making up theories about her murder. Since you have an in with law enforcement…I figured you might know the real skinny." Her face turned beet red. "Guess I'm digging a bigger hole for myself."

"Yes you are." I glanced down at the desk for a second before returning my gaze to her. "But you can stop digging. I honestly don't know anything except what was on television."

She started to back out of my office. I remembered to ask about the couple from Martinique.

Sandy looked at me with curiosity. "I'm not positive but I believe they were both employed by Claire Gallagher. May I ask why you're interested?"

Not wanting her to get the impression my interest had anything to do with Celina's murder, I waved my hand nonchalantly. "I was curious because I interviewed them. I never heard anything concerning their whereabouts."

She smiled. "Oh, yes. I remember the day they came to us to get food. Good thing you could speak French. I'm ashamed to say I can't speak it, especially since I come from a long line of Frenchmen."

"I don't speak the language well. Luckily I knew enough to understand what they needed."

"You might ask Belva Hernandez about that couple. Seems like she mentioned that Claire's daughter-in-law Marcie told her Claire needed some extra help."

I frowned. "Doesn't Claire have all of her family living out there on that big compound of hers? I wonder why she needed more help."

"Last I heard two of her sons and their wives lived out there, along with one or two other men who are divers with Gallagher Salvage."

"She probably needed a woman to help her personally, since she is confined to a wheelchair. Perhaps to give her family members some relief," I suggested.

Sandy came close to rolling her eyes. "Not the Claire Gallagher I know. She was always the most self-centered woman I've ever met."

"Maybe being confined to a wheelchair made her a better person."

Her laugh sounded nervous. "How do you manage to always think the best of everyone?"

I plastered a smile on my face. "Sometimes it's extremely difficult."

After Sandy left the office, I pondered what she said about Claire and thought about the tragedy this woman had experienced. A number of years ago, the Gallaghers—Claire, her husband Walt, and her two sons, Gary and Mike—were scuba diving off a group of Caribbean islands. In what was rumored to be an attack on their boat by modern-day pirates, Walt and Gary were killed and she was seriously injured. Claire and the other son managed to get back to Jamaica where she was hospitalized for a short time.

I couldn't imagine losing my husband and my son, plus knowing I would be confined to a wheelchair for the rest of my life. Claire was known around here for being a tough cookie, while Miriam Baum, Celina's adopted mother and the parish's other wealthy widow, from all accounts seemed to be more upper class. Surprisingly in the nearly nine years I've lived in Cypress Lake, I'd never met either woman personally, but had seen both around town, or else their photos when they appeared in the local newspaper.

I shook my head to rid myself of thoughts of loved ones lost, but images of dead Celina led me to wonder how I could write about such an awful crime like murder. But then, my mysteries were basically cozies. I didn't go into gory details about the body, and the killer always got arrested and properly punished, not shot and killed by the police.

Hopefully, whoever killed Celina will be caught and sent to prison. Miriam Baum needed some sort of resolution, even though the loss of a child could never bring true closure. If smugglers were involved, justice might be not be achieved either.

<h1 style="text-align:center">Six</h1>

As their ads extolled, Cypress Gardens Cemetery and Mausoleum offered a peaceful setting for deceased loved ones. I've always thought most cemeteries were peaceful, but this one seemed especially true.

Many grave sites held large above ground crypts containing the remains of Allemand Parish's wealthiest citizenry. Trees of several different species like oaks and cypress dotted the well-kept grounds. A slight breeze made July heat a little more tolerable.

I pulled over to the side of the narrow road and parked so I wouldn't block any access. The sound of another vehicle rumbling over the cemetery's gravel lanes caught my attention as I exited my car.

Two men got out of a white van. One of them walked around to the rear and opened the doors. A ramp automatically lowered with a whirring sound. Out of the back a woman emerged riding a motorized wheelchair. I knew immediately she was Claire Gallagher. The men must be her sons.

I felt drawn to the scene. Was this coincidence or fate? Next I expected to see Miriam Baum show up here. I couldn't imagine any connection between Celina's murder and the Gallaghers. However, one never knows about a person's private life.

The Gallagher party stopped at a gravesite where I assumed their people were buried. I left them to grieve and continued to the mausoleum to do my own.

My only consolation was that justice had been served in Jim's case. All the participants in his murder were going to prison with no chance of leaving except in a coffin unless they're found not guilty at their trials. Highly unlikely, so I'm told. The Gallaghers might never be able to find justice. Modern day Caribbean pirates were as elusive as their historical counterparts.

Drug smugglers and human traffickers were about as hard to pin down as the pirates, so Celina's killer might never be caught either.

I stared at the wall that held the vaults of Jim and six other people. All the other names blurred as I focused on my husband's neatly engraved in white marble.

My dear sweet Jim, I miss you so much. I sniffed, willing the tears to stay put. I concentrated on exchanging the dusty artificial roses and replacing them with the live daisies. I'd need to return in a few days to check on the flowers' condition.

I didn't want to leave, but knew staying longer wouldn't contribute anything to my well-being. Matthew and Caroline would be home in a few days and they depended on me for support.

Back in my car, I took a covert look at the Gallagher party. One of her sons leaned against their vehicle, an expression of animosity molded to his face. His sibling and mother Claire remained at the gravesite.

As usual my curiosity went into overdrive. Did he have a problem with his deceased brother or father? Or was his hostility directed at his living relatives? I shook off my inquisitiveness about the Gallaghers and drove away.

Visions of Celina's murder scene crept back into my head. The image of her in a body bag angered me. I didn't know if she was into some illegal activity or not, but no one deserved to be murdered.

On my way home I thought about the couple from Martinique. Why would people from that island want to come to Louisiana? I shrugged mentally. Probably for the same reason any other immigrant wants to enter the United States…to start a new life.

Maybe this was an idealized view, but Martinique seemed like the last place in the world someone would want to leave. Was it really an island paradise, or just a paradise for tourists and wealthy residents? Caribbean islands are noted for fancy hotels and beautiful beaches, but many island natives lived in dire poverty in places tourists never see.

My inquisitiveness pulled me in the direction of Claire Gallagher's home. Legitimately I would be checking up on a couple I helped out. I wanted to know how they were getting along.

Yikes! I'm being drawn into another murder investigation. How could that be? The murder victim wasn't even a member of the Gallagher family. Yet I still felt the force of curiosity luring me into what could turn out to be another dangerous situation.

Seven

I stopped the car at a security gate in front of Claire Gallagher's home and peered through the windshield at the sign hanging on a wrought iron arch over the gate. The words *Elena Plantation*, written in flowery script, danced in mid-air as an erratic breeze swayed the wooden sign. My stomach felt queasy with anticipation, but I couldn't imagine why.

A female voice from a black box on the gate post startled me. I hadn't even noticed the intercom. Too busy trying to decide whether I should be here or not.

"Can I help you?"

How did anyone know I was here? Of course, I'm such a dummy. A surveillance camera was attached to the fence post. The woman's voice seemed pleasant enough. Why should I be nervous about coming here? Except for the fact I really didn't have a legitimate reason for my visit...only my incessant curiosity.

Clearing my throat, I answered with my name and my intent to see how Lucie Celestine and her husband Octave were getting along. There was no response for a few seconds. Maybe I should have waited until Claire and her sons returned from the cemetery.

To my relief, the woman on the intercom permitted me to enter. Shortly, the gate opened with a soft whirring sound and I drove onto the grounds of Elena Plantation.

Thick trunked oak trees lined the winding driveway, their gray beards of Spanish moss waving in the breeze. I spotted a group of large pecan trees to my right.

The house was what's known in architectural terms as an Italianate raised American cottage. I knew this due to recent research into the different styles of New Orleans area houses needed for my current work in progress about murder on a plantation. *Hmm...could that be why I had the feeling of being drawn into a real life murder mystery*?

A gallery stretched across the front of the house with a center stairway leading to a recessed front door. I climbed the stairs and stepped onto the gallery. My gaze settled on the wheelchair ramp that emerged from the left side of the porch—Claire's pathway to a future rolling around in a chair.

I raised my hand to knock but stopped when I heard voices inside. A rather heated discussion about one of them allowing me into the compound was in progress.

"I don't understand why you object to her coming inside," one woman said. "It's not likely she'll be staying long anyway." Her voice sounded like the one on the intercom.

"Maybe not, but you know how Claire gets upset with us for inviting people in the house when she's not here."

"Oh for heaven's sake, Marcie, you're being ridiculous. She's here now so drop it."

"Suit yourself. Don't blame me if you get your butt chewed."

My goodness, I never thought my stopping by would be such an ordeal or cause any kind of commotion. I knocked, hoping my welcome would be a little warmer than the discussion indicated.

A woman answered with a smile. It appeared genuine.

"Hi, I'm Jill Doucet." She waved me inside. "I'll take you back to the kitchen where Lucie is right now."

I wondered about her last name. Maybe she wasn't one of Claire's daughters-in-law. She seemed pleasant enough, easy going. Actually I liked her, which was more than I could say for the other woman. And I hadn't even been introduced to her. Something about her irritated me.

Jill introduced her to me as Marcie Gallagher. She barely nodded. Her expression suggested her opinion of me was pretty low. Well, okay, guess that makes us even. *Gosh, what is wrong with me? I don't even know her, or for that matter, I didn't know Jill either.*

Although monochromatic, Marcie's apparel made quite a splash. She wore denim shorts, a tank top, and sandals all in hot pink. Even her nails were painted neon pink. A pink heart-shaped pendant hung at her throat. Matching earrings dangled from her pierced ears.

The two women were a study in contrast—Jill, a friendly brunette to Marcie's blond snobby persona. I could tell that Marcie's clothes, while casual, were expensive; Jill dressed more like I would at home— blue denim shorts and a red tee-shirt.

"Lucie is in the kitchen," Jill said. "I'll take you back there. O.J. helps with the yard work and other odd jobs."

"O.J.?"

"That's what we call Octave."

From the living room she led me through a formal dining room, and into the kitchen. Lucie stood talking to someone at the rear door with her back to us. She and the other person were totally engrossed in conversation. Not realizing anyone else had entered the room, the pair continued talking.

Lucie spoke in a French patois so I only picked up a few words. I could have sworn she said '*bad as Macoutes.*' Could she be referring to the *Tonton Macoutes*, the former paramilitary police of Haiti?

Jill either didn't know any French or she was a great actress. Her expression remained the same as it had been since she invited me inside the house. "Lucie? There's someone here to see you."

Lucie turned to us, her eyes wide. Her companion, a light skinned black man, appeared equally startled and quickly walked away.

I tried to sound relaxed and reassuring. She obviously was frightened. "Hi, Lucie. I don't know if you remember me. I spoke to you at the food pantry when you first arrived in the area. I'm Susan."

Lucie managed a brief smile and said in halting English, "Yes, you helped me and my husband get food."

"I see you've learned some English since we last met. I wanted to see how you and Octave were doing."

"We are fine. Miz Claire and everyone here are good to work for." She appeared relieved. Maybe she thought I was coming to arrest them for being in the country illegally. I was pretty sure they were. But illegal from where? Martinique? Or Haiti.

Lucie and I made small talk for a short time, then I bade her and the Gallagher household good-bye.

On the drive home I thought of several more questions concerning the presumably illegal pair. Mainly the queries had to do with my own future actions. Should I report my suspicions to law enforcement?

Did the Gallaghers know Lucie and Octave Celestine had arrived in Louisiana with false papers? I have to assume they did know. From all accounts, Claire Gallagher wasn't naïve or stupid. Did she believe she was helping them? I must feel the same way since I'm pretty sure a number of people we help at the food pantry are here without papers. I still want to help them.

I have such mixed feelings about people who come into this country illegally. Many flee violence and poverty in their countries and escape anyway they can. Criminals prey on the immigrants' dreams of a better life and transport these poor people here under horrific conditions. Quite a few die before they arrive. Yet they are breaking the law by sneaking into the country.

I decided to keep my doubts about the Celestines to myself for a while longer. The possibility they were legal did exist, although the chances of that were pretty slim. I went over in my mind the information I knew about the *Tonton Macoute*.

The *Macoutes* were a much feared and hated group of paramilitary police created by a nineteen sixties Haitian dictator known as Papa Doc Duvalier. His son Baby Doc Duvalier continued the group's operations. I couldn't recall this militia's official moniker. Locals referred to the group as *Tonton Macoute*, meaning Uncle Gunnysack, a Creole bogey man, who reportedly kidnapped unruly children, catching them in a gunnysack and carrying them off, never to be seen again. I shivered at the thought.

I didn't know whether *Macoutes* still existed these days or if the group had morphed into another equally frightening organization. Regardless, whoever Lucie Celestine referred to as 'bad as a *Macoute*' must be a terrible person.

Eight

Pulling into my driveway, I spotted Rachel coming out of her house. She started walking toward me. She certainly seemed to be overly interested in the possibility of illegal Haitian immigrants.

"Did you find out anything on the French-speaking couple?" she asked.

A mixture of curiosity and suspicion came over me. "I did uncover a little information." I purposely waited to see her reaction.

She frowned. "And?"

"Why don't you come inside with me so I can relax a little bit."

Her shoulders sagged slightly. "I'm sorry. You probably went to the mausoleum after leaving the food pantry. No doubt that was a distressing visit."

I nodded. She followed me into the house.

Shedding my shoes, I left them by the kitchen door. "I've begun to hate wearing shoes lately. They make my feet feel confined."

Rachel made a face. "I've seen your closet. For someone who hates shoes, you sure have a lot of them."

"Guilty as charged. I keep trying to find a pair that doesn't smother my feet."

I ushered her into the family room and sank into my favorite chair, an overstuffed wingback which I consider my security blanket chair. She sat on the sofa across from me. "If I tell you what I discovered about them and where they ended up, you have to tell me the real reason you are so interested in them."

Reluctantly, she agreed.

"This couple, Lucie and Octave Celestine, supposedly from Martinique, were hired by Claire Gallagher." I noted Rachel's surprised expression. "I dropped by to see them at Elena Plantation. O. J. as they call Octave helps with yard work and carpenter jobs around the house."

"What does Lucie do there?"

"She cooks, cleans, and sometimes assists Claire with dressing or getting around."

Rachel frowned. "I can't imagine Claire ever needing any help. She always acted like she could do anything she set her mind to. Being confined to a wheelchair after being such an active and independent woman prior to the incident on their boat must be horrible."

"It makes me feel bad for complaining about my feet feeling confined." I studied Rachel for a short moment. "Do you know Claire personally?"

"Several times over the years, I've met with her during social events. Those occasions were before her husband and son were killed. She still goes to the Gallagher Salvage office, so I've heard, but other than that she rarely leaves her estate except to go to the cemetery."

"Speaking of cemeteries, I saw her there when I went to the mausoleum. She was with two men I presumed to be her sons."

"Most likely. One has red hair, like Claire did in her younger days. His name is Rick Gallagher. The other man would be Mike Doucet, her son from a mysterious previous relationship. Did he have dark hair?"

I nodded. "Why is the relationship mysterious?"

"No one knows the identity of his father. Mike was adopted as an infant by the Doucet family. Thus his last name is legally Doucet. From what I understand he didn't know Claire was his mother until recently."

"So Jill is married to Mike. Marcie must be Rick's wife."

"What was her color du jour?"

I laughed. "Hot pink. I gather her clothing is always color coordinated?"

"Every time I've ever seen her she's been dressed in different shades of the same color. Sometimes it's the same shade, but never two different colors."

I wasn't sure I should reveal my suspicions about the Celestines' immigrant status, but she evidently suspected I knew more than I told her.

"Did you have any inkling about the couple's origins?"

"If I tell you about my doubts, are you going to go to Danny?"

"Not if you don't want me to," she said slowly. "I figured you had rooted something out about them."

"Don't say anything yet. I'm not certain about what I overheard."

She agreed.

"When I walked into Claire's kitchen, Lucie was talking to her husband in a Creole patois. She had her back to me and Jill and didn't notice us standing there. I thought she said someone was a 'bad as a *Macoute*'."

"The *Tonton Macoute* of Haiti?"

"They're the only ones I know of."

Rachel looked thoughtful. "I doubt Martinique has the same group. That pair could be illegals from Haiti. I had hoped they weren't."

"Okay now you tell me why you're so interested in the Celestines."

"I'm not interested in those specific immigrants per se, who may or may not be illegals. My interest lies in something that happened day before yesterday. I returned home from shopping to find Danny on the patio talking to a man I'd never seen. I felt certain he was law enforcement by his mannerisms."

I chuckled softly. "After so many years fraternizing with law enforcement and being married to cops, we wives can generally spot them. Did Danny introduce you to him?"

"That's the odd part," she said. "Danny was in his secretive police business mode with the guy, so I didn't even go out there to see what was going on. I caught a few words like illegals, Mexico, and Haiti."

"Hmm, I would've at least stuck my head out the door and said hello," I said. "But what's so strange about Danny discussing confidential police business?"

"Nothing as far as the police business goes. The newly elected or appointed department heads like Chief Ken Wallace and especially Brad often consult with Danny. This guy left around the back of the house, presumably as not to be seen. Another oddity—he must have parked his vehicle a long way from the house. None was in sight. "

"He might be an undercover officer. Maybe he's with ICE"

"That's kind of what I figured. But it worries me as to why Danny might be involved."

"Maybe this guy was consulting with him. After all, he was sheriff for years and knows the area like the back of his hand." I really didn't quite believe that, but hoped Rachel's worries might be calmed."

"When Danny came back inside, I asked who the guy was, but he told me it was a need to know situation."

I groaned. His words reminded me of statements Jim had made to me a number of times during our marriage. "Don't you hate it when they say that?"

She rolled her eyes. "It irks me to no end. He's basically saying he doesn't trust me. Or worse, he's wants to protect me."

I decided to change the subject. "Tell me about Miriam Baum and her daughters."

"She adopted both girls together after the real killer of her husband Ellis was convicted for his murder…not my brother."

"I understand from Celina that she and her sister have some Native American ancestry and also Hispanic."

"That very well could be the case," she said. "All I know is that Miriam's paternal great grandmother was a full blooded Apache from New Mexico."

Several years ago I had seen Miriam Baum briefly at a social function and had viewed her photo in the newspaper a number of times after several different charitable events. She was a stunning woman. Come to think of it, her long dark hair and turquoise jewelry she wore for each photo could easily depict her Native American heritage.

"I'd like to find out more about Miriam and Celina's sister Willow. Maybe gain some insight into why Celina was out in the middle of nowhere."

"Are you going to the funeral?" Rachel asked.

"I plan to go."

"Then I'll introduce you if I do. I might attend. 'Might' being the operative word. You can ride with me then."

I frowned. "Why would you not go?"

"I don't know how many bad memories will be drummed up by seeing Miriam at her home."

Bringing up bad memories by visiting certain people or places happened to me a lot. I understood her reasoning. "I assume Danny knows Miriam from the investigation of her husband's murder. Will he be going?"

She nodded. "I know he'll want to go to the post funeral gathering. Brad will be there and most likely other deputies and police officers."

"Who knows? They might pick up important clues to Celina's killer." A thought occurred to me. "Isn't her home the big antebellum house with the columns?"

Rachel smiled. "And maybe you can glean some interesting tidbits for the novel you're working on now. Doesn't your story have something to do with a plantation home?"

"Yes, coincidently, it does." I tried to look innocent. Maybe I was being disrespectful of Celina and her family by having a second motive for attending the funeral, but my interest in this whole case was taking on a life of its own.

~ * ~

Dusk settled on the bayou near a spot where Alex Narcisse sat hidden among the trees. For the sixth day since he arrived, he'd been trying to find his way out of this swamp. He had finished eating the crackers he'd found in the dead woman's backpack, but even rationing the water he only had a few swallows left. His hunger pangs returned.

He needed money to survive since the person he was to meet never arrived at that drop-off site. Could the dead woman have been his contact? He dismissed that idea. According to his instructions, he was to meet a man and give him the package he had carried with him from the island.

His thoughts went back to that night. When the gunshot rang out, his fellow passengers ran toward the second boat. Most made it onto the vessel as her crew, startled by the gunshot, tried to make a fast escape. Others did not make it aboard and those few jumped into the water swimming after the boat in desperation. No doubt those people were all dead by now.

He should have attempted to climb aboard that boat. His situation might have been better if he had. Swatting mosquitoes and watching out for snakes and alligators wasn't his idea of the freedom he'd been promised. Now that he knew what the package contained, he realized his life would have been simpler if he had thrown the package in the water. He'd have to bury it now.

~ * ~

Back home from the cemetery, Claire Gallagher maneuvered her wheelchair up to the door of her safe room. She leaned forward and punched in the combination on the hanging pad. Pausing a moment before she went inside, her thoughts strayed back to her first love.

Andre, a handsome diver who worked for her father back then, had charmed his way into her life when she was fifteen. He was the love of her life. She loved him even more than Walt. Andre was dead, the same as Walt and Gary. Nothing would bring them back, but finding those emeralds, especially the other cross, would ease the pain.

Shaking off her recollections, Claire moved her chair into the room, closing the door behind her. Her gaze moved over the glass-paneled showcases filed with valuable artifacts from other shipwrecks discovered by her and Walt. Gallagher Salvage had been the front operation. Amazingly they had been able to smuggle all these into the country by disguising the artifacts as tourist items—souvenirs from their travels.

She moved her chair to one particular showcase and unlocked the panel. Retrieving a plain wooden box from the shelf, she carefully opened the lid and removed a small bag. She untied the drawstring and pulled out her most treasured object, an ornate emerald cross with gold filigree on the end of each arm. She squeezed her eyes shut as she clutched the jeweled relic.

Months before he died in a diving accident, Andre had given the cross to her in secret, along with a seventeenth century journal he bought from an old man in Jamaica. Andre never revealed from which shipwreck he had recovered the cross, but the journal told the story.

All those other shipwrecks they had previously located weren't the right ones. According to the journal, there was a mate to the cross on one vessel in the fleet, a ship that has proved to be quite elusive. She had begun to wonder if perhaps the journal was a forgery—a ruse to throw them off the trail.

Nine

Saturday, July 25

Our Lady of Lourdes Chapel in the hamlet of Foretville was packed with mourners for Celina's funeral service, mostly people who volunteered or worked at the food pantry, various members of the town council, and Foretville's police force of two officers.

I had expected a Mass at St. Paul's Church, a much larger facility in Cypress Lake. In a way I'm glad the funeral wasn't held there. Too many memories of Jim's funeral were housed in that church.

Holding a funeral at such a tiny church did surprise me. This old wooden chapel had been originally built around eighteen hundred and rebuilt some sixty years later after a fire partially destroyed the building. Every so often the congregation talked about putting in air conditioning units, but with such a small congregation the expense wasn't an option. They decided on ceiling fans.

There were several women who appeared to be of Hispanic origin seated two rows ahead of me and Rachel. I remembered seeing them a few times at the pantry. Periodically the women glanced around anxiously. Were they worried about their immigration status? I shook off my question about these women, and scolded myself for possible racial profiling.

The packed building made breathing difficult due to the stifling heat. Even the priest sounded breathless as he spoke. Mercifully the service only lasted thirty minutes. Rachel and I left the church as quickly as possible and headed to Miriam's home for the post funeral reception.

"Did you happen to notice when Danny left the church?" A worried look crossed Rachel's face.

"I saw him sitting close to the front with Brad and some other deputies, but I didn't see him leave."

I figured she must be thinking about the possibility of him working with the sheriff's office again. She kept her gaze ahead for the remainder of the drive.

The Baum property looked like the setting for a movie about the Civil War. A long winding driveway edged by towering moss-draped oaks led to a huge plantation home, Greek columns and all. Viewing this antebellum home and its surrounds left me in awe.

Completing the scene, a man dressed as a butler answered the door. "Please come in," our greeter said.

I discovered later that the "butler" was part of a crew hired by Miriam to cater the reception.

With Rachel lagging behind me, I followed him inside. Considering all the antebellum light fixtures and furniture in the entryway, I half expected to see a woman in a hoop-skirted dress descending the curved staircase in the center hall.

The butler led us to a large room furnished in a contemporary style that ended my visions of the Civil War era. A big impressionist painting in what I consider to be Southwest colors hung on the wall over the fireplace. Several other smaller pieces were displayed around the larger one. The bright hues of the group captured my attention.

I turned to comment to Rachel, but she seemed to have disappeared. Then I caught sight of her speaking to Margaret De Silva, Cypress Lake's first woman mayor, newly elected like a number of other parish and city officials.

I returned my focus to the paintings.

"Beautiful, aren't they?" Willow, Celina's sister, stood next to me.

"I love the colors. They're hypnotic." I continued to study the art work.

"Everyone who sees those paintings can't stop looking at them," she said, her own eyes trained on the scene. "Todd Hunter, a Navaho from Santa Fe is the artist."

"You and Celina were born near Santa Fe?"

"Yes, in a town a few miles west of there. I don't remember anything about the place. I was eighteen months old when Celina and I were adopted. You're Susan Foret, I believe."

I smiled. "Yes, I knew your sister from the food pantry. She was dedicated to helping every person who needed assistance. I'm so sorry for your loss."

Willow averted her gaze for a short moment. "Sometimes she may have been a little too dedicated."

"How so?"

Her reply was interrupted by Miriam, who walked up to us accompanied by Sheriff Brad Theriot.

Miriam was close to the same height as Brad, who stood six feet tall. Her exquisite face with high cheek bones, her slim figure, along with her regal carriage would put any high fashion model to shame. Hard to believe she's in her sixties.

I greeted her by extending my hand. "I know you've heard this more times than you can count, but I'm so sorry for your loss. Words are inadequate at a time like this."

Her lips moved in what might pass for a smile and she took my hand. "Thank you. The difference is that I know you're sincere. You understand what it means to lose a loved one. I believe you knew Celina."

"I knew her from the food pantry, although not very well. We spoke a few times." I had to bite my lip to keep from blurting out the ultimate question. What was Celina doing out there in the middle of the night? The question still gnawed at me. Maybe I'm paranoid, but Miriam seemed to sense my unasked question.

Her dark eyes watered. "Excuse me. I need to visit with other guests." She walked away toward two couples and stopped to converse with them.

I forced myself not to start crying, but my eyes still teared up. *Losing my husband was difficult, but the death of a child must be even harder.*

Brad placed his hand on my arm and said in a low voice, "Any death of a loved one is difficult, especially when he or she dies violently."

I smiled at him, and then turned to Willow. "It was nice to meet you. I'm sorry it's under these circumstances."

At that moment, a slim, but athletic-looking man with dark hair appeared in the doorway. He scanned the room and seemed to settle his gaze on Willow. She uttered a low gasp.

"Is something wrong?" A stupid question...obviously there was. I suspected he and/or his presence here was a problem.

"No, no, nothing is wrong." Despite her denial, Willow made a quick retreat out the French doors leading to the patio.

Brad and I exchanged a glance. He shrugged. "Ex-boyfriend, maybe?"

When I checked the doorway, the man had disappeared. Rachel came into the room a few moments later and walked over to us.

"Are you ready to leave?" she asked.

I wasn't, but I knew Rachel felt uncomfortable here. So I acquiesced. I wanted to know the identity of that man and why Willow had such a strange reaction to him. And also I didn't get to hear the reason Willow thought Celina might be a little too dedicated in her work.

"I'll walk you ladies out to your car," Brad said.

As soon as we arrived at Rachel's car, I asked my question. "Who was that guy that Willow wasn't so happy to see? I got the impression you were familiar with him." I tried to sound nonchalant, but I'm not a good poker player. From the expression on Brad's face, I should have folded my hand.

At least he answered. "His name is Kenny Verrett. He's a professional diver who used to work for Gallagher Salvage."

"Interesting. You said used to work for Gallagher? What's he do now?"

"I don't happen to have his resume on hand so I don't know what he does for a living now."

He provided me with info but I should have known there'd be repercussions. Brad shot me that look…the one Jim or Danny used to give me when they suspected I was about to jump into the middle of their investigation. The difference was Brad's 'look' didn't seem to be out of concern for my safety.

"What?"

"Don't get involved in this case."

"I'm not getting involved." *Not really.*

He tried to look stern. "A time or two Jim told me he had to go on alert whenever you found something 'interesting.' He knew he needed to be prepared for trouble."

"I don't believe Jim told you any such thing," I huffed. "Danny more than likely jokingly told you something similar when he was giving you advice after you were elected sheriff."

His mouth moved into a tiny grin. "Well, maybe Danny did warn me about your penchant for investigating on your own." His expression turned serious. "There could be life-threatening consequences if you stick your nose into this case. We suspect some dangerous individuals are involved."

I arched a brow. My first thought…*aren't those kinds of people always dangerous*?

"Okay?" He stared at me, waiting for my promise to stay clear of their investigation.

I raised my hands in front of me in a defensive manner. "Okay, I'll try to control my curiosity."

Feeling completely reprimanded, I opened the passenger-side car door and slipped into the seat. Rachel remained speaking to Brad. She must be asking him about Danny's sudden exit from the services.

Finally, she came around the front of the car and got into the driver's seat. A few moments passed before she started the engine.

"Did Brad know why Danny left?" I had gotten the impression from his body language that he told her no.

"He either knew what was going on and wouldn't tell me because he'd be revealing sensitive information. Or else he really didn't know."

I heaved a sigh. "Probably he knew but didn't tell you because he figured you would tell me."

"Maybe so. I'll have to keep after Danny until he tells me."

My reputation has preceded me. But I resented someone like Brad, ten years my junior, forbidding me to get involved. I know I'm being childish. However, everyone has the right to act like a spoiled brat at least once in a while.

Rachel and I remained silent the rest of the drive home. Steven's car was parked in my driveway, meaning the children were back from Gulf Shores, so I had to go back to being an adult. That didn't mean I had to curtail my curiosity.

Ten

Matthew and Caroline ran to me with cries of "Mom, Mom!" as soon as I walked through the door. They both talked at the same time, describing the "ocean," aka the Gulf of Mexico, collecting seashells, and all the other exciting details of a vacation at the beach, including a group of dolphins they spotted one morning. I wouldn't have minded seeing those playful creatures myself.

"My goodness, y'all have such wonderful tans. I'm jealous. Now I'll have to go to a tanning salon."

"No, no, Mom!" Matthew shouted. He talks extra loud when he's excited. "You should have come with us, and then you would have a natural tan."

I couldn't help but laugh. His enthusiasm lifted my spirits.

"Hey," Steven said. "I'm starving. What's for lunch?"

Megan punched him lightly on his arm. "Really? You sound like a kid. After the huge breakfast you ate, you can't possibly be hungry."

Steven grinned. "I'm just a big kid."

My brother seemed a lot more lighthearted than he had been in many years, even if he sounded a little corny. I was glad he found someone special like Megan to spend his life with.

I didn't feel much like eating, but the kids probably were hungry. "Why don't we order pizza?"

"Aah, one of my favorite foods," Steven said.

"Mine too," Matthew agreed.

Caroline smiled. "Pepperoni, of course."

Fifteen minutes after Steven called in the order, the pizza delivery guy arrived. We all sat together at the dining room table. This informal meal seemed like a holiday feast to me. Even though we were missing Jim, the little group assembled here was my family. Plus I actually ate two slices of pizza. I didn't think I could eat anything after such a depressing day.

After we finished eating, I walked into the family room with Steven. Megan insisted on clearing the table.

"So how was the funeral?" Steven asked.

I shrugged. "How is any funeral?"

He looked a bit sheepish. "Stupid question, but I thought you appeared to be more upset than you would normally be about a person you didn't know well."

"You might feel the same way if you had been the one to discover her body."

He widened his eyes. "Geez, not again. Why didn't you tell me?"

"I didn't want to ruin your vacation."

Steven eyed me with suspicion. "I hope this doesn't mean you're considering an investigation of your own."

I averted my gaze for a short moment. "I haven't decided yet." *Not exactly true.*

He exhaled and shook his head. "Why would you want to get involved after everything that's happened to you in the past?"

"Old habits die hard," I said, trying to sound matter-of-fact.

Megan came out of the kitchen and walked over to me and Steven. "All the silverware is washed and in the dish rack. Paper plates and cups in the garbage."

"Thanks so much for doing that. I appreciate it."

"No problem," she said. "You looked as if you could have used a break."

I widened my eyes. "You two are the ones who should need a break after dealing with two eight year olds."

She smiled. "They were active, but nothing we couldn't handle. It was fun."

"They were well behaved," Steven said. "Anything we asked them to do or not do, they always complied...after the third time we told them." He grinned. "No, seriously, we didn't have any problems with them. Maybe if you had come with us you wouldn't have..." His voice trailed off.

Megan looked back and forth between me and Steven. "Did something happen while we were gone?"

"Susan discovered another murder victim."

"Oh, my goodness. What happened?"

I relayed the story of how Rachel and I discovered Celina Baum's body.

Megan looked at me sympathetically. "The experience must have been doubly difficult since the spot was the same place where Jim was shot."

"Discovering a body is always traumatic and the location made it more so." I shrugged in an attempt to dismiss Megan's anxious look. "But then I'm a magnet for murder victims. I either discover their bodies or they end up dying in front of me."

Steven shook his head. "But then you start trying to solve the mystery of their murders and almost get killed yourself. You don't have nine lives like your cat."

Megan cringed. "Please tell me you're not thinking about investigating this one."

"I've been going back and forth with the idea. Maybe I'll keep up with the investigation and use the info for a plot in my next book."

Both she and Steven looked at me in disbelief. I know what they thought. I was not being honest with them or myself.

"Try to stay out of the investigation if you can," Steven said. "But I know you all too well. Even if you start out following the police work, something will happen to draw you in."

I hated to admit he was right. Finding the body plus knowing the victim created the first step in making me want to delve right into the mystery of who killed Celina.

Megan and Steven left about four in the afternoon. For a while after they left, I felt at a loss. I chalked my feelings up to separation from my twin brother and his wife. Then the kids started squabbling over something silly. I chuckled to myself. Things are back to normal. At least what has become normal over the last year.

That night after I got the twins settled into their beds, I retired to my bedroom and sat on the side of the bed for a while. I looked up when I heard a soft meow. Katy, my cat, peeked in through the crack in the door. I called to her. She ran in and hopped onto the bed. She wanted some petting which I gladly afforded her. Eventually she curled up at the foot of the bed and fell asleep.

If only I could fall asleep so easily. I lay wide awake in the dark, thinking about Celina's murder. Everything that occurred at the post-funeral reception and the identity of the man from whose presence Willow tried to escape raced through my mind. A former diver for Gallagher Salvage...looks like there could be a connection between Celina's murder and the Gallaghers after all.

Something had drawn me to the Gallagher place. Maybe I missed my calling. Am I psychic? All the events beginning with the discovery of Celina's body seemed to be leading me to investigate the murder.

But I hesitated to get overly involved. A year ago my children lost their father. They couldn't lose me too. Investigating on my own had put me in some dangerous situations in the past. Sticking my nose in another case like those could easily end my life. Perhaps I should make an appointment for a session with New Orleans psychic Taylor Evans sometime soon. She wasn't just a psychic, but a good friend. She'd never steered me wrong in the past. I shook off the idea for the present. She couldn't make the decision for me.

Eleven

Sunday July 26

Rachel called me at ten in the morning to invite me and the kids over for a barbeque. "That sounds great. Count us in."

"Brad's going to stop by for a while. He started to decline but when he heard Remi would be here, he changed his tune real quick."

"Hmm, sounds like you might be playing matchmaker."

"Sort of," she said. "Remi admitted she found him attractive and I can tell he feels the same way about her."

"So you decided to force the issue."

"It couldn't hurt. Who knows whether anything will come of the match?"

I suddenly recalled the last barbeque I was invited to at Rachel's. "Are any other single males invited to this shindig?"

"Are you interested?" she asked with faux innocence.

"Don't you dare try to fix me up again like you did the last time. When or if I return to the dating scene, I'll find my own man. Now did you invite someone to match up with me?"

"No, I did not. But I hate to see you alone forever."

"I'm not alone. I have the twins."

"The twins aren't going to be with you when they get to be adults. Believe me, they will fly the coop before you realize it."

"Rachel, let's not talk about this anymore. What time do you want us to come over?"

"About noon-ish. Don't worry about bringing a dish or anything. Come on over and have a good time."

After we ended the call, I thought about the barbeque the Marchands held back in May. The man Rachel invited over for me was a deputy who had previously been a NOPD police officer. Another officer, who like Jim, had wanted to get away from the problems inside that department and the crime which continuously kept escalating in New Orleans. I can't even remember his name. He was a nice guy, but that was all I felt. Of course I was miffed at Rachel for trying to push us together. I sure hope she told the truth and had not invited a "date" for me.

At noon I walked next door with the twins. The delectable aroma of meat cooking on a grill floated toward us. The smell made me hungry and reminded me of my meager breakfast of two slices of toast and a cup of coffee.

Sounds of voices and laughter greeted me when I opened the gate to the back yard. Matthew and Caroline spotted kids they knew and rushed over to them. Rachel saw me and motioned me over to a half-circle of chairs where she and two other women sat drinking wine and munching on the usual array of snacks from the small table in the center of their gathering.

I recognized both women—Margaret de Silva, the mayor, and Remi Granger, Danny's granddaughter.

"Susan, you know Margaret and Remi, don't you?" Rachel said.

"Of course I do." I greeted each one with a smile. "Good to see you both. Madam Mayor, you must be enjoying some relaxation from public office today."

She laughed. "I sure am." She lifted a Nike clad foot as an example. "I was expected to show up to work at City Hall in a dress and heels. That was the dress code set by previous mayors, but I sent out a memo

Friday to my staff concerning office apparel. Office casual is now appropriate. I don't mean jeans and tees, but dresses and heels for women, suits and ties for men are now optional."

"You really stirred up the system since you became mayor."

"That was my intention. But please call me Margaret. Strictly for town business am I addressed as Madam Mayor. And only the men who lost the race call me by that title. Sometimes I detect a bit of sarcasm in their voices."

My turn to laugh. She really didn't mince words. I liked her. Despite her casual attire, her hair was perfectly coifed. Who would've thought a woman and a former hair stylist would ever be elected by the traditionally conservative people of Cypress Lake? But over the years since we moved here, a strong majority of the parish had evolved into a much more liberal society. It was about time for women to push out the 'good ole boys.'

I pulled up a chair next to Remi. "So how's the TV news business?"

"With the rising crime rate in our multi-parish area, the news business is booming. This is my first day off in a while. I told them I was also taking tomorrow off."

"Good for you," I said. "I'm sure the station has other investigative reporters on staff, don't they?"

"There are two others." She grimaced. "But we're all vying for the choice assignments. I'm probably going to lose out on at least one, but I needed some R and R."

"How about a glass of wine," Rachel offered me. She reached beside her chair into a small ice chest and pulled out a bottle containing a tiny amount of liquid. "Oops, I didn't realize we'd already drunk so much. Come with me inside to get another bottle and more glasses."

Rachel seemed a little unsteady on her feet when she rose from the chair. Was she the one who had drunk so much? This wasn't like her at all. I followed her inside the house.

"The air conditioning in the house feels wonderful," I said, trying to make conversation. "I love these barbeques, except for the heat. Oh, and the mosquitoes, but they have the decency to wait until the late evening to join the party." I'm usually pretty straight with Rachel, but for some reason I felt awkward asking her about how much she'd had to drink.

She pulled a bottle of Pinot Noir from the refrigerator and set it on the counter.

I grabbed a glass from the cabinet. "How many more glasses do you think will be needed?"

"Oh, three or four. A few of Danny's deputies and their wives or girlfriends are supposed to be coming over. You can leave the glasses sitting on the bar for now."

"Are you okay? You seem to have had more to drink than usual." There, I finally said it.

She heaved a deep sigh. "It's that obvious?"

I nodded. "Did something happen?"

"Danny and I got into an argument this morning. He's definitely signing up to be a reserve deputy."

"I'm not sure why you're so against his going back into law enforcement. Are you afraid of something happening to him?"

She remained silent for a long moment. "I suppose I am."

I couldn't remember her ever mentioning her anxiety, even when Danny was the sheriff. Every spouse of a law enforcement officer has fear in the back of his or her mind about their loved one getting killed by a criminal. Police work is a dangerous occupation. Danny had been with the sheriff's office in one position or another from the beginning of their marriage.

"I admit I always feared Jim getting shot, but I knew he'd never work at any other occupation. As you know, I didn't want to move out of New Orleans to live in Cypress Lake, and fought the move with all my might. I finally came to the decision that he and I would end up in a divorce if I didn't."

It occurred to me that this conversation was somewhat of a role reversal for me and Rachel. She was old enough to be my mother and had always been the one to give me encouragement about life as a police officer's wife and other situations. Another thought struck me.

"Does your concern have anything to do with the anniversary of Jim's death?"

She leaned against the kitchen counter and looked at me with surprise. "I ought to be shocked you would suggest such an idea. But you and I think so much alike, I should have known you would come to the right conclusion." She glanced away for a short moment. "Miriam's connection in this latest murder has stirred up bad memories. I'm also worried about you."

I jerked my head back and stared at her. "Me? Why are you concerned for me?"

"The fact we discovered Celina's body at the same place and on the anniversary of Jim's murder affected you greatly. I'm afraid this will reverse the progress you've made getting back to your life."

"Was that the reason for our conversation concerning the empty nest?"

She nodded.

I reached over and hugged her. "My advice is to not worry about something happening to Danny and forget about Miriam and me. That's easier said than done, believe me, I know. But it makes life a whole lot less stressful. If Danny stays around the house doing nothing, both of your lives will be miserable." I held out my glass. "Now pour me some of that vino."

She uncorked the bottle. "But no more wine for me."

Despite my upbeat words, an empty feeling worked its way through me. Maybe she was right. But I wasn't ready to start dating again. Who knows? I might never be.

We walked back out into the yard and joined the others. To my relief the food was ready. If I drank any alcoholic beverage on an empty stomach, I would have to be carried home, not to mention being a bad role model for my kids.

"We were about to send out a search party for you two," Remi said, setting her plate of food on the table now devoid of snack food.

I smiled. "We're here now. Looks like we need to get over there before the men scarf up all the food." I started to check on the twins to make sure they had food, but my help wasn't needed. Either they or one of the other kids' moms had already fixed them each a plate. What was that Rachel warned me about...? They would fly the coop before

I realized it. I dismissed that thought. There's at least ten more years before I have to worry about them leaving me.

Remi was sitting by herself so I walked over with my plate. "Mind if I join you?"

"Of course not. It appears I've been deserted." She gave a faux look of indignation. "Rachel and Mrs. De Silva would rather sit with their husbands than with me." A troubled look crossed her face. "Susan, I'm sorry. I didn't mean…"

I waved off her apology. "That's not the reason I wanted to join you. I have to compliment you on the wonderful job you did reporting on the discovery of Celina Baum's body. I know you weren't on the scene, but I've seen a couple of your other reports where the victim hadn't been removed yet. It's so disturbing when reporters do their best to show the body *in situ*. I can't understand why they believe it's necessary to display a lot of blood and gore."

She nodded in agreement. "Most stations' management believe the more blood and violence is televised, the higher the ratings. Our owner and a few others are trying to back off to a certain extent. Thank goodness changes are beginning as far as local news shows go. However, in New Orleans it's kind of hard not to report murder and other violence." She eyed me with caution. "You knew Celina, didn't you?"

"I knew her from my volunteer work at the Cypress Food Pantry. We weren't close friends or anything like that, but she was a really nice person and felt strongly about helping people."

"Does anyone know why she happened to be out in the middle of nowhere? I tried to get information from Brad, but he's pretty closed mouth about the case."

She kept watching me as if to determine when I would get upset talking about a murder victim. Or maybe she was afraid talking about this murder would bring back bad memories about Jim's death.

"As far as I know, no one has found out why, or else the sheriff's office knows and isn't releasing the information." I added, "I've been trying to figure out why she was out there myself."

"Do you know anything about the rumor that the area is a drop off spot for illegal immigrants?"

"Nothing, except that I've heard the rumor." I wondered if we were both trying to see how much information we could get out of each other without actually asking. I'm normally a little more open to a person with whom I feel comfortable, but I wasn't sure how much info I could safely dole out and not get into trouble. A decision was made for me. Brad strolled towards us.

"Ladies, y'all seem to be having a pretty serious conversation. It's too nice a day for depressing talk."

Remi seemed to force her smile. "Serious is not necessarily depressing."

Brad glanced at me. "I have the feeling y'all were discussing Celina Baum's murder."

What is his problem? I jumped in with both feet. "So what if we were? Her murder is news. Why can't we talk about it?"

His face reddened. "Because I don't want the case jeopardized because of civilian meddling."

I was really angry now. "First of all, I don't know any information to tell that would put the case in danger. Even if I did, I certainly wouldn't divulge classified info to the press. I used to be married to the chief of police. I know better."

He glared at me. "What I'm worried about is you investigating on your own and my office having to use valuable resources to rescue you."

Apparently the conversation had become louder than I thought. Out of the corner of my eye I saw Danny walking fast in our direction. Other guests turned to see what was going on.

"Is there a problem?" At six-four, Danny loomed over all three of us. His piercing blue eyes studied each of us in turn as if we were children in a school yard conflict...which I suppose, in a way, we were.

"Brad seems to think I'm trying to take over his job." I immediately regretted my barb.

Danny arched an eyebrow. I couldn't determine whether he found me annoying, or if he was amused and trying not to show it. "I can't imagine you as the sheriff."

My anger started to subside. I even managed a laugh. "That would be a sight, wouldn't it?"

Remi started laughing and the atmosphere lightened. Even Brad smiled.

I turned to him with a repentant look. "I apologize for my remark. I'm touchy about criticism of my past…uh…adventures."

"Apology accepted. I'm simply looking out for both of you." He turned his attention to Remi. "Investigative reporters have also been known to get into trouble."

"I'm always careful," Remi said, her expression amiable. "Like in your job, I have to go to the news or crime in this case. Most of us follow guidelines for our safety. Come, I'll tell you all about the unofficial rules so you can relax." She crooked her arm inside Brad's and led him off toward the rest of the crowd.

Danny waited until the pair was out of earshot before questioning me. "What's the deal between you and Brad?"

I blew out a deep breath. "I resented being ordered not to do something. I may had gotten into trouble in the past with my snooping around, but I wasn't wrong about who the bad guys were. You might not believe this, but sometimes events happen to me, or I meet a person that draws me into the situation. Murder seems to follow me around." I shook my head. "Maybe Brad thinks I'm leading Remi astray."

He chuckled at my remark. "I'm not sure that's possible. Calm down and tell me. What brought on all these warnings?"

I relayed the story about the incident at the Baums' and about Brad chewing me out, cautioning me about not getting involved even after he identified this fellow to me.

"Who was the man?"

"A former diver for Gallagher Salvage named Kenny Verrett."

He pursed his lips. "I would give you the same advice that Brad did, but I know you aren't going to pay any more attention to my warnings than his." He eyed me with fatherly concern. "Do you have a particular interest in Gallagher Salvage?

"Not really." *Should I mention my visit? No, too risky for the Celestines and their suspect immigration status.* "I'm more interested in Claire's house. My latest mystery in progress involves a plantation home. I enjoyed seeing Miriam's home also." *That wasn't really a lie.*

Danny hesitated a long moment before speaking. "Be careful with any dealings you have regarding Claire or Gallagher Salvage and try not to get involved...if you can help it."

"Why?"

He blew out an exasperated breath. "I'm advising you, not demanding, that you leave well enough alone. I suspect you have already visited her place for your novel research and discovered some interesting tidbit. I hope if whatever you uncovered or find out on any future visits that you believe to be possible illegal activities you'll report them to Brad. At the least, give the info to me and I'll pass it on."

"I will."

A sliver of guilt stung me. I couldn't believe he had been halfway open with what I interpreted to be concerns about the legality of Gallagher Salvage's operations, especially since I neglected to tell him about my visit to the house. Of course he suspects I did. Guess I should have told him the real reason for my visit. Danny knows me too well. He should also know that by giving me that small suggestion of illegal activity, my curiosity would make me want to know more.

Law enforcement might not be tailing me per se, but if suspicion is warranted, the sheriff's office or a government agency could be staking out the Gallaghers.

There must be a lot more going on at the salvage company than hiring illegal immigrants. Maybe that's the reason Marcie Gallagher didn't like the idea of my unexpected visit.

Twelve

Monday, July 27

Sandy Dugas phoned me around eight in the morning from the food pantry in panic mode. Several charitable organizations had generously donated two semi-trucks loads of non-perishable food and a refrigerated truck containing perishables like meat and seafood. All donations had to be logged in right off the truck. To top it all, our warehouse manager was out of town on vacation with his family and couldn't be reached.

Linda Cutrer, the person who normally volunteered at the same position as mine, but on opposite days, couldn't come in until noon today. Besides, this sounded like a two or more person job.

"My kids are back from Gulf Shores now. I'll have to find a sitter for them. I'll be there as soon as I can."

I hadn't planned on spending the day logging in supplies, but duty calls. Of course none of my usual teenage sitters were available. I phoned Rachel who agreed to watch them at her house.

After a hectic hour of making myself presentable and the twins squared away at Rachel's, I drove the five miles from my house to the food pantry.

Sandy sighed with relief when I checked in with her. "Thanks so much for coming. I managed to get Grace Henderson to start logging in some of the non-perishable foodstuff."

I couldn't imagine a more implausible scenario. Grace was the type of person who never wanted to do anything that wasn't *"in my job description."* I was positive that as soon as she saw me she would hand over the clipboard and disappear back inside the air conditioned office. That's exactly what happened.

Linda arrived shortly after noon along with another volunteer, so I took a well-deserved break. Walking back to the office, I spotted a familiar-looking man exiting his vehicle, a white Ford pick-up.

He wore jeans, western boots, and a black tee-shirt. It took me a few minutes to put a name to his face. Josh Broussard? What would a private investigator be doing here?

Josh stood next to the pick-up's open door with a surprised look on his face. "Susan Foret?"

"The one and only." I walked closer to him.

"No one ever made a truer statement."

"Oh, come on now." I met Josh through Megan during the time I searched for proof that Jim was murdered. He knew how stubborn and persistent I could be. "What in the world are you doing at a food pantry?"

"Working a case." A lopsided grin tipped the corner of his mouth. "I might ask you the same question."

"I've been volunteering here a couple of days a week for about six months." I tilted my head to one side. "The only case that would bring you here would be Celina Baum's murder."

He shrugged and tried to look innocent. "I could be looking into a case of embezzlement of food pantry funds."

I arched a brow. "Really?"

He cleared his throat. "You got time to talk?"

"Sure, I'm on a break. Come into my office."

He shut the pick-up's door and followed me. "Is anyone else in there?"

"Not that I know of. Everyone is out back unloading supplies from three semis."

My imagination ran wild trying to figure out why he would be working on a case the sheriff's office was handling. The curiosity building inside me nearly drove me crazy. His visit was too much of a coincidence to not be a sign. But a sign of what? That was the million dollar question.

Once inside the office, I sat in the chair behind my desk and he took a seat opposite me. Josh leaned forward and rested his arms on the desk front.

He wasn't exactly handsome, but attractive in a rugged way. I did notice a scar on his right arm an inch or so above his wrist that I didn't remember seeing when we first met. Of course at the time I was in turmoil after Jim's murder, so that didn't surprise me. A wound he suffered in Iraq? Or as a result of a case he worked in the past?

"Now tell me what's up with you?"

"I've been asked to look into Celina Baum's murder."

"But the sheriff's office is handling the case. As far as I know, they haven't given up trying to solve her murder."

"The family isn't happy with Sheriff Theriot's progress."

"Does Brad know they hired you?"

"That I don't know. And I'd prefer he didn't." He lifted his hands palms up. "Regular law enforcement doesn't like PIs like me nosing into their case."

"So why are you telling me stuff I didn't think PIs were supposed to divulge?"

He stared at me for a long moment. "You mean, like who I'm working for? Why do you think I am?"

"Because you believe I can give you information Brad and his deputies won't?"

He nodded. "Maybe you could. Besides, it's nice to see you again."

I sat up straight. "I didn't think you liked me very much."

"Didn't at first," he admitted. "As I recall the feeling was mutual. We did end our association on a cordial note."

I agreed. Too bad he didn't leave his reminiscence about our association at that.

He continued, "I thought you did a hell of a job ferreting out information after your husband's death."

I flinched.

He averted his eyes for an instant. "I'm sorry. I didn't mean to bring up a sensitive subject. Not too many women I know would have kept on pushing the cops to pursue the case as a homicide. You never quit."

I moved the subject away from Jim's death. "So what do you want to know? If I can help I will. Celina was a nice person."

"What did she do here?"

"Mostly she dealt with Spanish speakers, assessing their needs."

"Does anyone in charge here ask whether these people are here legally?"

I shook my head. "To the churches, they are people in need of food, clothing, and lodging."

He looked thoughtful as if contemplating his next question. "Could Celina have been involved in some way with smuggling illegals into the country?"

I leaned back in my chair. "It's an idea I considered at first. Now my inclination is toward a more humanitarian reason for her being out in the middle of nowhere at night."

"You mean, she thought she might be able to rescue some?"

"Exactly. There have been so many stories that have come to light about the horrific conditions the people endure after giving up their life savings to those criminals. She always said she wanted to do as much as she could to help the immigrants."

"I gathered as much when I spoke to her sister. Do you know Willow?"

My answer was interrupted by Sandy bursting into the office, a flustered look on her face. She stopped short when she saw Josh.

Regaining her composure, she announced, "Your services as a French speaker are needed right now."

"There's no one else here who can speak French better than me?"

"Not at the moment. A man stumbled in through the gate, weak and almost delirious. He's mumbling in some kind of pigeon French dialect. I did get a name out of him...Alex or Alec. EMS is on the way."

Thirteen

Josh followed me and Sandy to the location, much to Sandy's obvious discomfort. I couldn't figure out why. Maybe she thought he was a cop or maybe an undercover ICE agent. He did have the appearance of law enforcement.

The ailing man in question had been placed on a cot in the warehouse manager's office. His clothes and hair were wet and smelled of bayou water. With his closed eyes and his shallow breathing, I didn't believe he would be able to speak again.

Looking at this stranger lying there in such serious condition brought back cutting memories of Jim in the hospital. My throat constricted. I took in a deep breath and willed myself not to break down.

I checked the man's pulse and then glanced back at the others. "His pulse is almost non-existent."

A mumbled sound came from the man's mouth. I couldn't understand what he said. I moved my face closer. He uttered one word that sounded like *emeraude*, French for emerald. As with the Celestines I suspected him to be Haitian, but didn't know if the word was the same in their dialect.

His eyes fluttered open briefly. He squeezed my hand with a weak grip.

"Alex?" I said softly. "*Je suis* Susan. *Aide arrivee bientot.*" My French grammar wasn't great but he seemed to understand and closed his eyes again.

Sirens from emergency vehicles sounded in the distance. The wails grew louder as EMS approached.

"I'll go out and direct the EMTs to our location," Josh offered. He turned and left the room.

I kept holding Alex's hand until two EMTs rushed into the room and forced me out of their way. I noticed three deputies from the sheriff's office standing outside talking to Josh. I can't imagine why that many men were sent for a seemingly ordinary medical call. One of the deputies was Ronnie Hart, another neighbor of mine.

He motioned me and Sandy over to speak to him and the other deputies who I didn't recognize.

"What happened here?" Ronnie asked.

"The man in there stumbled into the compound," Sandy told him. "He appeared weak. I suspect he must have been wandering around for several days without food or water."

"Was he able to say anything?"

I glanced at Sandy. "She got him to give his first name—Alex. But that's all he told us about himself."

"Didn't he say something else to you?" Sandy remarked.

"He did, but it didn't make much sense. I thought he said *emeraude*, which is French for emerald."

The EMTs wheeled Alex out on a stretcher. Ronnie asked one of them about the man's condition.

"Serious," he answered and rolled his patient out to the waiting ambulance.

Soon after the EMS left for the hospital, the deputies departed in their vehicles. I decided it was time for me to do the same.

"Sandy, I'm sorry, but I've had enough. I hate to leave you in a pickle with so much left to do."

"Don't worry about it. I understand," she said.

I got out of there as quick as I could. I couldn't handle another dead or dying person.

~ * ~

The day's events continued to haunt me way into the evening. The kids were in bed so I didn't have them to occupy my mind.

I could still see Alex lying on the couch weak from dehydration and exposure. His milk-chocolate colored skin looked ashen. Mosquitoes had eaten him up. Could he have witnessed Celina's murder? If he were a passenger on a boat load of illegal immigrants, he very well could have seen her and her killer. What did he mean by *emeraude*?

All the trampled grass and foliage at the scene didn't seem right. A herd of wild pigs couldn't have mashed the grass down like that. It had to be a crowd of people.

The land surrounded by Bayou Jean Baptist was accessible only by boat. Dense swamps lay beyond the point where Celina's body was found. If people had flattened the area after being unloaded from a boat, they would have either been headed toward water again or straight into the swamp. Another boat had to be there to pick any people up.

Pigs also would end up in the bayou unless they turned around and ran back the other way. Maybe feral pigs can swim. Too bad there aren't any surveillance cameras in the swamp.

The unexpected appearance of Josh Broussard served up more food for thought. Was he really glad to see me again or was his statement a ploy to find out information?

Our association had been strictly business last year and it did end on a cordial note as he stated. I sensed something more amorous when he said it was nice to see me again. I wasn't sure if I liked the idea or not. *Forget it. I misinterpreted his tone.*

Emeraude surfaced once again in my head. If Alex was indeed referring to an emerald or emeralds, what connection did these gems have to him? Are jewels being smuggled into the state along with people?

In the New World, emeralds were mined in Colombia and to a lesser extent in Brazil. If I remembered world history correctly, the emerald was sacred to the Incas. There were also other places in the world where emeralds were mined.

Unfortunately, none of this information helped answer the questions about Alex and his *emeraude.*

Jewel smuggling presented an interesting possibility. Did Alex have them hidden somewhere on his person?

~ * ~

Danny answered the knock on his front door to see Brad standing there.

"We need to talk about Susan."

A frown wrinkled Danny's brow. "Does this have anything to do with the hoorah over here on Sunday?" He suspected as much before Brad even answered.

Brad nodded. "You could say that."

He ushered the younger man into the living room with a wave of his hand. "I know it's hot outside, but it's a safer place to prevent eavesdropping, if you know what I mean."

Rachel walked into the room and greeted him with a surprised, but pleasant look. "Hi Brad. How are you?"

"I'm good, and you?"

"Fine," she said. "Would you care for a cold drink? How about iced tea?"

"No thank you, ma'am. I need to speak to Danny about a couple of things. I won't be here but a few minutes."

The two men left through a sliding glass door at the rear of the house.

Danny felt a mixture of curiosity and unease. *What's Susan done now?*

"What's this all about?"

Looking ready to explode any minute, Brad fisted his hands at his side. "I'm pretty sure she's digging into Celina Baum's murder."

"She probably is interested in the case because she knew the woman. Look, she's a mystery writer. What has she done to suggest she's gotten involved?"

"At the Baums' house after the funeral, she questioned me about Kenny Verrett who is a diver with Gallagher Salvage."

Danny raised his eyebrows. "And you told her what?" He knew Susan's version, but he needed to hear Brad's.

"She asked who the guy was because Willow, Celina's sister, had a negative reaction to him being there. I kinda brushed her reaction off. I told Susan he must be an ex-boyfriend. When I walked her and Rachel out to their car, she started questioning me about him again. Who was he? She claims to have detected that I knew him."

Danny chuckled. "She doesn't miss much."

Brad blew out a deep breath. "I don't see how you can be so calm about this. She's either going to get herself killed or mess up our case… or both." He paused for a short moment. "I told her he used to be a diver with Gallagher's, but that was before I discovered she had visited the Gallagher place a day or so after Celina's murder."

"How'd you find out she went there?"

"An agent passed it on to me. At the funeral I didn't know that she'd been there so I simply warned her not to get involved because there might be dangerous people connected to Celina's murder."

"Have you asked Susan about the visit since then? If so, what did she say was the reason? It could be totally innocent."

"I didn't speak to her until Sunday. And no. I didn't ask her, but I doubt her visit was innocent."

"What makes you question her visit?"

"You know Claire Gallagher never lets anyone through that gate unless they're family or close friends. Susan drove up to the gate, spoke into the intercom, and was granted entry right away. So when I saw her and Remi with their heads together, I figured they were up to something."

"My granddaughter would like nothing better than to be right in the middle of the action. Together she and Susan would make a dangerous pair. But demanding either one of those women not investigate is like trying to get a bone from a hungry pit bull." Danny cocked his head to one side. "What else is causing you grief? Are you having doubts about your ability to solve this murder?"

Brad averted his eyes toward the patio floor for an instant. "No, this is a high profile case so I don't want anything to go wrong. The whole deal with ICE has gotten more complicated since Celina's murder."

"You ought to know there is no such thing as a completely smooth running case. There's always going to be hiccups." Danny placed his hand on Brad's shoulder. "Don't sell yourself short. You can handle any of those bumps in the road if you have patience and keep a lid on your temper. I have the utmost faith you can achieve your goals."

Brad smiled and seemed to relax. "Thanks. I appreciate your confidence in me."

"I'll talk to Susan and see if I can find out what her intentions are about the murder. In the meantime, I suggest you discontinue warning her to keep her nose out. She'll be curious to find out more."

After Brad left, Danny sat for a while on the patio thinking about the conversation. He remembered Jim's brief lack of confidence about handling his first big case...the murder of Teddy Berthelot at Mardi Gras several years earlier. Jim turned out to be the best chief of police Cypress Lake ever had. Maybe too good. And it got him killed. Danny shook off that line of thought.

Having a few doubts about their ability to handle big cases was normal for good young law men like Jim and Brad, whether they wanted to admit it or not. He did himself when he first became sheriff. And he wasn't so young. However, Brad seemed overly worried about his abilities. He may have bitten off more than he could chew.

By all accounts, Brad had been a pretty good officer during his time with Cypress Lake PD. Although he'd given him encouragement, Danny wasn't sure this young law man had enough self-confidence to lead the sheriff's office. Brad's older brother Dave Theriot, one of his own deputies, would have made a better sheriff. To Allemand Parish's detriment, Dave had found a higher paying job in Texas. Too bad he couldn't have talked Ronnie Hart into running for the office.

Danny wondered if Brad did feel threatened by Susan. Maybe she hit the nail on the head when she remarked that he was afraid she was trying to take over his job.

Something Brad said about Susan's visit to the Gallaghers' house bothered him. Federal agents don't usually pass along information to local law enforcement. He spoke from experience on that note. Of course it was possible not all federal agents were like the ones he had come in contact with while working on Jim's murder. Unless...

The sliding glass door swished open. Rachel appeared with two glasses of iced tea and handed him one.

"What's wrong with Brad?" she asked.

He smiled. "Oh nothing. He's having a few doubts about being able to handle Celina Baum's murder. You know...first big case after being elected. It's nothing for you to worry about."

"Hmm, whenever you say that it makes me worry more."

Fourteen

Tuesday July 28

An anchor for Channel 7 interrupted the network morning show with breaking local news. Lost in my own thoughts, I hadn't been paying attention to the program, but the dramatic music accompanying the announcement caught my interest.

"Early this morning, the bodies of five people were discovered floating in Bayou Jean Baptiste in Allemand Parish. None of the victims has been identified yet, but they are all suspected to be immigrants who entered the country illegally. As soon as we have further information, it will be passed along to our viewers."

My stomach clinched. I knew it…*people* had trampled the grass and not feral pigs. Alex could have been among the group, perhaps the only survivor. I wondered if there was any possibility of finding out his condition?

I phoned the hospital, but got nowhere. The woman I spoke to was not authorized to give out information on him, but she did tell me on the sly that there were armed deputies guarding his room.

Maybe Danny knows how Alex is doing. Hopefully he'll tell me what I want to know. I peered out the window to see if his truck was in the driveway. I was in luck.

I checked on the twins who were both still asleep and walked next door. Rachel answered the door and invited me inside. "I need to speak to Danny. Is he up yet?"

"Of course he is. In fact he's on his second cup of coffee."

I followed her into the kitchen. "Sorry to intrude on your breakfast, but I want to ask you something."

Danny chuckled. "You must have seen the news about the bodies."

I nodded. "That's part of what I want to know. I assume you heard about the man who arrived at the food pantry yesterday and was taken to the hospital."

"He's suspected of being in the country illegally. I understand you were there when he turned up."

"Yes, Sandy Dugas and I tended to him until EMS came in and took over. Do you know how his condition is now?"

He took a sip from his coffee cup. "Last I heard he's in serious, but stable condition."

"Then he's expected to survive?"

"Yes, but as soon as he's released from the hospital he'll be taken into custody and prepared for deportation."

I didn't know whether to be relieved or not. I was pleased he would recover, but not happy he would be sent back to a dangerous life in his country of origin. "He's from Haiti, I believe."

Danny appeared surprised. I glanced at Rachel, who sat with her elbows on the table, and hands steepled in front of her mouth.

"Did he tell you where he was from?" Danny asked.

"No, it's an educated guess."

"Not being privy to everything going on at the office since I retired, I'm not sure whether his country of origin has been verified."

"I don't know, Danny," I said, trying to sound lighthearted. "You seem to be pretty well up on things if you heard I was at the food pantry. Do you know if he has any connection with the victims who were found this morning?"

"It's highly possible." He shot me the *look*. "If I ask you not to get involved with this, will you listen?"

"I believe I'm already involved. Remember what I told you Sunday about events that happen to me, or people I meet drawing me into a case?"

"So you believe because you found Celina's body and you tended to this illegal immigrant, you are destined to solve her murder and take care of him?"

I pursed my lips. "Something like that. Don't you believe in fate?"

"On occasion I have experienced an event or two that seemed like destiny." He reached across the table and caught hold of Rachel's hand. "The way she and I met felt a lot like fate."

Rachel smiled at him. "I believe you called it kismet."

"Oh my, y'all are so romantic. That's my cue to leave. I left the twins asleep. They might be destroying the kitchen in search of breakfast."

Rachel and Danny must have settled their differences and appeared to be the same great couple they've been since I first met them.

The phone was ringing as I walked inside my house. I glanced at the caller ID and saw Sandy Dugas' number on the display. *Please don't let her be calling me to come in to the food pantry.*

"Susan, you're not going to believe this." She sounded excited and even a little frightened. That woman is going to have a nervous breakdown. But who am I to talk? I'm not exactly the calmest person in the world.

"What is it?"

"I know who killed Celina."

My heart took a dive. I could hardly speak. "Who?"

"Alex killed her." Her voice went up in volume.

"You mean the man who turned up yesterday? Why do you believe he's Celina's killer?"

"He had her backpack. I know it's hers."

None of this made sense. "Calm down and tell me the whole story."

"He came into the compound carrying a backpack. The bag got left behind when EMS transported him to the hospital. With all the excitement over him and the huge amount of supplies we were trying to unload, it wasn't noticed until this morning when I went to straighten up the warehouse manager's office. I knew right away it was hers."

"What did you do with the backpack?" I held my breath.

"I didn't know what to do," she said.

"Have you checked inside the bag?"

"No, I was so shocked at finding it. Hold on. I'll look."

I heard soft rustling and what sounded like a zipper opening. *Oh no, I forgot about her fingerprints messing up evidence.*

"There's nothing in here except an empty water bottle and a bunch of cellophane wrappers from those crackers Celina used to carry with her."

"It sure sounds like the bag belongs to Celina. Call the sheriff's office and tell them. A deputy will come out there and pick it up." *Brad may go out there himself to get it.*

She agreed and we ended the call.

The news was a lot to process. Why did he have Celina's backpack? Did he have a gun on his person? I didn't think he did. He could have gotten rid of the gun somewhere out in the swamp.

Alex was a complete stranger, but for some reason I didn't believe he was a killer.

Fifteen

Caroline absentmindedly stirred her cereal with the spoon. "Mom?" She looked at me sympathetically. "Are you okay?"

I did my best to appear fine. "Of course. Why do you believe I might not be?"

"You look unhappy. Not like when Daddy died, but lightly sad."

My heart broke at the mention of her father dying, but I concentrated on being amused at her wording. When Jim died, I must have been heavily sad to her. "Well I suppose I am kind of down, but I'll be alright in a day or so. A lady I knew died last week. She volunteered at the food pantry with me. I feel bad about her death because she was young."

"It's always sad when someone dies, isn't it?"

I sat at the table next to her. "It is for the person's family, but once they realize their loved one is in Heaven and is at peace, their sadness starts to go away." I didn't dare tell her the unhappy feeling lasted a long time.

My cell phone rang and I grudgingly got up. *Who's calling now?* This time Rachel was on the line. Relieved it wasn't Sandy, I answered.

"Hey, what's up?"

"Danny got a phone call from Brad and he left out of here in a hurry," she said. "Do you know what that's all about?"

"I can make a good guess." I told her about the call from Sandy.

"That sounds like bad news for that poor man. What I don't understand is why Brad has to call Danny for every little thing that happens. Even though this isn't little. Can't he make decisions on his own?"

"Danny might as well still be sheriff," I said.

"You took the words right out of my mouth."

"I plan to call Megan to see if she'll consider representing Alex when he's arrested."

"Aren't you jumping the gun here? He hasn't been arrested yet."

"No, but I'm confident he will be as soon as he's released from the hospital. Brad is anxious to get this homicide solved so he can look good in the eyes of the people who elected him. I hate to admit I voted for him."

"Me too," she said. "But it was either him or George Reynolds who is as old as Methuselah."

"Our options weren't great."

"Let me know if you hear anything else."

I promised and ended the call.

Matthew came running down the hall with his bicycle helmet in his hand. "I'm going bike riding with Reed." He referred to Reed Hart, the son of Ronnie Hart, the deputy who came to the food pantry when Alex was taken to the hospital.

"What happened to 'Mom, can I please go bike riding with Reed'?"

He pouted. "Sorry, can I please go?"

"Yes, you may, but stay inside our subdivision."

He didn't look happy, but agreed to my terms. I had the feeling Matthew would soon be testing the limits of my authority.

I phoned Megan and got almost the same reaction from her as I did from Rachel.

"Has he been arrested yet?"

"No, but if the backpack does turn out to be Celina's, Alex is going to be arrested for her murder," I argued. "Not to mention he's in the country illegally."

"I'll think about it and get back to you. I know an immigration attorney with whom I can consult."

"Please don't think too long about taking his case or he'll be assigned some young inexperienced public defender."

"Okay, I promise I'll get back to you soon."

Caroline was still dawdling over her breakfast when I got off the phone. "Who's Alex? Is he a bad man?"

Hmm...little ears hear a lot. "He's a man who came into the food pantry. He had been lost out in the swamp for a few days and was very sick. EMS came and took him to the hospital. I don't believe he's a bad man."

"Then why is he going to be arrested?"

"Sometimes things happen that make the police or sheriff believe a person has committed a crime when he or she really didn't. There is a trial and a jury decides from the evidence whether or not the person is guilty."

"I heard you say he was in the country illegally. Is that why he'll be arrested?"

"If he's found not guilty of the other crime that he's being accused of, he will be sent back to his country." *Why so many questions from an eight-year-old?*

"There was a girl who came to our school a few days last year. She couldn't speak English good and some older kids teased her at recess and said she came here illegally. What does that mean?"

"To come to the United States from another country, a person must have legal papers stating our government is allowing them to come here. There are a lot of poor countries and places that are dangerous and the people from those countries want to come here so badly that they sneak into the US without having the proper papers."

She looked thoughtful for a long moment, and then got up from the table.

"Bowl in the sink," I said.

"Yes, ma'am." On the way to the sink she turned to me. "When I grow up I want to help those people."

I felt a lump in my throat. "Good for you." *I hope when she does, she doesn't get into as much trouble as her mother usually does.*

<h1 style="text-align:center">Sixteen</h1>

For the third time this morning, my cell phone rang. The name Josh B. and his number on the display confused me. How did he get my cell number? Then I remembered putting his info in my contacts last year when he did some investigating for me. He got straight to the point after I answered.

"Looks like our friend Alex might be in serious trouble."

I started to question how he knew, but he didn't give me time to ask.

"I spoke to Megan earlier this morning."

Here we go again. Just like last time. "For heaven's sake. Don't tell me she asked you to babysit me."

"No, she said you told her I was there and wanted to know what if anything I could tell her about Alex."

"Sorry, I didn't mean to be so defensive. I've been getting a lot of flak from people I know. I did mention to her that you were present when he came to the pantry. By the way, I saw you talking to the deputies before EMS transported Alex. Did they ask why you happened to be there?"

"I'm not sure those particular deputies knew what I do for a living. They asked me what happened and I told them what I knew. Then I left before they could ask any more questions."

"I figured that's why you didn't stick around."

"They most likely ran my name through the system and have found out by now."

"What does that mean as far as your investigation goes?"

"I'll try to stay out of their way. Besides, if Alex is arrested for Celina's murder, the Baums may terminate my contract." He paused. "I got the impression from Megan you don't believe he's guilty. What makes you think he's not?"

"Woman's intuition."

"You know that's not going to fly with the cops or the court. You've seen the guy once."

"Yeah, I know." I sighed. "I feel sorry for him because he went through so much to get to this country. I want to help him."

"I understand how you feel. There was an incident a while back about people packed in the trailer of an eighteen wheeler and some died. That hacked me off. Those coyotes don't have any feelings. All they think about is getting the money."

His anger at those people who prey on the immigrants surprised me. I wasn't expecting his response. I also wasn't expecting to feel comfortable enough to tell him about my conversation with Caroline.

"Sounds like she takes after her mother. Hold on, I'm getting another call...from Miriam Baum. I'll call you back when I find out what's going on."

Josh called back in a few minutes. "Miriam said the sheriff called her and asked if he could come by her house. A backpack had been located and he wanted to see if she could identify the bag."

"I guess that settles it. If she identifies the backpack as Celina's, then Alex will be arrested whenever he can talk. Did Miriam ask you to come to her house?"

"Not right away. She said she would call me after the sheriff leaves and let me know the details. I might be out of a job."

He ended the call with a promise to let me know if the backpack belonged to Celina.

I thought back to the times when I was present at the pantry at the same time as Celina. She did have a backpack in which she kept packs of peanut butter crackers and handed them out to people who stopped by for food. Many times she offered them to children, along with a small candy bar.

If Alex had possession of her bag, he obviously witnessed her being killed and may even have seen her killer...unless he was the killer.

Seventeen

A loud boom of thunder startled me. Was rain forecast for today? I peered out the sliding glass door at the increasing darkness. Huge black clouds loomed overhead. Matthew hadn't returned from his bike ride.

I phoned Renee Hart to see if perhaps the boys returned to her house.

"No, they haven't gotten back yet. Reed knows to come home when the weather gets threatening," she said. "But I don't see them anywhere on the street. We should go look for them before this storm arrives."

"I agree. I'll go up a few streets on the other side of the subdivision to see if I can locate them."

"Good. I'll take this side. Give me a holler if you find them."

Caroline was in her room reading. She looked up when I entered.

"I have to go searching for Matthew and Reed in the car. You'd better come with me. I don't know how long I'll be gone."

She appeared hesitant to stop reading.

"Bring the book with you in the car," I said.

Minutes later we left the house and began the search. I drove up every street on the right side of Cypress Avenue, the main street in our subdivision. No sign of the boys.

My cell phone rang. I stopped the car and answered.

"Did you find them?" Renee's usual calm voice was starting to sound unnerved.

"No, I haven't seen them or their bikes. Do you think they went out of the subdivision?"

"That's possible. Maybe we..." A clap of thunder drowned out her words."

A few large drops of rain splashed on the windshield. Another boom of thunder, a flash of lightning and the bottom dropped out of the sky. Rain poured down so hard I could hardly see past the hood.

Renee and I had been disconnected, but she phoned back. "I spotted them riding down the street from the direction of Richard Road."

"I'm on my way. Matthew's definitely in trouble now."

"So is Reed."

She referred to the road leading out of the subdivision past the grove of trees a short distance behind my house. The land beyond is heavily forested and in some spots marshy, an area I imagined to be full of snakes and other assorted critters. Not a safe place for kids to play. Boys are more adventurous and want to explore, but dangerous is dangerous.

Caroline pretended to be reading, but I saw a 'serves him right' smile on her lips. Her expression reminded me of my own reaction as a kid whenever Steven got into trouble.

The rain had slowed by the time I reached Renee's house in time to see her ushering the boys into her garage along with their bikes. I told Caroline to stay in the car. She happily agreed.

I didn't want to say too much to Matthew while I was so angry with him, but I let him know by the look on my face and the tone of my voice. "I did tell you not to leave our subdivision, didn't I?"

Matthew looked down at the garage floor. "Yes, ma'am, you did."

"Where did you go?"

He glanced at Reed as if asking for backup. Reed stood silent.

"Where did you go?" Renee repeated my question to her son.

"We rode down Richard Road way out to where the woods end," Reed said, shuffling his feet.

"That's way too far away from the house for you to ride," she scolded.

"Aw, it's not that far. Besides, I've been there before and nothing happened."

Renee's eyes widened. "Get in the house now. Stay in the laundry room with those wet clothes and muddy shoes."

He opened the door leading to the laundry room and stepped inside.

I escorted Matthew to the car and made him wait while I put a plastic sheet left over from some gardening purchases on the back seat. Then got his bike and stowed it in the back of the SUV. I should have made him ride his bike back to the house.

Neither I nor the twins spoke on the ride around the corner. I unlocked the door and returned to the car to remove the wet plastic from the seat. By the time I got inside the house, Matthew had gone to his bedroom and even locked the door.

I could understand him being upset with me for reprimanding him in front of his friend, but he and Reed were in the same boat. I've never known him to lock himself in.

"Matthew, unlock the door," I said as calmly as I could manage.

"I'm changing clothes right now."

I decided to back off a little. "Okay, when you're finished, bring your wet clothes to the laundry room. Thank you for leaving your muddy shoes in the laundry room."

"Okay," he answered. "I'll be out in a minute."

Maybe I was jumping to conclusions, but I wondered about his actions. What was the real reason he rushed to his room and locked the door? Could he be hiding something? But what sort of terrible stuff could an eight-year-old boy be hiding in his room? A frog? A turtle? I guessed I'd find out sooner or later. Whatever it was I hope it didn't end up in my room.

Megan's phone call interrupted the musings about my son and his possible hidden treasures. "What's up?" I asked, hoping she'd decided to represent Alex. She had.

"Things have been moving fast. Josh informed me that according to Miriam Baum, the sheriff was headed to the hospital to read Alex his rights."

"Wow, Brad is moving fast. A little too fast, if you ask me. I gather Miriam identified the backpack as Celina's."

"I agree. Miriam also moved too fast, in my opinion. Since she has terminated Josh's contract, he'll be working with me on this case. Her loss is my gain." She paused. I could hear paper shuffling around. "As soon as I can get everything together, I'm going up to the hospital. A local attorney in Cypress Lake has gone up there to make certain Alex doesn't speak to the sheriff."

"Who is the local attorney?"

"Carole Bordelon," she said. "She speaks French and has experience dealing with Haitian immigrants and also some Vietnamese who speak the language. She'll be working with me on his case."

"Great. I'm relieved."

"Don't uncross your fingers yet. I'm not a miracle worker. I'll talk to you later."

Matthew emerged from his room carrying his wet clothes. I noticed he left the door open. Maybe whatever he tucked away in there wasn't alive and able to get loose in the house. Or else I misconstrued his behavior. Somehow I didn't believe I was mistaken. Mother's intuition?

Eighteen

I walked next door to speak to Rachel. Danny was still not back from his support mission for Brad. I couldn't help being sarcastic. I have two role models for the head of a law enforcement agency—Jim and Danny. Brad didn't even come close to either of them.

Granted, Danny no doubt enjoyed his return to law enforcement, but Brad was sheriff now. He should make his own decisions inside of relying on Danny.

Rachel greeted me at the door. "Do you know what's going on?"

"I know a good bit, but I haven't been able to find out more."

"Don't keep me in suspense." She sat at the kitchen table.

I pulled out a chair across from her. "Megan agreed to represent Alex. As she put it, things are moving fast." I relayed the call I received from her about Brad rushing to make the arrest.

Rachel shook her head. "And I accused you of jumping the gun to think his arrest was imminent. Surely Brad doesn't have enough evidence to make an arrest. I hope Danny was able to talk him out of making such an impulsive decision."

"Well, if he can't persuade Brad, the district attorney will decide they do or don't have a case."

"Would you like some coffee? Or how about hot tea?"

"Tea sounds great. I need something to relax me after the crazy morning I've had dealing with eight and nine year old boys who don't follow the rules. Thank goodness only one of them is mine."

She looked more curious than alarmed. "What in the world happened?"

I told her about Matthew's bike ride with Reed Hart and my suspicion about Matthew hiding something in his room."

"Did you ask him?"

"No, I didn't want to accuse him of something he might not have done. After Jim's death, he began acting up. Then for a while he appeared to be dealing with school and summer activities much better. He didn't argue with me when I told him to do or not something. Ever since he came back from Gulf Shores with Steven and Megan, he seems to be regressing."

Rachel looked pensive as if recalling old memories. "My daughter Jessica rebelled for a while after my husband and I divorced. Then when he was murdered, her behavior became worse."

I knew her daughter was from a previous marriage, but she had never mentioned her first husband to me. I hadn't realized he was murdered. "How did you handle all of that?"

"I left my job at the University of New Mexico and moved back to Baton Rouge to be close to my family. My brothers all became surrogate dads to her. We went to several counseling sessions."

"It certainly worked wonders. Jessica turned out great."

Rachel smiled. "Yes she did."

The sound of a vehicle pulling into the driveway alerted both of us. Minutes later Danny came through the door. From his expression, I'm sure I was the last person he wanted to see.

Fatigue mixed with frustration pulled at his face. He joined us at the table. "I think I should have stayed on as sheriff for at least another year. I might have been able to train one of my deputies for the job."

"What did Brad do this time?" I blurted out.

"He's trying too hard to prove himself." Danny shot me a menacing glare. "And if you repeat what I said I'll say you're lying."

I leaned forward in my chair. "Danny, as much as I would love to prove Brad is not up to the job, I'd never repeat anything you said to me in confidence."

He rubbed his hand across his face. "Sorry, I didn't mean to take my frustrations out on you."

"Tell us what happened," Rachel urged. "You were up at the hospital?"

"I won't ask how you guessed that," he said. "I finally talked Brad out of trying to get a warrant to arrest Alex Narcisse in his hospital bed. Possession of Celina's backpack isn't enough evidence to get an arrest warrant. The DA would have denied the warrant anyway and Brad would have looked foolish."

It might sound silly, but hearing Alex's full name seemed to make him more of a real person. As far as Brad being made to look foolish, I wanted to say...have at it. Rachel said it for me, but in a much nicer way than I would have.

"Honey, you aren't responsible for him. Doesn't he need to learn to do the job without your help? There's only so much you can do to keep him from looking foolish."

He exhaled. "You're right. I guess I'm not really retired, am I?"

I couldn't help myself. I wanted to know everything. "So what's going to happen now? Does Alex have an attorney?"

He eyed me with annoyance. "I believe you already know the answer to your second question."

"Megan?"

"And Carole Bordelon. So he's well represented. By the time we arrived at the hospital the two of them were in the room and wouldn't allow him to make any statements."

"I need to go check on the twins. Well...Matthew anyway."

"Is something wrong with the kids?" Danny asked.

I told him about the bike ride episode.

"He seems to have reverted back to his rebellious ways like he did right after Jim's death. His behavior after I found him and took him home was highly suspicious."

"Susan thinks he may have hidden something in his bedroom," Rachel explained.

"Kids these days are a lot savvier than back in the day, but he's a little young to be hiding drugs," Danny mused. "Maybe he caught a frog or a turtle and hid it in his room."

"That was my first thought. When he finally came out of his room, he left the door open."

"Maybe he thinks he's too old to have his mother watch him change clothes," Danny said with a teasing tone."

"Hmm, I never considered that." I thought for a moment. "It seems there's more to it than pre-puberty modesty. Besides, he's a little young for that, too. In a year or two I'll take that scenario into account."

Rachel studied me for a short moment. "You've been on edge lately with everything going on. The anniversary of Jim's death, finding Celina's body, and all this business with the food pantry are enough incidents to give anyone a nervous breakdown. He could be picking up on your distress."

"You might be right. Caroline asked me this morning if I was okay."

"If you suspect Matthew is hiding something in his room, I say find an excuse to go make a search," Danny said.

"I think I will. If nothing turns up, I'll have a long talk with him to see if I can find out what's bothering him. In the meantime I'll try to calm my nerves. Yoga? Meditation?"

As I walked out the door, I heard Danny say to Rachel. "Hon, I think you hit the nail on the head about her nerves."

He didn't know I heard him. I didn't hear the rest of his remarks. However, I agree with the statement. I couldn't figure out how to put a positive spin on all the negative events piling up on me daily.

My psychic friend Taylor Evans popped into my head. I had intended to set up an appointment with her a few days ago, but never got around to doing so. I'll call now and see if she can fit me in. The premonition of a future event bothered me, but I couldn't put my finger on what it would be. That crazy feeling of impending doom. Will there be another murder? Or something from my past coming back to haunt me?

Nineteen

Wednesday, July 29

At nine-thirty in the morning, I left for New Orleans to visit Taylor. One of my usual sitters agreed to come in even though the time was quite early for most teenagers while summer still lingered. This late in the season they wanted to squeeze every minute of sleep out of the short time before school begins in August.

I had managed to locate a photo of me and Celina along with two other volunteers taken at a small get-together not too long after I started volunteering at the food pantry. Taylor would use the picture in her reading. I felt more comfortable seeing her than I would by being analyzed by a psychologist or any other sort of counselor for my shot nerves.

The opinion of most of my friends and acquaintances was always the same whenever I mentioned Taylor, or the idea of seeing a psychic. So-called psychics are out to scam people, they tell me. How could they know all the things they reveal to a person? Their answer: 'Fortune tellers' researched the client on the internet. Everyone knows you can find out anything you want to know about a person by Googling them.

Originally I picked Taylor from the list because she had a normal sounding name. She wasn't Sister Barbara or Gypsy Rose. As it turned out, she didn't even wear a turban, or look into a crystal ball and tell me I was going to come into some money.

Forty-five minutes later I spotted the Superdome from the interstate. The Dome, now known as the Mercedes-Benz Superdome, was a New Orleans icon and home to the beloved Saints football team.

I've always been a football fan, but I secretly hoped Matthew wouldn't play the game. There has been so much concern lately over the serious consequences of head injuries. Of course if he wanted to try out for a team, I probably wouldn't forbid him from doing so. Being a single parent is no picnic.

I turned off at the Poydras Street exit and drove down the ramp to street level. This part of the roadway beneath the elevated highway with its dim lighting even in day time always seemed spooky to me. Good thing I wasn't traveling through here at night. I'd be more of a nervous wreck than I am now.

Driving through the city brought back many memories, some good, a lot bad. How ironic that Jim survived the high crime of New Orleans while serving with NOPD, at the time a notoriously corrupt police department, and then died in a small town that hadn't had a murder in at least five years before we moved to Cypress Lake. His murder was committed by a fellow cop and a childhood friend who was a public official. It was as paradoxical as a soldier who served three or four combat tours in Iraq or Afghanistan, and came home safely, only to be killed in a traffic accident or a drive-by shooting.

Before I realized, I had turned the corner onto Taylor's street. Another New Orleans staple, shotgun houses with their tiny front porches and gingerbread trim, along with the ubiquitous corner grocery store were prevalent in this section of town. Although I grew up in an upper class neighborhood, this older part of the city and the historical buildings of the French Quarter were the New Orleans I loved.

Taylor greeted me at her front door and ushered me back to her office. I settled into a chair in front of her desk, waiting while she conducted her usual study of my aura.

"I feel a lot of negative energy coming from you. Recently many unfortunate events have happened. You have worries about getting involved."

"Yes, I need to figure out what to do in relation to those recent events. Hopefully your insight can put me on the right track."

"You know I can't make a decision for you," she cautioned. "I can only tell you what I see. You have free will to choose your path. I don't need to use my psychic abilities to know you want to investigate a murder. Again, this is a decision for you to make after my reading."

"Understood." In a way her statement disappointed me. I wanted someone's permission to get involved in a murder investigation.

"Tell me a little bit about the event all this negative energy stems from."

"I discovered the body of a murder victim. Her name is Celina Baum. She—"

"No more information," Taylor interrupted.

"I have a photo of her." I pulled the picture from my purse and handed it to her. "She's the one to the left of me."

Taylor placed two fingers on Celina's image. Closing her eyes, she breathed in and out several times. "There are many people, foreigners. They appear frightened. Many are running toward a boat." She paused a long moment. "I see Celina, lying on the ground. There's blood on her. She doesn't appear to be part of the group of foreigners.

"The discovery of her body disturbs you because you know her," Taylor continued. "Your friend is acquainted with her also. The victim wanted to help these people. I see a man, one of the foreigners, kneel down next to her. He picks up what looks like a backpack." She paused again. "He's still kneeling beside her, but something startles him. He runs away into the swamp, taking the bag with him."

Taylor opened her eyes. "That is the incident that bothers you most. The reason you were in the area had something to do with your husband's death."

She always assured me she didn't keep up with crime news, local or national, because many times she worked with law enforcement and didn't want the information to affect her readings. Besides that, the information given out for public consumption was that Celina's body was discovered by fishermen who were never identified. If I hadn't told her I discovered the body she might not have known. She definitely didn't know about Rachel's presence at the scene.

"Did the man who took her backpack shoot her?" I prayed she would say no.

"I couldn't get a picture as to whether he shot her or not. I detected the presence of another person close by. Perhaps this was what startled the man."

"There's another incident—"

"Concerning the same foreign man," she answered before I could finish. She closed her eyes again. "He fell ill from being in the swamp for days. He came to your workplace. He spoke to you."

"Only one word which didn't make sense."

"I'm not picking up anything he said to you. If I had an item that belonged to him or even a photograph of him I might be able to tell you more."

"There's no chance of me obtaining any of his possessions at this point in time."

"I feel there are several other problems troubling you …something closer to home," she said, studying me with her gaze.

I nodded. "My son has started acting out again like he did right after Jim's death." I thought a moment. "I do have a picture of him in my wallet." I retrieved the photo of Matthew and handed it to her.

She placed her index and middle fingers on his photo. Staring at the image, she said, "He's hiding a valuable item in his room. An item he and a friend found by accident. He didn't steal it. You need to find the item before the wrong people discover he has it. This object is somehow connected to the woman's murder."

I shouldn't have been shocked because she knew all this, but I was. Stunned might be a better word, but also terrified about the prospect of my son being in danger. Who were these wrong people? The idea that Matthew had property connected to Celina's murder flooded me with chills.

"You are troubled by a future event, but you have blocked this occasion from your mind because of a painful incident connected to it."

I frowned. "I guess I'll discover what this feeling of impending doom is all about sooner or later."

"There is one other vibration I picked up from you concerning a man who seems to have a connection to the foreign man," Taylor said. "He will appear to have a romantic interest in you, but I feel he's not honest about his feelings."

Twenty

Anxiety and panic made my drive home a grueling trip, mentally and physically. By the time I arrived, my hands ached from gripping the steering wheel so tightly. I sorted through everything Taylor had said, including the painful future event and the man who appeared to have a romantic interest in me. Josh? I would worry about him later. Right now the most pressing item was my son.

My first thought was to rush inside and confront Matthew about his hidden item. Then I took a few deep breaths and recalled Danny's advice. Find an excuse to go make a search.

What could be a better excuse than to put away his freshly laundered clothes? Then if Taylor's prediction turned out to be wrong—which I didn't believe possible—I wouldn't look like an over protective mother and make our relationship worse.

I walked inside and forced a big smile. "I'm back."

Both kids and their sitter looked up from a book she had been reading. I wondered why she was reading to them. They both could read well. Caroline's statement explained the reason. The sitter wanted to make sure the books were returned to the library in one piece.

"Tina checked out some books from the library. This one is a real good story about unicorns."

Matthew grunted. "Unicorns are for sissy girls. They're not real anyway."

"But Matthew," Tina said. "You like robots. Technically they aren't real."

"Yeah, but they're more for boys, and robots and drones are here now. Unicorns won't ever be."

I tried to recall any conversation like this one between Steven and me at the same age. He and I always seemed to be on the same page about our likes and dislikes until we were at least ten. At that age, Steven didn't want me hanging around him and his pals. They wanted to do boy things which they couldn't do with a girl tagging along. Mostly, I stayed home and made up stories I hoped to turn into a book. Of course I had a few girlfriends, along with my cousin Melanie, who would join me for an occasional sleepover at our home or theirs.

"I checked these books out of the library a few days ago," Tina explained to me. "I sat for the Doiron kids night before last. They loved the stories. I thought maybe Matthew and Caroline might also enjoy them.

I paid Tina extra money. She always was the best of all the sitters. After she left, I went into the kitchen to fix lunch for me and the twins. It was all I could do to restrain myself. Finally, I couldn't stand it any longer. This is ridiculous. I should have trusted my own intuition in the first place. I'm the parent and if he has an item in his room that might lead to dangerous consequences, I have to act. Tough tootsies if he gets mad at me.

"Matthew," I said with amazing calm. "There's a matter I need to discuss with you privately in your room."

He frowned. "Are you going to yell at me again about not obeying your rules?"

"That all depends on you."

Once in his room, I closed the door and sat on the side of his bed. I patted the spot next to me. "Come sit with me."

He looked confused and with a lot of caution sat on the bed.

I cleared my throat. "I have to ask you a question. It's very important that you tell me the truth. If I'm wrong about what I'm going to ask, I apologize."

"Okay," he said slowly. "I didn't do anything wrong except not follow your rules."

"We're past your disobedience. There's something else." I eyed him with a stern expression. "Are you hiding anything in your room?"

His eyes widened. "No…"

"Tell the truth, Matthew."

He lowered his head. "Reed told me that the other day he rode his bike over where we went and he saw this man throw something shiny into the swamp. He wanted to see what it was then but he had to be home soon so he left. And he didn't want the man to know he'd seen him. We rode over there and started looking around. That's when we found the gun."

My heart skipped a beat. "Gun! Where is it?"

"It's in the drawer where I keep my jeans."

I rose as calmly as I could manage and went to the drawer he indicated. I didn't see a weapon at first. "Where?"

"I stuck it in those torn jeans you said you wanted to throw in the trash," Matthew explained.

Careful not to touch the gun, I unwrapped the denim bundle. Most likely the gunman's prints and any DNA had been washed off by rain and from sitting in swamp water for days. But Matthew and Reed had both handled the weapon.

A chrome-plated revolver with a black grip lay inside the jeans. Having been in dirty swamp water and wet from the rain, moisture from the gun had soaked the denim. The whole drawer smelled to high heaven.

My visual inspection indicated the weapon wasn't loaded, but I wasn't taking any chances. I left it *in situ*. "Go in the family room and sit. Don't move."

I followed him down the hall and grabbed my cell phone from the lamp table next to my security blanket chair. I punched in Rachel's number. As soon as she answered I spoke. "Is Danny there?"

"Yes, he's right here."

"Tell him to come over now and you too. The item Matthew hid in his room was a gun." I disconnected before she could respond.

I checked out the twins' reaction. Caroline looked worried and confused about what had happened. Matthew stared at me with a frightened expression.

Minutes later Rachel and Danny walked in to the house. Rachel went over to Matthew and sat in a nearby chair. She spoke to the twins in a low voice, words I couldn't hear. She appeared to be consoling them.

"What's going on," Danny asked. "Rachel said Matthew found a gun."

I led him to Matthew's room. "It's in the open drawer."

He studied the revolver for a short moment. "A three-fifty-seven," he said, turning to me. "This could be the weapon that killed Celina."

I hoped Alex's DNA wasn't anywhere on there.

Danny pulled his cell phone from his pocket and keyed in a number. "Brad, you need to get over to Susan's house. We may have the murder weapon... No, it's not what you think."

I could imagine what Brad thought about the idea of the murder weapon ending up at my house. For all I knew he probably figured I went snooping around and kept evidence from him.

"Listen," Danny continued on the phone. "Is Ronnie Hart on duty?...Good, he needs to be in on this...I'll explain when y'all get here."

The thirty minutes it took for Brad and Ronnie to arrive may as well have been three hours.

Brad glared at me as soon as he walked into my house. "What have you been up to now?"

"I haven't been up to anything," I snapped. "Matthew and Reed discovered the gun yesterday when they went bike riding." I glanced at Ronnie. His jaw muscle tightened. "Matthew had it hidden in his bedroom."

Danny motioned to the men and led them to the gun. I didn't follow them. Instead I walked over and sat next to Matthew on the sofa.

"Mom, is the sheriff going to arrest me?" His lip quivered.

"No, but you can expect a lecture. I don't understand why you and Reed didn't tell his dad or even Mr. Danny. Your father told you and Caroline about this. I was sitting right there when he said, 'If you ever find a gun on the ground or hidden in the bushes, tell an adult and leave it where you found it. The police will handle it.' I'm sure Reed's dad gave him and the other kids the same instructions." I glanced at him. "Where did you hide the gun before you put it in your jeans drawer?"

"Under my shirt behind my back."

"What were you going to do with the gun?"

"I don't know. We thought it would be awesome to have a gun like Reed's dad...and mine."

"Honey, your dad was an adult and in law enforcement as is Mr. Ronnie. They are allowed to carry guns."

Ronnie strode out of Matthew's room talking on his cell, his voice concise. "Brad is coming over there to speak to Reed...Yes, without me...I'm going to talk to Matthew...Because we decided it would be better for me not to interview my own son. I'll talk to Reed later."

I assumed he was speaking to his wife, Renee. He was not happy. I tried to imagine how Jim would have handled this situation. I couldn't remember him ever raising his voice while correcting either one of the twins. No doubt he would be angry, but his handling of the situation would have been better than mine. I wondered about Matthew's actions. Would he have even attempted such a thing if Jim were still with us?

<h1 style="text-align:center">Twenty-one</h1>

I was relieved that Brad wouldn't be interviewing Matthew. Ronnie would be more understanding, since he does have children of his own. My reasoning also included the fact that Brad seems to have it out for me so he might transfer his dislike for me to my son.

"Is it okay for Caroline to stay or should she go to another room?"

"If she wants to stay, it's fine." Ronnie smiled at her. "It's up to you."

"I can tell that Matthew doesn't want me to stay," she said. "That's why I am."

Ronnie appeared to force back a laugh. I covered my mouth with my hand.

"Okay, then let me get some answers from you, Mr. Matthew," he said. "Now it's important for you to tell me everything. Understand?"

Matthew nodded.

"Why did you go bike riding way out there to that particular place?"

"Reed told me he saw a man throw something shiny into the swamp, but he couldn't stay to go check it out. So we went back there to look around."

"So y'all found the gun, then what?"

"We decided to keep it. Reed said it would be safer at my house so I took the gun home with me."

"Why did he think the gun would be safer here rather than at his house?"

I suspected Ronnie knew the answer already.

"He said you or his mom might find it."

"But not your mom?"

Matthew made a quick glance at me. "Mom doesn't usually go through my private stuff."

His statement reflected either an indication of his approval of me as a parent, or afforded me the distinction of being a parent who doesn't keep a close eye on her children…or both.

"Anyway it wasn't loaded," Matthew mumbled.

A brief frown flitted across Ronnie's brow. "This gun wasn't loaded, but that's not always the case. I can't count the number of times there's been kids playing with a gun they *thought* wasn't loaded and it turned out there was one bullet in there. In all those times somebody got hurt or killed."

Matthew's eyes widened.

"Do you understand why we're upset about you and Reed handling this gun?" He paused for emphasis and met Matthew's gaze. "Whether it's loaded or not?"

He hung his head. "Yes, sir. Only grownups are allowed to use guns. Kids can get hurt."

"That's always a good reason for someone your age not to fool around with any kind of weapon."

"I'm sorry. I won't do anything like that again."

"Good," Ronnie said, extending his hand. "Shake on it?"

Matthew shook his hand. I could almost hear a sigh of relief coming from him. I suspected he still worried about being arrested.

"One more thing. Do you remember where y'all found the gun? Could you take us there?"

"Yes, sir, I can take you over there."

"Okay, you and I will go pick up Reed and Sheriff Theriot so you boys can take us to the place." He glanced at me. "If that's alright with you."

"Of course, maybe there'll be some other evidence y'all can use." *I hope any new evidence doesn't point to Alex.*

"It would be great if we did." Ronnie added in a low voice, "But I doubt there's too much of a chance for us to find any more evidence."

"Miracles do happen."

He eyed me with suspicion. "Are you praying for a miracle to prove Alex Narcisse is guilty, or that he didn't have anything to do with Celina's murder?"

"The latter," I admitted.

"I heard you made arrangements for him to have an attorney."

"News travels fast around here." I couldn't tell whether he approved or not. "I asked my sister-in-law to represent him. In my opinion, he's being railroaded."

Ronnie didn't respond for a long moment and then said in a low voice that was pretty close to a whisper, "Brad does have a serious case of tunnel vision." He gave a small grimace.

I'm sure he regretted his emphatic statement.

Twenty-two

Thursday, July 30

Everything is back to somewhat normal status today. The gun had been removed from my home and neither twin seemed worse for wear after yesterday's uproar over the weapon.

Ronnie didn't have to worry about me repeating his statement. I didn't plan on telling Brad, that's for sure. I wasn't going to repeat his words to anyone, not even Rachel.

I wondered about Reed's description of the man he saw tossing the gun into the swamp. Was he black, white, or Hispanic? Who was he? Another question came to mind. Did he have any connection to Gallagher Salvage operations?

All those questions raced through my head, plus the subject of Alex's *emeraude*. Either he had emeralds on his person and the stones weren't mentioned by the sheriff's office, or he didn't have the gems on him. Could he have hidden them somewhere in the swamp? Maybe he didn't ever have them, but someone he knew did. More questions and not any answers.

I went into the kitchen to take stock of the groceries on hand and discovered I was out of quite a few items. Grocery shopping looked like my job for this morning. The store might be crowded because some people like to get a head start on Thursday for their weekend get-togethers.

The twins balked at accompanying me to the store, but I managed to get them into the car. Minutes later we were on our way.

I drove past a little strip mall housing a convenience store, a barber shop, and Marie's Diner, an eatery which hardly anyone seemed to frequent. How they were still in business I'll never know.

I did a double take. I could have sworn I saw Brad entering the diner. A black truck was parked outside. Of course quite a few people around here have black pick-ups.

Granted Brad did have the right to eat wherever he chose, but this area had recently become rundown, and the crime rate in this part of town was on the rise. His presence here seemed strange. I suppose he could be talking to an informant.

Who knows? I may be mistaken about who I saw. We passed by so quickly. I shook off further thoughts and concentrated on to the job at hand.

Turning into the parking lot of Four Brothers' Market, I lucked up and spotted a place close to the entrance. As the name implied, the market was owned by four brothers, this store being one of three locations in Allemand Parish. I was determined to go in, buy what I needed and get out quickly.

I achieved my goal. An hour later we left the store with only essentials except for a package of popsicles which was the kids' reward for not bugging me for everything sweet in the store.

On the way back home, I drove past the strip mall again, hoping to verify my sighting of Brad. The black pick-up was no longer parked outside the diner. Guess I'll never know why he was there, or who he met with earlier. Or if the man I saw really was Brad.

With the groceries stored, I walked out to check the mail. As I made my way down the driveway to the street-side box, I recalled the first time I had checked the mail here almost nine years ago. That day I received one of those oxymoronic good rejection letters for a manuscript I had submitted. Good, in that it wasn't a form letter, but an encouraging personal note about my writing style. But it was still a rejection. I smiled at the thought. I now have one published novel to my credit and on the way to finishing another. Not that I won't ever receive another rejection letter in my career, but I hoped it wouldn't be anytime soon.

However, there was a letter in the box, not from an editor, but from the school the twins attended. Two school supply lists were enclosed. Oh, gosh, I forgot about the date. School starts again on August fifth—a week from yesterday. Classes seem to start earlier and earlier every year.

I didn't know whether to be happy for school starting or not. On the one hand, a more structured environment would be good for the twins, especially Matthew, but I hated to think about the possibility he might act out at school.

~ * ~

He answered his cell phone as soon as it rang. The number on the caller ID suggested there could be a problem. This person didn't call unless trouble was imminent.

"I heard they found the gun," his caller said.

His heart raced. He paced back and forth in front of the window, clenching his phone tightly. "What the hell are we going to do now?"

"What do you mean *we*? You're the one who lost the package, among other things."

"Yeah but you're also in this up to your eyeballs. We need to stick together."

"Unfortunately you're right. Our partner is not happy with you at all. I regret getting involved with that guy."

"You and me too." He was surprised to hear the other man admit a mistake. He never liked this so-called partner from the very beginning. "Have the cops confirmed it's the murder weapon?"

"I don't know whether they have or not. Rumor is some kids found it where I assume you tossed it. Susan Foret's son hid the gun in his room."

He didn't like the sound of this development, but tried to make light of the situation. "One good thing, the cops didn't find the package on Narcisse."

"There are three reasons why."

He clenched his jaw. *The SOB always has to show he knows better than me.*

"One, Narcisse wasn't the carrier," the caller continued. "Two, he was, but hid the package somewhere out in the swamp. Three, the cops don't always give away all the details."

"Well, that's just great. Susan Foret should be taught to stay out of business that doesn't concern her."

"I agree, and there's also another person who needs a lesson or two. I'm sure you know who. He's getting a little too close to the truth. Besides that ICE agents have been snooping around here. So no more screw-ups on your account. Do we understand each other?"

"Yeah." He ended the call before he said something he would regret.

Twenty-three

Megan phoned me about two that afternoon. "I'd like to meet with you if you're available."

"Is this to discuss Alex's case?"

"Yes, I have some questions about your encounter with him."

"Sure, when do you want to meet? Can you come by the house?"

She hesitated. "I'd rather meet at a more private location. Can you get a sitter for the twins?"

"I don't think so. I had a hard time locating one on Monday when I unexpectedly had to go to the food pantry. My favorite sitter Tina told me when she last sat with them she would be visiting out of town relatives until a few days before school starts next week."

"Hold on a minute," she said. "Steven's on another line."

I suppose I could get Rachel to watch them for a short time, but I hated to ask her since she took care of them on Monday.

Megan came back on the line. "I have you a sitter. Steven agreed to come and stay with them. In fact he was on his way to see me when he called. He should be there in about twenty minutes."

"Okay, where do you want to meet?"

"At Carole's office. She's letting me use an office while her colleague is on vacation. Do you know how to get to her office?"

"I believe I can find the place. It's on Cedar Street, right?"

"That's it. I'll see you in forty-five minutes or so."

I changed into a nicer blouse than the one I'd worn earlier to go grocery shopping and then freshened my make-up while I waited for Steven to arrive.

Changes in my attire and using cosmetics again began in earnest about three months ago. I realized that Jim wouldn't want me to let myself go. I shook off my self-pity and pulled out of the spiral of depression I had fallen into after his death. While I searched for his killers, adrenaline kept me going, so it was a big letdown after they were all arrested.

My heart skipped a beat. I knew what future event had been making me feel impending doom. I'd soon be required to go to New Orleans for the federal trials. Reliving the trauma will be devastating.

No! I didn't allow those criminals to defeat me then and I won't let them do it when I face them at trial.

Caroline came out of her room when Steven walked in. He had arrived a little sooner than expected to which I teasingly commented, "My goodness, I can't believe you're early."

He feigned an annoyed look. "I can always go back out and wait five more minutes." He pretended to start towards the door.

Caroline giggled. "You can't leave again, Uncle Steven." She tugged on his arm to pull him back. Of course, Steven pretended to give in.

"See, she doesn't mind if I'm early." His expression clouded. "Where's Matthew?"

"He's in his room." My shoulders sagged. "You heard?"

"Megan told me." Steven walked over and hugged me. "I hope you weren't too hard on him."

"I tried not to be, but he knows better than to hide a gun in the house, especially under the circumstances. So he's grounded until further notice. No bike riding or other outdoor activities with his friends and no friends inside either."

Steven nodded in agreement. "I'll try talking to him. I might be able to find out what's going on with him."

"I would appreciate any insight into his thinking."

"Okay you better get moving. Megan's anxious to speak to you about her case."

I left the house and drove toward an older section of town. The area where Carole's office was located had street names of trees, even a Cypress Street, which sometimes led to confusion since the main street in our subdivision held the name Cypress Avenue.

Professionals like attorneys and CPAs had turned old frame or stucco houses on Cedar Street into offices. Not exactly sure of the building's location, I slowed the car until I spotted a shingle identifying the offices of Bordelon, Stanton and LeBlanc, attorneys-at-law. White gravel covered a small space intended for client parking next to the quaint bungalow style house.

Carole had another office in New Orleans as most of her cases tended to be heard in the federal court house there. She was originally from Allemand Parish and continued to maintain this office with her partners Tim Stanton and Sharon Leblanc. On occasion she took on a local case not related to immigration.

Inside the office, Carole greeted me and led me back to the room where Megan had set up her work space. I sat in an upholstered chair close to the desk.

"I take it Steven arrived in a timely manner," Megan said.

"He did." I smiled at what was a family joke. My brother has never been known for arriving on time for anything, including his birth. He was born almost twenty minutes after me. Another ten minutes and we would have different birthdays. "I really appreciate everything you and Steven have done for me and the kids. I would have had to bring them with me." I glanced at Carole. "I know that we wouldn't have any privacy. Caroline overheard a conversation I had earlier with Megan and asked all sorts of questions like 'was Alex a bad man because he came here illegally?'"

"I'm sure you explained everything to her satisfaction," Megan said.

"I must have. When she grows up she wants to help those people."

"Excellent," Carole said, clapping her hands. "The next generation of immigration attorneys is in the works."

We all laughed.

"Okay, let's get down to business," Megan said with authority. "Susan, I'd like to go over what happened the day Alex arrived at the food pantry."

"Josh and I were talking in the office I use there. Sandy Dugas came running in saying my limited French was needed to speak to a man named Alex who stumbled into the compound in bad shape. She had already called EMS. After I saw his condition, I didn't think he would make it much longer. He kept mumbling something that sounded like *emeraude*."

Megan nodded. "I thought that's what you told me. What happened after he mentioned it?"

"He didn't say anything else. I assured him help was on the way. Did he mention *emeraude* to you?"

"He refused to answer after I asked him what he meant."

"I advised him to be completely truthful with us if he wanted our help," Carole said. "I'm not sure I got through to him. He appeared frightened."

"What is his current condition? I tried to find out but no one would give me much information. I asked Danny and he said serious but stable."

"This morning he was much improved. Either Brad or ICE will be arresting him soon, depending on whether there is enough evidence to charge him with Celina's murder."

"The backpack doesn't prove he killed her, that's for sure."

Megan tapped her fingers on the desktop. "It is circumstantial at best, but considering Alex's immigration status, a jury might vote guilty."

Carole snorted. "Of course, you know how all illegal immigrants are murderers and rapists."

"The DA could make it appear as though Alex wouldn't have possession of the backpack unless he killed her and took it from her." I sighed. "And now the murder weapon has possibly been found. The prosecution could make a connection to Alex."

"True," Megan said. "I don't see how they can prove Alex was ever in possession of the gun. I'm certain any fingerprints on the weapon were wiped before it was tossed into the swamp."

"Is there any way for me to speak to Alex? I might be able to get him to confide in me."

Megan exchanged a look with Carole who nodded. "I'll see what I can do."

Carole's cell phone buzzed. She glanced at the display and rose from her chair. "Excuse me, I have to take this. It's another client." She walked out of the room.

"Have you heard whether the gun is the weapon used to kill Celina?"

Megan shook her head. "Not yet. I expect to hear soon."

"I'm sure Brad put a rush on ballistics testing."

She rolled her eyes. "You can count on it. He certainly is anxious to arrest someone for murder."

"He has reprimanded me and warned me about getting involved in the case. But I feel I'm already caught up in it. Rachel and I discovered Celina's body. Alex showed up on a day I wasn't supposed to be at the pantry. Now Matthew had the possible murder weapon hidden in his room. I'd say it's fate."

"This is not to encourage your involvement, but it's beginning to look like fate." She studied me with her gaze. "You will be called on to testify if he's charged with murder."

Butterflies flitted around in my stomach. "I may be in for continuous court visits then."

She widened her eyes. "Oh, trials for the men who killed Jim…is that soon?"

"Yes, I'll have to check my paperwork for the exact date. They postponed the trial once already. Seems like the date is sometime in September. I'm not looking forward to having old wounds reopened."

~ * ~

Jill Doucet's phone rang. The number on the display indicated her husband Mike was the caller. "Hey, where are you?"

"Can you talk?"

She glanced around the room. Claire was in her collection room. Marcie didn't seem to be around, but she could be lurking in another room listening to every word. "I'm going to walk outside to make sure the two you-know-whos can't eavesdrop."

"Good idea," he said. "Have you seen Rick this morning?"

"No, but I heard his truck leave about an hour ago." She walked down the front steps and down the path toward the driveway. "Okay, tell me where you are."

"I'd rather not say over the phone. I'll be home in about thirty minutes so I'll fill you in on how things went."

"I'll be glad when this is over."

"Soon, hon," he said. "How'd your meeting go with Claire?"

"Nothing out of the ordinary. She chewed me out again for allowing Susan Foret access to the house. I don't know what set off her alarm this time. She already called me on the carpet for the incident right after I allowed Susan to come inside."

"You ought to know Claire by now after all these years. She's so worried about outsiders learning about her collection."

"You mean her ill-gotten gains? But you and I are privy to how she obtained those items. Her obsession with the damn emeralds and that shipwreck are going to be the death of her and us too."

"Don't worry. We're going to be alright. I hate to turn on Claire, but I have to think about us and our future son or daughter. You need to stay calm for the baby's sake."

She placed her hand on her stomach. Anything could happen in the next seven months, especially for a forty year old woman in her first pregnancy. Her heart raced at the thought.

~ * ~

"I've been trying to get hold of you." Brad eyed the undercover agent from across the table at Marie's Diner. "Your boss Agent Gorman and his partner Jackson came to see me."

Holden took a swallow of his coffee, and then leaned closer. "He's not my boss. Somebody higher up on the chain is who I report to. In fact we're working on different cases. Those two might mess up mine. So why did Gorman call you in?"

"He informed me that Mike Doucet had agreed to cooperate with them on their case against the Gallaghers. They told me to back off from the Baum murder investigation. They've taken custody of Narcisse.

"According to them, their case was much bigger and more important because it involved international affairs, the murders of American citizens, and smuggling of jewels and other artifacts as well as illegal immigrants. I figured they referred to the attack on Claire Gallagher's boat among other things." Brad studied him, anxious to hear his response.

He rubbed the five o'clock shadow on his face for a long moment before answering. "You figured right. What'd you tell them about backing off?"

"I told them I would unless I saw they were fixing to deport Narcisse without trying him for murder. He's guilty of Celina's murder and he probably hid those emeralds he was carrying down in the swamp somewhere."

Holden nodded. "No doubt. But unless he tells somebody where he hid them there's no chance of locating the jewels."

"Well, he's not talking. I thought he might have buried them around the spot where he tossed the gun, but we couldn't find anything. I wouldn't put it past Susan to have the stones in her possession." He waved his hands angrily. "I mean, look, her son had the gun hid in his room."

Brad left the diner angry with himself for his stupid remark about Susan. She didn't have any reason to hold on to those emeralds if she had found them. She might be too curious for her own good, but she wasn't crooked. In hindsight, he was beginning to wonder about Holden's statement. If he's working a different angle, seems like there ought to be more coordination within ICE.

This case was not going the way he wanted. If he couldn't prove beyond a shadow of a doubt Narcisse killed Celina, he would be stuck in this backwoods forever.

Twenty-four

The meeting at the law office had drained me. The thought of appearing in court to face those men who killed Jim, plus the present situation with Alex, sapped my strength. A cup of espresso or even a latte could put some energy back in me.

A new coffee shop had recently opened its doors in town. I decided to stop by and check out the place. Coffee Heaven—a cutesy name—was located on Main Street not far from City Hall. I had reservations about driving past another place which held so many memories, but I had avoided it as long as I could. The last time I saw Cypress Lake City Hall was over a year ago. Today I drove past the building as fast as I could legally do so.

Inside the coffee shop, I inhaled aromas of fresh brewed coffee and sugary treats that reflected the business' name—Heaven. To me coffee and a doughnut or sweet roll seemed like perfect comfort food.

I ordered a latte and selected a sweet roll covered with white icing from the glass-fronted counter at the register. A booth next to the window was empty so I slipped onto the green vinyl seat with my order.

After taking a sip of the hot latte, I savored a delicious bite of the roll. As I finished eating, I remembered I should have told Megan about my visit to Claire Gallagher's home and the conversation between Lucie and Octave.

I left the shop with a second latte in a to-go cup, planning to drive back by Megan's office and fill her in. I stopped to pull my phone from my purse and started to key in her number.

Out of the corner of my eye I saw a man walking toward me, a cell phone in his hand. I didn't pay too much attention to him until he walked straight into me.

My coffee cup and phone launched out of my hand. Coffee splattered on the sidewalk. My phone ended up in the grass next to the concrete. I would've followed coffee and phone to the ground if he hadn't grabbed me.

"I'm sorry, ma'am," he said with a heavy Southern drawl. "Are you okay?"

"I think so," I said, mentally checking myself. "But my coffee isn't. Oh, there's my phone."

"Here, I'll get it." He bent over and retrieved the phone. Handing it to me, he added, "Let me buy you another cup of coffee."

"That's not necessary. That was my second cup. I probably didn't need more caffeine anyway."

"Come on. It's the least I can do for being a distracted walker."

His drawl and gorgeous blue eyes made it hard for me to refuse his offer. "Okay, let's go back inside."

He opened the door and stepped in behind me. Two women seated at a nearby table eyed him boldly. I had to admit he was good looking and that five-o'clock shadow positively sexy.

At the register, he paid for another latte for me and ordered a cup of coffee for himself. I asked for mine in another to-go cup.

"By the way, my name is Jack Holden." He smiled and his expression suggested I should tell him mine.

"Susan Foret."

"Would you care to sit awhile?"

Fast mover, this guy. I think I'll pass. "Sorry, but I was headed to an appointment. Thanks for the coffee."

He looked disappointed, but nodded. "Again, I apologize for running into you, but not sorry I met you."

My laugh sounded nervous even to me. He was very attractive and charming, but I felt guilty about thinking so.

My car felt like an oven after sitting in the sun. Heat build-up doesn't take long in ninety-five degree weather. I put the air conditioner on full blast and drove back to Megan's office.

The small parking lot had available space for four vehicles. There were presently three. In light of the close quarters, I decided to park on the street across from the office.

After locking my car I started to cross the street. A black pick-up truck seemed to appear out of nowhere heading straight for me. The deer-in-the-headlights syndrome came over me. I couldn't move. My heart raced. The driver wasn't slowing down. *Move! Get to the office.*

I heard a scream. My adrenaline kicked in. I scrambled across the street, ending up on the curb. The truck sped away with tires screeching.

I lay on the sidewalk with eyes closed trying to slow my pulse and my breathing. Seconds later I heard voices both male and female.

"Susan, are you hurt?" I felt a hand on my shoulder.

I opened my eyes to see Josh stooped beside me. "I don't think so."

He helped me to my feet. "What happened? We heard your scream and tires squealing."

My scream? At the time I didn't realize the sound came from me.

"Black truck...tried to run me over," I panted.

"Come inside," Megan said, leading the way up the front steps. "Do you want me to take you to the ER?"

"For heaven's sake, no," I insisted. "I'm not hurt except for a couple of scrapes on my hands. I'm shook up...and mad. Staring at the front grill of a truck is not fun."

"You should call the cops." Josh said. "They won't be able to do anything without a license number, but a report will be on file."

I thought a moment. This happened in the city limits. "Okay, I'd rather talk to Cypress Lake PD than Brad's crew."

Josh nodded in agreement. I phoned the police station and asked for Ken Wallace, who held the position of chief. He had worked for Jim for several years and was of considerable help to Danny in apprehending Jim's killers and rescuing me from their clutches. I trusted him.

"Someone tried to run me down and almost made it. The driver left the scene. I'm not hurt, but I want to file a report." I told him my location.

"I'll be over there in fifteen minutes," Ken said.

The chief arrived with Toby Hahn, another officer who had worked for Jim during his tenure as chief. Despite the fact Toby was in his late twenties, he looked like a teenager. He probably didn't seem like much of a threat to the bad guys with his cherubic face. According to Jim, Toby's innocent look was a great advantage to his crime fighting skills.

We all settled in a conference room down the hall from the three private offices. I sat across the table from him and Toby. The others gathered around in the remaining seats except for Josh who moved his chair back against the wall. Guess he wanted a full view of the group.

Ken's nickname 'Bulldog' had a double meaning. His short stocky frame and his square jaw with a slight overbite resembled his namesake, but his resolve in going after criminals also brought to mind the tenacity of a bulldog.

"Tell me exactly what happened."

I provided the details. "Sorry I couldn't get a license number." I glanced at the others. "Did anyone else?"

Negative responses came from the group.

"The truck had disappeared by the time we ran outside to see what had happened," Josh said. A frown creased his brow. He looked disgusted, most likely at himself for not being fast or vigilant enough. As I recalled from our past association, he was proud of his skills as an investigator.

"Can you describe the truck?" Toby Hahn asked.

"The truck was a black GMC. I'm positive of that, but I couldn't tell you the model. It looked fairly new."

"What about the driver?"

I shook my head. "With the windshield tint so dark, I couldn't tell what he looked like."

Toby looked up from the notebook he had been writing in. "You referred to the driver as 'he.' You believe a man drove the truck?"

"I suppose the driver could be a woman. But I don't know of any women who have it out for me."

Ken almost smiled. "Maybe the driver didn't have a grudge against you. He or she could have been intoxicated and left the scene to keep from being arrested."

"The driver might have been drunk. However, I'm certain he or she sped up intentionally when I started across the street."

Ken turned to Toby. "Check out the neighboring offices and see if anyone else could give us more information."

Toby rose from his chair and smiled. "It's good to see you again, Ms. Foret. Sorry it's under these circumstances."

"Thanks Toby, good to see you too." *My circumstances always seem to be a bad occasion when it comes to speaking to police.*

Twenty-five

"Was there a reason you returned to the office?" Megan regarded me with a curious look as did the others.

I suddenly had second thoughts about revealing my visit to the Gallagher place. However, I couldn't very well blow off the question. "There was something I thought might be related, but maybe not."

"Tell me anyway. We can use all the help we can get."

"There was an odd incident at the reception after Celina's funeral. I was speaking to Willow, Celina's sister when a man came into the room." I furnished the details concerning Willow's reaction to this man and Brad's identification of Kenny Verrett as a former diver with Gallagher Salvage.

Megan looked at Josh. "What do you think? Could he be related to Celina's murder?"

He pursed his lips and nodded. "It's possible. Of course, this guy could be an ex-boyfriend of Willow's as the sheriff suggested. It can't hurt to check him out, though."

"Now that all the excitement is over for the day, I'm going to go home and relieve Steven of his babysitting duties."

"Be careful," Megan said. "I'll call to let him know you're on your way."

Josh insisted on following me home. He wouldn't take no for an answer. I could be accused of distracted driving, but as I drove toward my house, my thoughts turned to Taylor's reading. Is Josh the unnamed man to whom she referred?

He hasn't actually expressed any romantic interest in me. If so, I couldn't imagine what ulterior motive he could have for pretending to have feelings for me. Maybe I hadn't met this man yet. Or Taylor could be mistaken about the whole business. There was no man.

Jack Holden suddenly came to mind. No, meeting him was a one-time deal—merely a pleasant episode designed by a Higher Power to make me feel like I was still attractive to men.

When I pulled up in my driveway and exited the car, I waved an invite for Josh to come inside, but surprisingly he declined. So much for appearing to have a romantic interest in me.

My thoughts turned to Jim. I felt guilty for even thinking about relationships with other men. If I did start to date again, how would I explain another man to the twins? Would they accuse me of being disloyal to their father?

Later in the evening after the kids were in bed, I tried to figure out why I changed my mind about telling Megan and the others of my suspicions about the immigration status of O.J. and Lucie.

What exactly did Gallagher Salvage do? Salvage operations usually recovered ships that had sunk or were damaged beyond repair. Was the Gallagher family working on a business operation when the pirates boarded their boat? Or was the family on a pleasure trip to the Caribbean?

I went to my computer to search for any newspaper articles about the incident. It would have happened before we moved to Cypress Lake. So that would be at least nine years ago. Considering the prominence of the family in Allemand Parish, I had to assume there would have been local newspaper coverage even if it was merely about the funeral. There could have also been television coverage on one or more New Orleans stations.

According to an article from the *Cypress Lake News*, the attack on the Gallaghers' boat occurred on July 23, 2007. So the visit I witnessed at the cemetery by Claire and her sons marked the ten year anniversary of the incident.

According to the article, the family was on a diving trip off several uninhabited islands south of Jamaica. There was no indication whether they were in search of a sunken ship to salvage as part of a business deal, or not. The craft they were on was listed as being a twenty-five footer which didn't seem large enough for a salvage operation. But what do I know about salvage? Hardly anything. I read further down the article which stated the pirates allegedly boarded the vessel and shot Claire and her husband, disabled the boat and waited for her sons to surface from their dive.

Curiously, Gary Gallagher was shot and killed upon boarding the boat. Maybe I'm reading in between the lines incorrectly, but it sounded like Gary went on board alone. Didn't he realize something was wrong?

Mike Doucet came away uninjured. Where was he when his brother was shot? It seems Mike fixed whatever mechanical problem the pirates had caused and managed to get Claire to a hospital in Kingston, Jamaica.

If I had been investigating this attack, I would have a lot of questions for Mike. It seemed strange the pirates didn't shoot him too. I thought these modern-day pirates were ocean versions of carjackers. Why didn't they take the boat instead of simply disabling it?

I looked up the Gallagher Salvage web site. A short history of the business was listed. The company, originally named Duplessis Marine Salvage, belonged to Claire's father, Robert Duplessis. Upon his death, the business passed to Claire and her husband, Walt, and they changed the business name to Gallagher Salvage.

Whoa! Wait a minute. A bio of Robert Duplessis included in the company history stated he loved to search for sunken Spanish galleons. He claimed he unfortunately never located any of those jewel-laden ships.

I recalled reading articles about so-called treasure hunters who discovered galleons sunk in the Caribbean and recovered immense riches. Emeralds were commonly in the cargo, along with gold, silver, and other jewels from the New World.

Could there be a story or video on a New Orleans television station in their archives that I might be able to view? I doubt a person like me who has no official connection to the story would be allowed to look at any such video…but Remi Granger would. Also I was certain Rachel knew more details about what happened from local talk.

I couldn't do anything this late tonight. Tomorrow is another day.

Twenty-six

Friday, July 31

The next morning I phoned Rachel and invited her over for coffee. She knocked on the door a few minutes later. I waved her inside.

She appeared upset. "Why didn't you tell me about almost being run down in the street?"

"How did you find out?"

"Steven called me this morning and asked me to check on you. I was getting ready to come over here when you called."

"I swear Steven is becoming an old lady. I'm perfectly fine."

"He wants to make sure you're okay. Don't be mad at him."

"I'm not mad, I'm annoyed. Come sit down and I'll tell you all about it."

I filled two mugs with coffee and brought them to the kitchen table. Seated next to her, I wrapped my hands around the warm cup. Thinking about the incident chilled me to the bone. I would have preferred to block the close call from my mind.

"Okay, tell me what happened," she said, her voice stern.

"Megan asked me to come to Carole Bordelon's office to talk about the day Alex came to the food pantry." I delivered a brief rundown of my interview with the two attorneys. "I left and went to get a latte at the new coffee shop by City Hall. I remembered another piece of information I should have told Megan and decided to return to the law office." By leaving out the part about Jack Holden, I felt like a school girl keeping secrets from her mother.

"So you went back and that's when the truck almost hit you?"

"Yes, their small parking lot next door was almost full so I found a space on the street across from the office. The driver never slowed down. In fact I believe he or she sped up. I barely made it across the street."

"I understand you called CLPD and Ken came with Toby to take a report."

I took a swallow of coffee. "That's about it. I have no idea who would try to kill me unless a family member of one of those who murdered Jim has it out for me for trying to send their loved ones to prison."

Rachel grimaced. "That's a scary thought."

"I'm fine now. I wasn't hurt, so let's drop the subject. There's something I am curious about and thought you might know more details than what was in the newspaper article."

She arched a brow. "I almost hate to ask, but what is it?"

"What can you tell me about the attack on the Gallaghers' boat? Was there any suspicion that Claire's or her son's account of the incident didn't happen exactly as they said?"

Rachel reflected on my question for a long moment. "There was some skepticism among the Jamaican police and local law enforcement here considering the fact Mike was uninjured and the boat wasn't stolen."

"My thoughts exactly when I read the newspaper account. Didn't the Jamaican authorities follow up on their suspicions and investigate?"

"Local gossip suggested Claire paid them off in order for her and Mike to be able to leave the country. She needed more extensive medical care than could be provided there. I guess she didn't want to stick around for all the red tape involved in an investigation. Eventually the case went cold; the attackers were never found."

I shrugged. "That stands to reason if they were your run of the mill pirates."

She looked at me inquisitively. "Why are you pursuing a ten year old event? Do you believe the Gallaghers have a connection to Celina's murder?"

I nodded. "I believe there is a link, but it's nothing I can pinpoint. I detected an aura of animosity when I saw them at the cemetery."

Rachel confirmed my feeling with a nod of acknowledgement. "According to people who know the family, Claire and Rick have been at odds a lot since the incident on the boat. And also bad blood between Rick and Mike."

"Rick wasn't with them?"

"No, he doesn't care about boats or the salvage business."

"I don't see how Mike came away uninjured. Maybe Rick feels the same suspicions I do about the account given by Claire and Mike.

"Quite possible," she said. "Rick may believe his brother and father were not killed by ordinary pirates. But could he truly suspect his own mother and/or his half-brother had something to do with the murders of Walt and Gary?

"The idea of people killing other family members has been around since time began. Remember Cain and Abel."

Twenty-seven

I peered out the kitchen window at the sound of a car door slamming. Megan walked around the front of her silver BMW toward my front door. She looked so cool and professional in her black skirt, long-sleeved white blouse and black heels complete with hosiery. I would be dripping with sweat in this heat. I unlocked the door and greeted her before she could ring the bell.

"You could have come through the side door like most people I know," I teased. "You're family."

She looked amused. "I'm here on official business so I decided to be formal."

"Official business? Is this about Alex's case?" I ushered her inside and into the family room.

Seated on the sofa, Megan took a sheet of paper from her briefcase and handed it to me. The note, written on Allemande Parish Sheriff's Office letterhead, allowed me to enter the hospital room of Alex Narcisse and speak with him for twenty minutes.

"I made arrangements for you to speak to him in his hospital room this afternoon at two. I hoped for a longer time, but didn't want to push my luck. He didn't want you involved at all."

I widened my eyes. "I can't believe Brad agreed to my visit. How did you get him to allow me access?"

"All I can say is what happened was strange."

"Strange?"

"I tried to convince him that you had gained Alex's confidence when he came to the food pantry. I felt like you would be able to get through to him to tell the truth. Of course he was skeptical because what I was asking would be the prosecutor's job to prove his guilt." Her tone of voice displayed her annoyance.

I forced a laugh. "I can imagine what he said to that."

"He turned my request down flat."

"Wait...he said no? I'm confused."

"This is where the strange part comes in," she said. "I left his office and was almost out of the building when he came running after me. He said he'd been hasty in his decision."

"So you went back to his office and he provided you with what amounts to a hall pass for me." Something didn't seem right about this. I said as much.

She looked thoughtful for a long moment. "I don't know whether this has any connection to his change of heart or not. When I left the first time, his phone started ringing. I didn't think anything about it."

"You think what or who changed his mind might be related to his phone call?"

"Something did," she said.

After Megan left, I couldn't help thinking about Brad's actions, today and in the days since Celina's murder. Why was he so intent on keeping me from having any connection to this case? Someone must have advised Brad to change his mind about allowing me access to Alex. But who was the person who had such influence over Brad?

Danny's advice to me about being careful when dealing with Claire and Gallagher Salvage came to mind. Depending on what their suspected activities were, a government agency could be keeping an eye on them. Hiring undocumented immigrants was against the law, but two undocumented employees didn't seem like a serious enough crime to warrant this much interest from immigration and customs agents.

I dismissed all my questions and concentrated on the meeting with Alex. I hated to admit that this venture might be for nothing. My contact with him had been about thirty minutes at the most and for the majority of the time he remained in a semi-conscious state. He might not remember me at all. I may have gotten in over my head by asking to talk to Alex. If I ask the wrong questions, my interview with him could make him more determined not to talk.

Perhaps Brad had the right idea about keeping me from injecting myself into this murder case. I shook off my self-doubt and concentrated on bettering my poor French language skills.

Speaking of French, now that I think about it, Alex seemed to understand pure French and not a local patois. Although I did recall Sandy remarking that he spoke in a French dialect she couldn't understand. I suppose his delirious state might have made his speech garbled.

Enough of these mind boggling thoughts. I needed to find a sitter for the twins. Luckily Tina had returned from out of town and agreed to stay with them for a couple of hours.

About one-thirty, Tina arrived and I left to meet Megan and Carole at the hospital. I dreaded entering the place where I had witnessed life slip away from Jim. I braced myself against a flood of bad memories.

According to the arrangement with Brad, I could go in without the attorneys, another odd element of this scenario. Could they have the room bugged? That's crazy and I think might also be illegal. Guess I am being paranoid.

Alex lay in bed facing the window. Probably wishing he were out there instead of in the hospital with one arm handcuffed to the rail. He looked up when I closed the door behind me. A frown creased his forehead.

Disappointment set in. *He doesn't remember me.* "Alex, *je suis* Susan."

A flicker of recognition showed in his eyes. "I thought you were a figment of my imagination," he said in slightly accented English. "It was your voice that calmed me."

Surprised, I wondered if Megan and Carole knew he spoke English. "Even with my terrible French?"

"Your French was not so bad." He managed a brief smile.

I took a seat in a chair next to the bed. "You look a lot better than the first time I saw you. How are you feeling?"

"As well as can be expected under the circumstances, physically, but otherwise…" He averted his gaze for a short moment. "My situation is tenuous at best."

"Tell me about yourself. Are you from Haiti?"

He hesitated a while before answering. "I was born there."

His answer piqued my curiosity. I didn't know what he had revealed to the attorneys, so I ad-libbed. "You speak English well. Any other languages besides French and English?"

"The island dialect."

"The dialect of Haiti?" I asked.

He continued with a short answer like the ones before. "Yes, Haiti." He eyed me with caution. "The attorneys have asked you to get information from me?"

"I won't lie to you. Both attorneys and I only want to find out what actually happened out there when the woman Celina Baum was shot. A friend of mine and I are the ones who discovered her body. The place is the same spot where my husband was killed a year before her murder."

"I am sorry about your husband," he said softly.

"Thank you." I didn't want to dwell on Jim's death. I don't know why I even brought up the subject. I continued my attempt to get him to tell me what happened. "Were you alone out there?"

"I did not kill the woman."

I glanced at my watch. My allotted time would soon be up. "Unless you tell us exactly what happened, we can't help you."

"You are a very nice lady and the two attorneys are also nice, but I don't see how I can be helped. They work with the laws." Despair in his voice was evident. "If I am found guilty of murder I will go to prison for life. If not, I will be deported."

Not much of a choice, I admit. I wasn't ready to give up yet. "Can you tell me about *emeraude*?"

He shook his head. "What I know will make my situation worse." His voice shook. "No more questions, please."

"I have one more question. Do you have any relatives in this area?"

His face blanched. "No." He turned away from me. I wouldn't be getting any more information.

"Good bye, Alex. I didn't mean to upset you, but I wish you well." I rose from my seat and walked toward the door, hoping he would call me back. He didn't.

I exited the room feeling glum. Guess I'd never make it as an interrogator. I nodded to the deputy who guarded the room. He acknowledged my action with a half-hearted wave of his hand.

Megan and Carole were nowhere in sight so I started walking down the hall. I spotted them seated in the waiting room.

"I gather from your expression you didn't get far," Megan said.

"You're right. He wouldn't give me any information." I glanced from Megan to Carole. "There's something I need to tell you… something I started to reveal to you at your office."

"You mean when you returned later?" Carole asked.

I nodded.

"I need to speak to Alex first," Megan said. "While you were in his room, the doctor told us he would be released from the hospital in the morning. After I return, we can go back to the office where we can speak in private."

"Before you go to his room, I have a question. Did you know he speaks English fluently with only a slight accent?"

Both attorneys exchanged a look of surprise.

"I thought he might understand a great deal, but every time I asked him a question, he looked confused. Carole would translate into French and back to English for me. He never really offered any information about how he got into the country or anything else or that he could speak English. A lot of vague answers were all we got. I will have to fuss at him for not letting on." Megan looked pleased. "You did good."

"Personally I think he spoke English to me because my French is so awful."

"Quit," Carole said. "You can't be that bad."

Megan smiled. "We'll discuss every detail of your conversation later at the office." She turned and walked off down the hall.

As I watched her converse briefly with the deputy, I wondered if Alex's possible residency in Martinique could provide a way out for him. That is, if he lived there legally or even at all. He might not be related to Lucie or O.J. A question for Carole to answer.

Twenty-eight

I studied the faces of Carole and Megan seated across the conference table at the law office. Josh took up his usual position away from us against the wall facing the door. I guess he liked having a good view of everyone and also never with his back to the door.

"I'm sorry I couldn't get any more information from Alex."

Don't worry about it," Megan said. "Usually my clients are all too happy to tell me every detail about their lives. Not him."

Carole creased her brow. "I understood from his conversations with us he was Haitian."

"I asked him if he was and he told me he was born there."

Megan's lips set in a hard line. "It was too much to hope for to have him tell you exactly how he arrived here, or who ferried him to Louisiana."

"I asked him about *emeraude*. He said, and I quote, 'What I know will only make my situation worse.'"

"That's a lot more than we ever got out of him," Carole said. "Maybe we should let Susan interview him from now on."

I shook my head. "I doubt he will open up to me anymore. We left on sort of a sour note."

"How so?" Megan asked.

"First I need to tell you what I started to reveal before. It's relevant to the way my meeting with him ended."

Carole gave a brief wave of her hand. "Okay, go on."

I had to wonder if she was unhappy about my semi success with her client, but I shelved the idea for the time being.

"About a month after I started volunteering at the food pantry, a couple, the Celestines, who supposedly were from Martinique, came in to our compound. They spoke nothing but French. My skill at the language is pretty limited, but if you can believe this, there are only a few people at the pantry can speak French on any given day. I was called upon to try to converse with them. I managed to figure out their needs.

"Right after Celina's murder, a friend asked me if I knew what had happened to those people," I continued. "I found out they had been hired by Claire Gallagher so I decided to stop by the Gallagher place and see how they were doing." I relayed the rest of the story to the group.

Carole leaned toward me. "So you believe this couple is really from Haiti, but used false identification papers indicating they were from Martinique."

"I believe they have a connection to Haiti, hence the mention of the *Macoutes*."

Megan pointed her index finger at me. "Did you mention this couple to Alex?"

"I asked if he had any relatives in this area. His face turned white. He said an emphatic no and turned his back on me. That's how we ended our conversation."

"Who is this friend who asked you about them?" Josh finally spoke.

"I'd rather not bring this person into the mix for now." I didn't want Rachel involved. If I disclosed her name they would want to know why she was asking. That might end up with me revealing Danny's warning about the Gallagher operations. I doubt he'd be happy if I divulged information that might compromise any ongoing investigation, if there was one. Suddenly I felt torn between the two sides of the law, prosecution and defense.

I steepled my fingers, keeping my elbows on the table. "Carole, I have a scenario to put forth. I want to know what would happen if…" I eyed the immigration attorney with caution. *She'll probably think I'm naïve or insane.*

She arched both brows. "If what?"

"Let's say either Lucie Celestine or her husband is related to Alex and for some reason they had become legal residents of Martinique. If their papers are valid and they arrived legally, there would be no problem with their being here, right?"

Carole nodded.

"What if Alex was also a legal resident of Martinique and if it's proved he didn't murder Celina, is there any possibility he would not be deported?"

"There are a lot of ifs in your scenario. First part regarding the Celestines." She held up one finger to stress her point. "If all that is correct, there should be no problem." Then two fingers. "Second part concerning Alex's status, the fact remains he obviously came to the US illegally. As far as we know, he didn't have any kind of identity papers on him. It might be possible to deport him back to Martinique instead of Haiti if we can prove the former was his last legal residence."

I tried to mask my disappointment with a half-smile. Megan wasn't fooled.

"I know you want to help him, but his choices are limited. First things first, we have to prove he didn't shoot Celina. And we can't help him if he doesn't tell us exactly what happened and how he arrived in Allemand Parish."

"Defense attorneys try to give a jury evidence to suggest reasonable doubt. My belief is that in order to prove a person is not guilty you have to find the real killer."

"That's not always possible." Megan's voice brimmed with exasperation. "From what I understand the murder scene may have been a drop site for undocumented immigrants. Any one of dozens of people could have shot her. They have all scattered to who knows where."

I wanted to continue arguing my point by telling her she wouldn't be married to my brother if I hadn't fought to find Anne's killer. It was extremely childish of me to even think about voicing those thoughts. I'm too wrapped up in this. It was time for me to go home to my kids.

I rose from my seat. "I'm going to head back to my house if there's nothing else to discuss."

"Susan," Megan said. "Don't…"

"I'm not angry or anything like that," I interrupted. "I need a break from thinking about murders. We'll talk later."

Josh followed me out to my car. "You really get wrapped up in these cases, don't you?"

I heaved a sigh. "Yes, I do when I believe in the person's innocence. Maybe if I quit discovering bodies, I could concentrate on fictional murder victims."

He placed his hand gently on my arm. "This is easier said than done, but try to relax and not think about this case. Megan and Carole are doing everything they possibly can do legally."

"I know they are." My shoulders sagged. "Ever since the anniversary of Jim's death and discovering Celina's body, I've been a wreck, snapping at everyone and not being a very nice person. That's probably why Brad doesn't like me."

Josh frowned. "What do you mean he doesn't like you?"

I tried to play down the significance. "Oh, every time I come in contact with him, he starts in on me about sticking my nose into his investigation."

He shook his head. "Sounds to me like he feels threatened by you."

"I told him something similar. It didn't go over well."

"Good for you," he said. "By the way, he knows about me working with Megan on Alex's defense. I'm not exactly his favorite person either. He's a…well, my name for him isn't nice for use in mixed company."

He made me smile with his remark.

"I'm glad to see you smile," he said. "Now go home and relax. Take a long soak in a tub full of bubble bath and drink a glass of wine."

"Actually that sounds wonderful. Thanks for the idea."

"I aim to please."

His voice sounded a bit husky. I wondered if he pictured me...and him in this romantic scenario. And did I like the idea myself?

The bubble bath and glass of wine would have to wait a little while longer for me. I decided to stop by the cemetery and visit Jim. I wished it were possible to really speak to him.

Twenty-nine

The peacefulness of the cemetery quieted my thoughts as I strolled along the sidewalk leading to the mausoleum. My spirits sank when I spotted the drooping gerbera daisy on Jim's vault. The plant needed water badly. I chided myself for never returning to take care of that. Hopefully it wasn't too late to save it.

The cemetery management preferred artificial flowers on the vaults. The reason seemed obvious. They didn't want dead flowers sitting in plain sight, not to mention dirty water dripping on the clean marble.

Removing the plant from its holder, I looked around for one of the water faucets for use of cemetery clients and located one nearby. After flooding the pot with water I dug around in my purse and managed to find a travel pack of tissues to wipe up the dripping water. *I'll bring it home and replace these flowers with artificial ones.*

I took a seat on a concrete bench facing the vaults. Staring at Jim's name carved in white marble, I tried to focus on relaxing for a while. Despite my effort to clear my mind, a slide show of thoughts and images raced through my head. So much for my meditation technique.

Jim, I need help. Foolish me, he can't help me. I'm on my own and if I don't get it together soon I'll end up having a complete breakdown.

I suddenly had the feeling of someone watching me and checked out the surrounding area. Jack Holden strolled toward me.

He grinned. "I'm not stalking you, I promise."

"Are you sure about that?"

"Well…maybe a little," he drawled. "I happened to be driving by and saw you turn in here. I wasn't going to disturb you, but you looked up and saw me."

His reason for being here seemed a little contrived. I looked around and saw a black pick-up parked behind my car. "I didn't even hear you drive up."

"You were concentrating hard on something else." He motioned with his hand to the bench. "Mind if I join you?"

"Not at all." I moved over to allow him to sit. I needed to know about this good-looking man who for all practical purposes was a total stranger.

"Do you have relatives in Allemand Parish?"

"No, my folks are from Miss'ssippi. I work offshore. Got to go back in a few days."

Even though his athletic physique fit perfectly for work on oil rigs, his explanation intrigued me.

"Most offshore workers, especially single guys who weren't headed for home, tend to spend their free time in Morgan City or even Lafayette where there's a lot more exciting places to visit."

"That's if you like staying drunk for two weeks," he said. "Actually, a guy who works with me on the rig lives over across the lake. In, uh, Beau Chene, is it?"

I nodded. Although Beau Chene was larger than Cypress Lake, the one and only time that town gets wild is during Mardi Gras. Then the place is really rocking.

"My buddy told me if I wanted to spend time in a quiet place, Allemand Parish was the perfect place."

"It used to be."

He cocked his head to one side. "Oh? What's going on?"

"Over the last several years, the parish has had a number of high profile murders including my husband, who was the chief of police in Cypress Lake."

His expression sobered. "I'm sorry. Is he the one you're visiting?"

"Yes, it's been a year since he died. But that's not everything going on in the parish. My husband was killed because he discovered a drug trafficking ring run by the former mayor. Now there's evidence of a group smuggling undocumented immigrants into the state."

"I heard about those folks they found on the bayou that didn't make it. Remote places like these coastal swamps are tempting spots for illegal activities."

"Where in Mississippi are you from?"

"The Kil'."

"The what?"

His blue eyes sparkled when he laughed. "The Kil' is what we've always called the area. The name is spelled K. I. L. N., pronounced Kil'. There used to be a lot of kilns around there which were operated by the timber industry."

"That's very interesting. I'm a mystery writer so maybe I'll figure out some way to use your town in a story if I set one in Mississippi."

"I enjoy a good mystery. Are you published?"

"Yes, I am. You should check out my website. It's under Susan Foret."

"I'll do that."

His intense eyes kept studying my face. They were almost hypnotic. I had to keep reminding myself that most men who had his particular physical characteristics of dark hair and big blue eyes always seemed to be the stereotypical bad boy. But oh how ladies loved outlaws! I wondered if Danny was one of those in his younger days. I'll have to inquire some time.

It's time for me to leave before I do something foolish.

"It's been nice talking to you. I need to get back to relieve the babysitter."

"How old is your baby?" he asked.

"Babies, plural."

His raised his eyebrows.

"Oh they're not infants," I explained. "They are a set of eight year old twins, a boy and a girl."

"Wow, you must have your hands full."

"Sometimes they are a handful. Nice seeing you again." I managed to pull myself away and walk to my car. I felt his gaze follow me until I drove out of his sight.

When I arrived back home, Tina informed me Megan had left a message for me to call her. I paid Tina and keyed Megan's number on my cell phone.

"What's up," I asked when she answered.

"I was worried about you, especially after I called your house and you weren't there."

"Why didn't you try my cell?"

"I did, but you didn't answer."

Boy I must have really been in a daze. "I guess I didn't hear the phone. Is that the reason you called?"

My words didn't come out as I intended. "Sorry, I didn't mean to snarl."

"Don't worry. I'm not offended." She paused for a long moment. "There is something I want to tell you concerning the case."

"What about it?"

"Carole is hesitant about revealing any more facts about what our plans are. In a way it's related to attorney-client confidentiality. So it's probably better if..."

"If I don't sit in on your meetings," I interrupted. "I had the feeling she resented my presence."

"Don't get your feeling hurt. Carole is all about being professional. You're not an attorney or a licensed investigator."

"There's another reason. Your life seems to be in danger," she continued. "I'm not certain if the police are brushing off your close call as a drunk driver who didn't want to be caught. However, I believe whoever drove the truck was intentionally trying to kill you, or at the least attempting to scare you."

My pulse accelerated. "I'm glad you confirmed my way of thinking about the incident and not that I'm crazy."

"Sometimes your actions are crazy."

"I'm the first to admit it."

"Anyway, I hope what I'm about to say will make you feel a little more optimistic about Alex's chances," she continued. "Although there are many possible snags involved here, there is one plan of action Carole's looking into as a possible way to keep Alex from being deported if he's found not guilty of murder."

I perked up. "Can you tell me about it?"

"The program is referred to as TPS or Temporary Protected Status. People who came to the US from countries in some sort of upheaval and are in danger of physical harm are granted TPS. After the earthquake in Haiti, the Haitian people were included in this because conditions there were so bad."

"That sounds promising," I said.

"As I mentioned before, there are all sorts of problems in Alex's case."

"Like the possibility he'll be convicted of Celina's murder?"

"Yes, but also the current TPS program for Haitians expires January of twenty-eighteen. And then there's his illegal status."

"I do feel a bit more optimistic, but I realize there are so many ifs involved."

"If TPS isn't in the cards for him, there's another program that might be," she said. "However, he'll have to be cleared of Celina's murder first."

"He hasn't been formally charged yet, has he?"

"Not yet, but my intuition tells me he will be...soon."

Thirty

Saturday, August 1

"Oh come on," Matthew shouted at the television. "Seriously?"

I came out of the kitchen to see what happened. A breaking news alert on TV had interrupted Saturday morning cartoons. I cringed as Channel 7 went live to a press conference in front of Cypress Lake City Hall.

The moment I saw Brad, I knew what this was about. My intuition was right on. Megan's guess was also correct as to the timing. Alex had been arrested for Celina's murder.

Brad stood at the microphone, looking quite pleased. Several other deputies and the DA, along with two men I didn't recognize, moved in behind him. These men were later introduced as Immigration and Customs Enforcement agents.

A smell of burning food from the kitchen drew my attention away from the news conference. I rushed to the stove and removed burnt pancakes from the skillet, dumping them into the garbage. *Looks like the kids are having cereal for breakfast.*

By the time I returned to the den, the news conference was over. Oh, well, I'll find out on my own what transpired. I was surprised Brad didn't have Danny on the podium with him to hold his hand. I scolded myself for being sarcastic and recalled the words I told Josh about my current bad attitude. How could anyone stand to be around me anymore?

Back in the kitchen, I set two bowls out for Matthew and Caroline, several different boxes of cereal so each could make a choice. I called the twins to breakfast.

"I thought we were having pancakes," Matthew said, frowning.

"We were, but I burned them. So these are your choices." I indicated the boxes displayed on the table.

"I want Fruitie-O's," Caroline said.

Matthew studied the boxes and finally picked one with loads of sugar and marshmallows in it. I usually give them one choice, but today I didn't feel like hearing a lot of moaning and groaning. I was surprised there wasn't more griping about the absence of pancakes.

After getting the twins taken care of, I poured a second cup of coffee and popped two slices of bread into the toaster.

With my meager breakfast fare, I sat at the table with the kids. They seemed pleasantly surprised by my action. I realized I'd left them with babysitters, or alone to their own devices while I either worked on my novel, or delved into the mystery of Celina's death, the complications of Alex's situation, and other seemingly connected events like what happened on the Gallaghers' boat.

Maybe I really do need therapy. There were only two things I should be concentrating on—my kids and my writing—in that order.

We talked about the upcoming start of school. It was hard to believe my babies would be in third grade this year. Naturally Matthew stated his desire for endless summer vacation.

"For a few weeks before my school started every year, I always wanted summer to last forever," I said, trying to start a discussion. "Then after classes started, I didn't mind too much. My friends and I were together again and there were all the after school activities."

"Oh I like soccer and playing with my friends," Matthew said. "It's the classes and homework I don't like."

"Is there any subject you like?"

"Gym class."

"Other than gym."

He thought a moment. "Science and math are okay."

His answer didn't surprise me. He always did well in those subjects. "That's great. What about you, Caroline?"

"I like history and English." She made a face. "But math and science are not fun at all."

Matthew shook his head. "Not me. History and English are boring."

"Well, maybe you could help your sister with your favorite subjects and she can return the favor." I waited for an explosion from Matthew. What a shock. None came.

"Maybe I might help you with math." Matthew's expression belied his reluctant tone.

Caroline smiled. "That would be nice. School's going to be good this year. I want to try out for the chorus."

This arrangement might work out. I hope and pray it does and there's a smooth running school year.

A soft meow came from under the table. Katy brushed against my leg. Like the rest of us she also needed attention. I reached down and scratched her head.

"Wow," Matthew said. "I can hear her purring all the way up here."

"That means she agrees," Caroline said. "We're going to have a great school year."

Rachel phoned and invited me and the twins over for a backyard barbeque this evening. These events had long been a Saturday tradition from Memorial Day to Labor Day at the Marchands' house. Tonight the other guests included Ronnie Hart and his family.

The twins, especially Matthew, were thrilled that his friend Reed Hart would be there and I released him from being grounded.

Around six we walked next door. I brought a dish of baked beans to contribute to the meal.

After placing the bean dish on the picnic table, I sat on the patio with Rachel and Danny while we waited for Ronnie and his family to arrive. The delicious aroma of meat cooking on the gas grill floated over to us, and reminded me of the many barbeques Jim and I attended here over the years.

I mentally sighed. My recollections of Jim that popped up every time I attended an event, or smelled a certain aroma would have to stop if I wanted to move on with my life. Not an easy task, but a necessary one.

"Danny," I said, finally summoning the nerve. "When you were younger were you ever considered to be a bad boy?" I made air quotes around bad boy."

He looked at me as if I had suddenly dropped out of a tree. "Where the devil did that come from?"

My face grew warm. "Sorry, I guess that did seem to come out of the blue. I met a guy and have seen him a few times..." I hurriedly explained to their surprised looks. "I don't mean seeing as in dating. He and I happened to be in the same place a couple of times and we talked." *Why did I feel like a teenager telling my parents about a new boyfriend*?

Danny looked confused. "What does this guy have to do with me possibly being a bad boy?"

"He has the same coloring as I presume you had when you were younger. I mean dark hair and big blue eyes."

He nodded, brushing his hand over his silver hair. "Okay, I'll admit my hair used to be dark. So what?"

"Every guy I've ever known who had those physical characteristics turned out to be prototypical bad boys...love em and leave em ladies' men."

"Hmm, were you one of those?" Rachel teased.

Danny leaned back in his chair for a long moment. Then he turned to us with a mischievous grin. "I might have been." His expression grew serious. "So who is this guy? Do we know him?"

He sounded pretty much like my father had whenever I was going on a date. "I doubt it. He told me he works offshore on one of the oil rigs. He's not from Louisiana, but from Mississippi."

"Oh, from the Coast," Rachel asked.

"No, he's from a town which he called The Kil'. The real name is spelled K.I.L.N. Have you heard of it?"

Rachel shook her head. "Like Louisiana there are so many wide spots in the road in Mississippi that aren't even on the map. What about you, Danny?"

He looked away briefly. "As a matter of fact, I have heard of the place. It's a small town north of Bay St. Louis. Years ago I met a man from there. I can't recall his name. What's this fellow's name?"

"Jack Holden."

He shook his head. "Name doesn't ring a bell."

His expression seemed odd, but I couldn't put my finger on what bothered me about it. "I'm sure if Kiln is such a small place, whoever the man was they knew each other."

He opened his mouth as if to reply. Whatever he intended to say was interrupted when Ronnie, Renee, and their three kids arrived through the side gate.

The evening passed with friendly dialogue and good food, a typical South Louisiana Saturday night. The one missing component was Cajun music.

The subject of Alex's arrest, Brad's tunnel vision, or undocumented immigrants didn't come up, at least not among me, Rachel, and Renee. Several times Danny and Ronnie had their heads together discussing what appeared to be a serious subject. Those men couldn't seem to completely leave their work at the office, so to speak. But I shouldn't talk. I couldn't leave a murder investigation out of my thoughts even for a few hours.

Around ten in the evening, the Harts left. Danny stayed outside to take care of the grill and clear all the paper plates and other trash with help from the twins. Rachel and I moved the leftover food and beverages inside.

She took a seat at the kitchen table. "Come sit here and tell me about this Jack Holden. You said you and he happened to be in the same place a couple of times and you talked."

I sighed. "Yes, Mother. I'm sorry I even brought up the subject."

"Too bad, dear," she said. "I want to make sure he isn't dangerous."

"He might be dangerous, but not in the way you're thinking." I sat in a chair across from her.

"I'm not letting this go. Tell me about the times you two met."

"Okay, okay." I proceeded to tell her about the incident at the coffee shop and the second time at the cemetery.

She didn't seem concerned until I detailed our meeting at the cemetery. "Running into him at the coffee shop sounds innocent enough, but not the second time at Jim's grave. He didn't have any reason to be there. Sounds like a stalker to me. For all you know, he could be the guy who tried to run over you with his truck."

I shook my head. "No, I don't think so."

My heart thumped. Jack Holden's black pickup parked behind my car at the cemetery suddenly came to mind.

Thirty-one

Wednesday, August 5

The first day of the new school year arrived sooner than I thought. Prior days had flown by, filled with shopping for school supplies and new uniforms as the twins had both outgrown last year's clothes. Then there were new sneakers. The brand name shoes were outrageously high priced.

This year, for the first time Matthew and Caroline didn't have the same teacher. I resigned myself to the fact they were probably old enough to be separated.

After leaving the kids at school I came home feeling depressed. The unfinished novel sitting on my desk should be my first priority, but somehow I couldn't bring myself to work on it.

What I really wanted was to do research pertaining to Celina's murder and figure out the connection to the confrontation on the Gallaghers' boat. I felt certain there was a link.

I could email Remi about the possibility of getting more info on the event. Her involvement with digging up this old information might be tricky because I wasn't certain about procedure. I didn't want her to get in trouble because of me.

Who knows? There may not be any problems with her opening an investigation into an incident like that one. Of course Claire Gallagher may object to reopening old wounds. From what I knew about her, she would have a lot of influence in shutting down any suggestion there was a need to reinvestigate.

I couldn't understand why she didn't follow through with the Jamaican authorities. If my husband and son had been murdered in cold blood, I would have stopped at nothing to find the killers. And it seemed to me the U. S. Coast Guard or even the FBI should have been on the case, since the deaths of American citizens were involved, even if the attack occurred in international waters or Jamaican waters.

I decided to email Remi after I spoke to Willow about Kenny Verret's connection to Celina and once I checked the *Times Picayune's* archives.

Hanging around the house wasn't getting me anywhere. I grabbed my laptop, opting to do my research in Coffee Heaven. Writing on laptops in coffee shops was common these days.

Or maybe I hoped to run into Jack Holden again. I shook off the thought. He's probably gone back offshore by now.

The anticipation of possibly seeing him again mixed with a nagging fear he might be the man who tried to run me down. I knew nothing about the man except for my attraction to him. For all I knew he could be a serial killer. He might even be Celina's killer.

I arrived at Coffee Heaven and went inside. Looking around the shop, I noted an unoccupied yellow booth-like sofa along the wall with small tables spaced periodically in front. I guessed people figured those spots were too close for comfort. Someone seated next to you could easily observe information on your computer.

The patrons mostly sat one person to a table in the center of the room, either engrossed in their phones or with a laptop open in front of them. There were two women seated at a booth by the window who were actually having a conversation. A young man about eighteen or nineteen occupied the other booth, his fingers clicking on his laptop.

I ordered a latte and a cranberry-orange muffin from the display case. The tables by the wall were still vacant when my order was completed so I grabbed a spot in the corner at the far right before any newly arriving customers could claim it. With my laptop booted up, I started searching for more info about the incident.

I took a few small sips of coffee and broke off a piece of the muffin. I nibbled on the tart cake as I surfed the internet.

The *Picayune's* archives, usually a treasure trove of information, surprisingly had a brief reference to the event two years later. In fact, the only item of interest in this piece was a mention that the assailants escaped in their own boat and the case had grown cold because authorities were never able to locate the aggressors. To what authorities were they referring? Jamaican or United States?

"Hello," he drawled. "We meet again."

Startled, I looked up into the big blue eyes of Jack Holden. My breath caught in my throat. Was it fear or desire?

"I figured you'd be back offshore by now."

He made a face. "Unfortunately, I will be by tomorrow afternoon. May I join you?"

"Sure, I'm happy for the interruption." I frowned. "My research isn't going well at all."

Jack slipped in beside me and regarded me with a curious expression.

"Research for a mystery novel?"

"You could say that." I should have closed the lid the moment he walked up. Don't know if he saw the article on my screen. I hesitated to reveal the subject of my search. Maybe I could improvise and pretend an attack on a boat was part of my plot. He's not from around here so he might not be privy to the real incident.

Bad idea. Like I told myself before, I have no idea of this man's past. I snapped the lid shut.

"So what have you been doing since we last ran into each other," I asked.

He shrugged. "Riding around enjoying the scenery mostly." He leaned back in his chair and smiled at me. "Including the ladies, one in particular."

Wow, was that a pick-up line or an indication he's been following me? I began to rethink my attraction to him and feigned ignorance to his come-on, or whatever he meant. Rachel's warning about him lurked in the back of my mind.

I glanced at my watch. "Time has gotten away from me. I need to get moving." I placed my laptop into its case and attempted to leave. The arrangement of the tables prevented me from leaving unless he moved over to allow me to pass.

"Be careful out there on the rig," I said, looking him straight in the face. His powerful gaze threatened to make me back down. I didn't.

He finally realized I intended to leave and moved over so I could pass without ending up in his lap. His expression seemed to be a combination of irritation and confusion. Obviously he had never been turned down by a woman and was still trying to figure out why I had brushed him off.

My next thought sent heart and mind racing. *"There is one other vibration I picked up from you concerning a man who seems to have a connection to the foreign man,"* Taylor said. *"He will appear to have a romantic interest in you, but I feel he's not honest about his feelings."*

Was he the man she meant? If so, what was his connection to Alex?

Thirty-two

The one black pick-up I saw parked in the vicinity of Coffee Heaven turned out to be a Dodge Ram. I didn't know whether to be relieved or not. If Jack Holden owned this one, he wasn't the person who tried to run me over unless he had another truck—a GMC.

People around here don't usually buy the same type vehicles of different brands concurrently, especially not someone who doesn't have a permanent home in this area. But if there were two drivers in the household…

Stop with the ifs. I'm making this situation more complicated than necessary. There was no way for me to find out if he really worked offshore and was leaving tomorrow as he claimed. I felt like an idiot for allowing myself to be attracted to him. Luckily, I never agreed to go on a date with him. My curiosity about his motives still intrigued me.

I needed to speak to Willow, but I didn't have a phone number for her. I could search social media sites and see if there was any way to get a message to her. If not, there were two other options. I could show up and ask to speak to her or I could mail a note to her by snail mail.

She may not want to speak to me if she and Miriam believe Celina's killer is in custody. My opinion differed from theirs. Any number of people present at the site could have shot Celina, but Alex conveniently happened to be the person with any connection that Brad could get his hands on.

I sat in my car for a short moment with the air conditioner on high. The walkway along the shore of the town's lake, also known as Cypress Lake, seemed like the ideal place for me to continue with the research on my laptop uninterrupted by Mister Romeo. Even if I got no results on my search, I could sit on a bench and enjoy the view.

After parking my car, I found an unoccupied bench and sat for a while staring at the scene.

The water was fairly calm, splashing gently against the trunks of a row of cypress trees. These trees marked a spot where the Allemand River flowed into the lake. A slight breeze ruffled beards of Spanish moss hanging from the trees.

I don't know why I hadn't thought of doing this months ago. The water and trees created such a peaceful atmosphere. I felt totally relaxed. Even the few joggers who ran by caused little interruption to this tranquility.

Rebooting my laptop, I made another attempt to locate more information on the boat attack. There didn't seem to be any. I couldn't understand why. I could say that Claire paid off everybody in two countries to let the whole incident fade away. An irrational idea at best. How would she explain the deaths of two people?

Any additional searching on the web this morning appeared to be a waste of time. The heat was beginning to get the best of me anyway. I felt perspiration forming beneath my tee shirt.

I shut my laptop down and put it away. What a disappointment. There didn't seem to be an answer forthcoming about Celina's murder or the attack on the *Claire G.*

I did a double take. In what could only be described as a contrived plot twist in a novel, the jogger approaching me turned out to be Willow Baum. She recognized me and trotted over.

"I see you're enjoying the view and the sunshine," she said. Her dark hair was pulled back in a ponytail.

"Definitely the view, but not the heat," I replied, wiping sweat from my brow. "I've wanted to speak to you ever since the funeral. Can you sit awhile?"

"Sure, I need a break." Willow sat next to me on the bench and pulled a small water bottle from her fanny pack. After taking a few swallows, she eyed me with suspicion. "Why did you want to speak to me?"

"You may not want to answer my questions. If you find them too painful to rehash, tell me and I won't bother you again."

A frown creased her forehead. "Questions about Celina, I presume."

"Yes, but my question is about a statement you made. I said Celina was really dedicated to her work at the food pantry. You replied she may have been a little too dedicated."

She averted her eyes for a brief moment. "I'm not certain how or why she happened to be out there, but I strongly suspect the reason had something to do with helping undocumented immigrants like our birth parents."

"Then your Native American ancestry is of Mexican or Central American origin."

She nodded. "Guatemalan."

Now for the big question. "I didn't imagine your adverse reaction to Kenny Verret. What's the connection to you? Or was there a relationship between him and Celina?"

Apprehension flittered in her eyes. "I can't discuss the connection between him and Celina." She jumped up and ran, not jogged, down the sidewalk.

Once again I've either made an enemy or hurt feelings or both. I never meant to do that, but my obsessive need to find answers always managed to get me in trouble physically or emotionally. Willow was a nice person. She lost her sister in an act of violence. I felt terrible for upsetting her.

Even though I didn't get a lot of information, I have a better understanding of Celina's mindset. She and Willow must have been born in the United States after their parents came to this country illegally. But the reaction I received from Willow about Kenny Verret did answer one question at least in my mind. He was not Willow's boyfriend, ex or otherwise.

Her reaction raised more questions. Why couldn't she discuss the relationship between Celina and Kenny? Did Celina know about the immigrants being dropped off there? And if so, how did she know?

I left a message on Remi Granger's cell. Hopefully she would be able to get back to me soon. Time was not in Alex's favor.

As I told Megan, I firmly believe that reasonable doubt is not a good way to find a person not guilty of murder. Sure, the defendant is cleared legally, but unless the real killer is found and convicted, the defendant is always going to be under a cloud of suspicion.

Steven is a good example. He never went to trial for the murder of his wife because there wasn't enough evidence to charge him. Then the case went cold for ten years.

For a decade the police still considered him the killer and his life was a living hell. He was eventually arrested after they reopened the case. If I hadn't risked everything to find Anne's killer, my brother would be in prison at Angola or on death row.

As I pulled into my driveway, my cell rang. The caller ID indicated Remi returning my call. I answered still sitting in the car.

"Thanks for getting back to me so quickly."

"No problem," she said. "What can I do for you?"

"I'm doing research on an incident that occurred ten years ago… an attack on a boat owned by Allemand Parish residents that happened in the Caribbean."

She spoke in a low voice. "You mean Claire Gallagher's boat?"

"Oh, you know about it." I shouldn't have been surprised. She is an investigative reporter.

"I heard about the attack years ago, but never thought too much about it until now."

How interesting. "Why now?"

"Rumors. I can't talk about it over the phone, but I would love to meet with you. When is a good time?"

"The kids are back in school now so any time during the day is fine."

"Can we meet for lunch in NOLA tomorrow?"

"Sure, that would be great."

I wasn't anxious to make a trip to New Orleans, but at least we would be away from the prying eyes of Cypress Lake people. We decided on a time and place and ended the call.

Remi certainly seemed eager to meet with me. I wondered if she knew that Rachel and I had been the 'fishermen' who discovered Celina's body. Could my intuition about a connection between Celina's murder and the Gallaghers have been right all along?

Thirty-three

Thursday, August 6

Remi met me at a little eatery on Canal Street named Cal's Place. Established sometime in the 1930s, Cal's looked like a dive, but I'd eaten here many times in the past and can attest to the delicious food.

Although I was anxious to hear what Remi knew, I couldn't help taking a few moments to drink in the ambience of the place.

Red and white checkered tablecloths covered each table. Voices buzzed, along with periodic bursts of laughter amid the aroma of beer and fried seafood. The walls were lined with photos of the cafe owner posing with New Orleans celebrity musicians and Hollywood actors in town to film movies. Over the years, Louisiana had become known as Hollywood South because of the multitude of movies being filmed in the state.

We managed to find a table toward the back of the crowded room and settled in to check out the menu. A waitress took our orders and scurried off to the kitchen.

Remi's expression seemed to be a cross between curiosity and caution. "First, let me ask you why you're researching this particular incident."

I leaned forward in order to speak low, so other diners wouldn't be privy to our conversation. One never knows who might be listening.

"I believe there is a connection between Celina's murder and the Gallagher family, either through the attack on their boat or some element of the family salvage business."

She smiled. "Straight to the point. I like that. So I'll do the same."

"Good, because I haven't been able to get much info about what actually happened on the boat."

Her expression grew serious. "Do you have any evidence to prove your theory?"

"Not really. I do know there's a connection between Celina's murder and illegal immigrants coming into the country. Plus, I'm pretty sure that a couple who claim to be from Martinique are actually from Haiti. These people are currently employed by Claire Gallagher."

She arched her eyebrows. "What makes you so sure they are from Haiti? They might originally be from Haiti and moved to Martinique."

I told her about my visit and the conversation I overheard. "It's still a possibility. However, from their body language after they discovered my presence, intuition tells me their papers from Martinique are false."

"I have to agree. Sounds like your instinct is right on." Her expression changed to one of frustration. "From what little I've been able to uncover about the pirate attack, the whole incident was swept under the rug. I find it hard to believe, since two American citizens were killed and another seriously wounded."

"Wouldn't Danny be in the know about it? I asked. "He was the sheriff back then."

"I asked him about it recently and he told me he wasn't at liberty to discuss the incident."

"What made you question him now?"

"My photographer…" The waitress interrupted with our food. After she left, Remi continued. "My photographer can read lips. He informed me after he lip read the conversation between Brad and a reporter from a rival TV station."

"How did this reporter come up with a connection between the Gallaghers and smuggling immigrants into the country?"

"Good question," she said.

"What did Brad say?"

"He turned his face so his lips couldn't be read."

To mask my frustration at hitting another roadblock, I concentrated on my lunch. Breaking off a piece of French bread, I spread butter on it and savored the taste. I love bread and rolls, sweet or otherwise. Seafood dishes with rice like the Shrimp Creole in front of me can be healthy, but all this white bread negates the benefits.

We ate in silence for a while until Remi's phone rang. She retrieved the cell from her purse.

"I can't hear you," she said. "I'm in Cal's. I'll go see if I can find a quieter place." She excused herself. "Station's on the line."

Breaking news? Sirens were going off in my head. Something told me Allemand Parish would soon be in the news again.

Remi returned a few minutes later. "I've got to go catch this story." She leaned closer to me and whispered, "Mike Doucet, Claire's son, has been shot."

"Is he alive?" I whispered back.

"The information we have is that he's been transported to West Lake Memorial for emergency surgery."

My breath caught in my throat. Her words brought back Danny's life changing announcement a year ago. *Jim's been shot. He's at West Lake Memorial in surgery.*

Remi grabbed her purse and left money with me to pay for her meal. "Let's continue this discussion soon."

"Definitely."

Had I been wrong in my assessment of Mike Doucet? Or had someone in the Gallagher family decided to take justice in their own hands?

<h1 style="text-align:center">*Thirty-four*</h1>

Heading for the hospital to find out Mike Doucet's condition was tempting, but not a viable option. In a couple of hours the kids would be out of school.

Rachel greeted me as I exited my car. "Have you heard about the latest shooting?"

"You mean Mike Doucet?"

"How did you know?"

"I had lunch with Remi at Cal's Place when she got the call."

She eyed me with concern. "What are you two cooking up? I'd hate to see either or both of you get into a situation you couldn't get out of."

"Come inside and I'll tell you about our discussion." I unlocked the door and stepped inside, followed by Rachel. "Did Danny go to hold Brad's hand?" I exhaled. "That wasn't nice. I've got to stop putting him down."

"In answer to your question, Danny went to the scene, but he heard about it from Ronnie."

"*Mea culpa*, Brad," I said. "Where was Mike Doucet when he was shot?"

"He was in his truck out on Richard Road. I don't know any other details."

"Remi told me he'd been taken to West Lake Memorial for emergency surgery."

Rachel sat at the kitchen table. "Okay, fill me in. Why did you have lunch with Remi?"

"We talked about Celina's death and a possible connection to the attack on the Gallagher's boat."

"So she thinks the two incidents are tied in some way?"

I nodded. "However, she's having as much trouble as I am finding out anything. She overheard a reporter from another station ask Brad questions about illegal immigrants and a connection to Gallagher Salvage."

Rachel arched her eyebrows. "How interesting. What was Brad's response?"

"She couldn't say. I suspect he either told the reporter he had no comment or he didn't have any information on the subject."

We talked for about fifteen or twenty minutes and then she went back to her house. Feeling restless, I paced around, not knowing what to do with myself. I rehashed all the details I knew about the events of the last several weeks since Celina's murder.

I jumped when the doorbell rang. Who could that be? I wasn't expecting visitors. Through the peephole, I spotted Josh standing on the doorstep.

"Hey," I said. "What's up?"

"I thought you might want an update on our friend Alex or other subjects."

"You know I do. Nothing bad has happened, has it?"

His serious expression upgraded into a smile. "It's a mixture of good news and bad."

I invited him inside with a wave. "Would you like some coffee?" I raised a finger in the air. "Or better yet, how about some iced tea?"

"Tea sounds great. It's pretty warm out there."

Opening the refrigerator, I turned to him. "Sweet or unsweet?"

"Sweet, of course." He offered one of those lopsided grins I'd seen him give a few times. "Someone once told me drinking unsweet tea in the South is heresy."

I laughed. Amazing what laughter can do to raise a person's spirits. "Oops, guess I commit heresy every time I drink iced tea. Most sweet tea is too sugary for my taste, which is why I make two pitchers, one of each." I brought the glasses of tea to the table. "Why are you still standing? Have a seat."

Josh pulled out a chair and sat. He took a large swallow from his glass. "Delicious. Now about Alex…he decided to cooperate with Megan and Carole about how he got to Louisiana. That's the good news. I'm not at liberty to divulge the details yet. Carole is trying to contact ICE about a number of things, including his immigration status. The bad news is we still need to prove he didn't kill Celina Baum."

"Brad isn't going to agree to drop murder charges against him, is he?"

He shook his head. "Neither is the DA They're out for blood." He gulped down more iced tea. "Would you be willing to talk about the day you and Rachel found Celina's body?"

I clasped both hands around my glass. A chill flowed down my spine, and not from handling the icy beverage. At the moment this was not what I wanted to do. Recalling the scene would dredge up bad memories not only of another body but of Jim's death as well.

He apparently sensed my apprehension. "If you'd rather not, I understand."

"No, I'll tell you what I remember." I told him everything I recalled, including my impression of a crowd of people trampling the grass.

Elbow on the table, he stroked his chin thoughtfully. "Your story corresponds with Alex's version. Locating one or two of those people will be next to impossible."

"I agree. Most would be afraid to come forward."

"True, but first we'd have to find any of the people who were smuggled in."

"Where do you suppose these people were taken after landing in Allemand Parish?

"Most likely New Orleans," he said. "They could easily assimilate and never be seen again."

"Sounds logical." Since I wasn't certain he would believe my claim of a link, I proceeded with caution. "On another subject I believe is connected. Have you heard about the latest shooting?"

"You mean Mike Doucet? A contact of mine told me he's in critical condition, but is expected to survive his injuries. Doctors have him heavily sedated so he can't be interviewed for a couple of days. The word is he was shot and also dragged out of his truck and beat up. He's got some head injuries."

I drew in a breath. "Someone really wanted him dead."

"Why do you believe these are linked?" He narrowed his gaze on my face. "Did you pick up on anything when you visited the Gallaghers' place? I mean, other than the two possible Haitians."

"I got the impression from the conversation between Marcie Gallagher and Jill Doucet I overheard that Marcie was upset Jill allowed me to enter their compound. She kept telling Jill in so many words Claire will be upset that a stranger was allowed to come inside the house.

"Several days after Rachel and I discovered Celina's body, I saw Claire and her two sons at the cemetery. The whole scene of them at the gravesite of Walt and Gary Gallagher exuded animosity among the three."

"How so?"

I explained how Rick stood back, leaning against their van while Claire and Mike appeared to be there to honor their deceased loved ones. "Maybe I imagined the dissention, but I don't think so. From what I've heard, there's been bad blood between the two brothers since the attack on their boat in the Caribbean."

He appeared to consider my version of the scene. "Might be something to look into. You haven't had any more close calls lately, have you? No one who seems to be following you?"

"No one's tried to run me down again, if that's what you mean. I haven't felt like anyone's been following me or stalking me either." *Unless Jack Holden qualifies.*

Thirty-five

Josh gave me the strangest look. "Is something wrong?"

I began to wonder if he was psychic. "No, why do you ask?"

"The look on your face suggested you thought of something pertaining to my previous question."

"There is a man…no never mind. It's probably nothing."

He leaned forward in his chair. "Uh uh, that's not going to work. Who is this man and what did he do to make you suspicious?"

"He says his name is Jack Holden. He keeps popping up at some of the same places I happen to be in, including the cemetery when I went to visit Jim."

Josh's eyes widened. "Sounds like stalking to me or close to it. What else can you tell me about this guy?"

Have I opened a can of worms? "He said he's from Mississippi, which I could have figured out without his acknowledgement because of his drawl. He claimed to work offshore on a rig and was on his days off."

"What's he look like?"

"He's about your height and build, but with dark hair and large blue eyes."

Josh's expression clouded. "Where else besides the cemetery did you run into him?"

"Twice at the new coffee shop—Coffee Heaven. Do you know him?"

"No, I don't think so. Whoever he is, you need to stay away from him."

I shrugged. "I'm curious to know if he's coming on to me because he truly wants to get to know me or if he has ulterior motives. I asked Danny if he'd heard of the town he was from in Mississippi. He said he had, but his reaction seemed strange."

His stern look surprised me. "Running into you at the coffee shop might indicate he's interested in you, but not the cemetery unless he has a relative or friend buried there."

Funny, that's almost the same words Rachel used. Guess I'm an idiot for not recognizing he wanted something from me.

The school bus rumbled to a stop in front of the house. I heard Matthew yell and another kid respond.

Josh perked up. "Sounds like a disagreement out there."

"Good heavens, I hope Matthew's not getting in a fight. It's only the second day of school."

Josh followed me outside to see what had happened.

I saw what appeared to be a stand-off between Matthew and an older boy who lived down the street. Matthew was smaller in size than that boy, who I thought might be a fifth grader.

"What's going on?" I asked, walking toward the pair.

The two kept attempting to stare each other down. Finally the older boy mumbled something I couldn't hear, and then started walked toward his house.

Matthew glared at me. "I could've taken care of him myself. I didn't need you to take up for me." He marched across the lawn and into the house after glaring at Josh. I stood there stunned without moving for a moment or two.

Caroline waited for me at the door. "I can tell you what happened."

"I'd rather have Matthew explain to me. It would be like tattling if you tell me the story."

She lowered her gaze. "I guess so."

I brushed my hand over her hair and gave a small smile. "Do you remember Mr. Josh?"

"I think so," she said. "It was a long time ago." Her expression brightened. "You came to our house with Aunt Megan."

"That right." Josh smiled. "It's nice to see you again, Caroline."

She didn't seem to mind his presence. At least she returned his smile.

"Go and get changed out of your uniform," I said. "I'll fix you and your brother a snack."

She skipped down the hall to her room.

"Cute kid," Josh said. "But your son definitely didn't like me."

"Well, he wasn't in the best of moods. He didn't like my interference into his business. That I stopped his fight."

"You really have your hands full. I take it your problems with him started after Jim's death."

I blew out a deep breath. "Yes, that's true. I need to go have a talk with him."

"Then I'm going to take off," he said. "I'll keep you informed when I can."

Long after Josh left, I kept rehashing what he said about the immigrants and their possible destination: New Orleans. If Lucie and O.J. Celestine were undocumented Haitians, how did they end up remaining in Allemand Parish and not being shipped off to New Orleans? Could there be safe houses near here?

I tried to visualize an area in the parish that might fit the bill. Nothing came to mind at first. Then I recalled a neighborhood near the outskirts of Foretville. Small wood frame homes, including a few shotgun houses lined a two street area and occupied by low income families.

~ * ~

Jill Doucet's gaze centered on her husband lying in the hospital bed. She reached for his hand and entwined her fingers with his. The doctors told her his chances for a full recovery were excellent. They wanted him sedated to allow his body to recover from the trauma of being shot and beaten. Talking to the police might upset him too much.

She understood their reasoning, but she feared, perhaps irrationally, he wouldn't wake up. A slight noise behind her startled her. She cringed.

Marcie, of all people. This irritating woman with her color coordinated outfits was not who she wanted to see. Every piece of clothing she had on today from her Capri pants and tee shirt to her sandals was bright teal, along with earrings and bracelet to match. Her nails were even painted the same color.

"How is he?" The look of concern on her face seemed fake.

"As well as he can be expected to be for someone who was shot and beat up." She met Marcie's gaze. "But don't worry, the doctors believe he's going to survive."

A flicker of emotion Jill couldn't decipher passed over her sister-in-law's face. Marcie always did have a thing for Mike. Was she truly concerned about his condition? Or was she sorry he was expected to live? Or both?

More questions bothered her. Why hasn't Claire been up here to check on her son? Did she send Marcie instead?

~ * ~

Jack Holden, my ass. Josh fumed all the way back to the law office. *I'm willing to bet my last dime he and Keith Parker are one and the same. But what was the former Army MP doing here? I thought he was Parker when I passed him on the street a few days ago. But he didn't acknowledge me at the time so I brushed it off as mistaken identity.*

One reason Parker may not admit knowing him is he's working undercover for a federal agency like ICE. Their agents were in the area. But what was his interest in Susan? He didn't blame Parker for being attracted to her, but following her to the cemetery seemed over the top. If Parker worked undercover, he might believe she had information he needed or else she was connected to their investigation here.

He also could have taken a new identity for some other reason like creditors or even the law. In which case he's out to get what he can from a beautiful and possibly vulnerable woman.

Either way, Susan would end up being hurt or in trouble with the law. Parker wasn't going to hurt Susan...federal agent or otherwise. Not if he could help it.

Thirty-six

I brought Matthew his afterschool snack in his room where he'd escaped to after rushing inside. I set the saucer of apple slices on his dresser. "I brought you a snack."

He pouted. "I'm not hungry."

"Matthew, will you tell me what that business out front was all about?" I tried not to sound accusatory.

He lowered his eyes for a long moment. Finally he looked me straight in the eyes. "Was Dad really murdered?"

Taken aback, I couldn't speak for a few seconds. "Of course he was. The people who killed him were arrested. I thought you knew he was murdered."

"Then why do other kids keep saying he killed himself? That he was a coward?"

The more he said, the madder I became. "Because they don't know any better." This didn't make sense. "Who are these kids who told you this?"

He hesitated.

"I know it's not cool to name names, but I really want to find out why they're doing this. It's bullying and that's not right."

"Mark Hernandez was the guy out front today," he said.

Hernandez? Joe Hernandez was one of the Cypress Lake police officers involved with the men who murdered Jim. "Do you know if Caroline has had problems, too?"

He nodded. "She told me a girl in her class and her brother who is in second grade keeps on telling her the same thing."

"Is their last name also Hernandez?"

"I think so."

"Mom?" Caroline stood in the doorway of Matthew's room. "He's right. Their names are Cindy Hernandez and her brother's name is Kirk. They keep picking on me too. Cindy said her father didn't kill my dad. He killed himself."

I didn't know how to answer her charge. Children take things so literally. Joe Hernandez didn't kill Jim. Jack LeBlanc and Bill Kaufman were the men responsible for the actual murder. Joe was involved in other parts of the illegal operations conducted by those two men who killed Jim, including kidnapping me.

"Mr. Hernandez took part in an illegal business that the two men who killed your father were operating. He wasn't arrested for murder."

Matthew frowned. "So why do they keep saying Dad killed himself?"

"The children are confused about what happened. I suppose they don't understand why he was arrested if he didn't kill your father."

"Well, I'm going to set them straight," he snapped. "Next time Mark tells me that stuff I'm going to punch him."

Oh, good heavens. "You will do no such thing. Fighting isn't going to solve anything. I know this is difficult to do, but when they start hassling you, walk away." I eyed each child to get an answer.

Caroline agreed, but Matthew found it harder to go along with my solution. Finally he said yes, he would walk away.

"Can we tell them their dad wasn't arrested for our dad's murder," Caroline asked.

I wasn't sure that would work, but…"It couldn't hurt to try."

I left them discussing the Hernandez kids and how to handle the hassling if the situation arose again, which I thought was pretty grown-up.

An adult like Mary Hernandez, their mother, needed to explain the situation to them so they understood the circumstances completely. I wanted to phone her and make clear what had been happening. Legally I couldn't.

Joe had been charged with several offenses including kidnapping when he and Jack LeBlanc took me to a deserted camp as a prisoner on orders from Bill Kaufman, the former mayor. They planned to get rid of me and then all escape. Luckily they didn't. I will be called upon to testify at the trial or trials if each were tried separately.

I wondered if my kids and I would be subjected to these painful reminders for the rest of our lives. My stomach lurched at the thought.

Thirty-seven

Friday, August 7

I waved to the kids as they boarded the school bus and then started to go back inside the house. Danny's voice stopped me.

"If you have a minute, I'd like to ask you a few questions." His tone sounded serious and his countenance matched.

I forced a laugh and tried to sound lighthearted. "Are you going to interrogate me?

His expression lightened. "Not unless you've done something criminal. Seriously, I wanted to clarify some info on the subject we talked about a few weeks ago."

I frowned. "What subject do you mean?"

"A while back you told me about the riff between you and Brad at the Baum's house."

"Oh, of course. What else do you want to know?"

"You said you were interested in the Gallaghers' home because of your current writing, but you didn't mention having already visited the place."

He wore the same look on his face that Jim always displayed when he knew I had omitted an important piece of information because I knew he'd be upset with me.

I held up my hands palms facing out. "Okay, you got me. I did visit the house, so what's the problem?"

"Claire doesn't usually allow anyone through that gate unless they're family or close friends. How'd you get her to let you in?"

"Claire wasn't at home. That particular day she and her sons were still at the cemetery when I left there after visiting the mausoleum. Jill Doucet allowed me to enter."

I had the feeling I might be in a predicament. His next question would surely be why were you really there? I was wrong.

"So you told her you were writing a mystery set in a plantation home and you wanted to get a feel for the place."

He appeared to be putting words in my mouth. Okay I'll play along. "Sure, that's what I told her." I narrowed my gaze on his face. "Danny, what is going on at the Gallaghers' house or their business?"

"I'm not at liberty to discuss that."

"I really hate that statement. It's been so overused lately."

"Sorry, but I can't tell you anything. I wanted to make certain you weren't involved and you didn't end up where you don't belong. You should know this, if you go nosing around there again, you will be suspected of being involved in criminal activity." He turned and strode to his truck.

Surprised, I stood frozen to the spot for a long time. Wow, I really hadn't expected him to provide me with a legitimate reason for being there. But in a way I was involved because the real reason I went there had nothing to do with my current work in progress.

Whoever had the Gallagher place staked out must have seen me go in. They believe I have a connection to whatever criminal activity is going on.

In the past I had gotten into serious situations with some bad individuals, but never with the law. Was being arrested a possibility? My riff with Brad didn't help matters. He might be happy to see me in trouble.

~ * ~

Danny sat on the park picnic bench across from the ICE agent. "Does the name Jack Holden mean anything to you?"

His face remained expressionless. "No, why?"

"Really? I know that's the name you furnished Susan on the occasions you *accidently* ran into her." Danny stared at him. "What's your interest in her?" Most likely he sounded like the father of a teenage girl asking about a certain young man's intentions with his daughter. True, but he felt the same way about Susan as he did regarding his own daughter, his step-daughter, and his granddaughter.

Keith Parker remained silent for a long moment. "I suspect she's involved in some way with the Gallaghers' operation. From what Brad told me, Claire Gallagher doesn't allow anyone in through those gates without being vetted first. Susan went right on in after the gates opened."

"Brad talked to me about her visit and made the same point. If he had spoken to Susan himself he would have discovered Claire and her sons happened to be visiting the cemetery at the time and Jill Doucet allowed Susan inside."

He frowned. "What business did she have there?"

Danny tilted his head slightly to one side. "I'm sure she told you she's a mystery writer. It so happens, the story she's working on right now is set in a plantation home."

Parker leaned forward as if to stress his point. "Then tell me why she's researching the ten year old attack on the Gallagher boat?"

He didn't know she was, but he faked it. "I'm not surprised about her looking into the attack, but I am surprised you didn't come to the conclusion that if she were collaborating with the Gallaghers she would have no reason to look into the piracy incident."

Danny studied Parker's face to determine if he was buying his story. "She's got an insatiable curiosity. It's gotten her in trouble a few times, but she's always been above board."

Parker's face remained without expression. "Maybe she's in a different situation now that she doesn't have a man to take care of her. Desperate people do desperate things."

Danny tensed his jaw. "She's not in financial straits, but a smooth talking man might be able to take advantage of her." He paused, waiting for his message to sink in. "Leave her alone. She has nothing to do with any illegal activity regarding Gallagher Salvage. She wants to find out who killed Celina Baum and believes there's a connection."

"Then you need to make sure she keeps her nose out of ICE business and your own sheriff's office's business. Let us do our jobs before she ends up ruining our respective cases or gets herself killed."

Easier said than done. "I'll see what I can do. In the meantime, as a professional courtesy, I'd appreciate it if you quit following her around."

Parker narrowed his eyes. "You must have a thing for her yourself."

Danny rose from the bench, his fists clenched at his side. "Out of respect for your late father, I'm going to ignore your comment and not dignify it with a response."

Thirty-eight

Today was one of my usual volunteer days at the food pantry. I should at least show up for a few hours even though I don't feel much like going. Danny's conversation with me earlier still weighed heavy on my mind. Why did he provide a reason for me to have visited the Gallaghers' house?

I decided to do my duty at the food pantry. The distraction would be good for me. I needed to stop thinking about making a fool of myself over Jack Holden. My description of him to Danny and Rachel must have sounded like some love-sick teenager.

Good thing I came to my senses before I did something crazy. Jack was merely looking for sex. In the future he should learn better lines when he tries to pick up a woman. Maybe those work on some women. They almost succeeded with me. Or else those big blue eyes did a number on me.

I had continuously told myself I wasn't ready to start dating again, but if I could be attracted to a man other than Jim, maybe I was fooling myself.

The man Taylor referred to as having an ulterior motive had to be Jack Holden. I considered the idea for a moment. If he was only after sex, why did he seem to be following me around? Come to think about it, Danny had such an odd look on his face when I mentioned Jack's Mississippi home town. Could there be another reason Jack tried to get close to me? A reason related to my conversation with Danny this morning? And what was Jack's connection to Alex?

I stayed at the pantry long enough to record some invoices and talk to a few people who came in to pick up groceries. Concentrating on numbers wasn't working for me today. I drove out of the compound and stopped at the street.

A sign told me Foretville was two point five miles down the road. Curiosity affected me like an addiction. The desire to know pulled me in the arrow's direction instead of toward my house. What could it hurt to check out the area I believe might have safe houses for illegals? I knew my question was like the alcoholic who asked, "What could one little drink hurt?" But I still drove there anyway.

Small frame cottages lined the two street neighborhood, including a few shotgun style homes. Many of the houses were in dire need of paint. Judging from the condition of some of the roofs, leaks were prevalent during rainstorms.

The area seemed deserted. I wondered if the sound of a vehicle driving down this street sent the residents into hiding.

Then I saw her. Lucie Celestine walked quickly toward the rear of the third house from the corner, carrying a large shopping bag.

Driving to the next cross street, I turned my car around and sat at the intersection with the engine idling, waiting for Lucie to return.

The sound of another vehicle approaching in the opposite direction drew my attention. A silver pick-up with two occupants advanced toward me. The driver glanced at me through his open window as he drove past. He slowed down to a crawl. I saw his face reflected in the side view mirror.

My heart skipped a beat. Kenny Verrett! He must have recognized me. I put the car in drive and turned the corner, driving away from him.

I glanced in my rear view mirror and breathed a sigh of relief. The pick-up had continued moving away.

At the next intersection, Liberty Road, I realized Miriam Baum's home was located about three miles to my right and Claire Gallagher's house a short distance to my left. I found it interesting that those two families lived so close to these houses possibly occupied by undocumented immigrants. Two families involved in some way to the same group of people.

After Danny's warning I couldn't turn left and drive by Claire's house. If I went to the right I would be traveling way out of my way to get back home. But I had no way of knowing whether Miriam's house was also under surveillance. For all I knew, this whole area could be on Immigration and Custom's radar.

On top of everything, the needle on my gas gauge pointed very close to empty. That's what I get for ignoring the low fuel warning light. What a dilemma.

My natural GPS kicked in then. I remembered a northbound side road about a mile before the Baums' house. I made a right turn and headed toward Joe Boudreaux Road.

To city dwellers, this may sound like a strange label for a street, but in most rural areas, the largest or sometimes the only landowner's name served as the street name, basically for EMS, police and fire services.

I breathed another sigh of relief as I pulled into the Exxon station on Main Street. I dug in my purse for my credit card and went through the usual procedure to start pumping gas. Filling up took over forty dollars. The car must have been running on fumes. I grabbed the receipt as it slid out of the slot on the pump and got back in my car.

Glancing at my watch, I realized I hadn't eaten lunch. A burger and fries from Ted's Burger House would have to suffice. Instead of the drive-thru, I opted to go inside and eat.

A long line of patrons waited to place their orders. The delicious aroma of grilled meat filled the air. My stomach growled in response.

As I approached the counter, I spotted Josh retrieving his order. At least he was already here so he couldn't be following me.

Paranoia took hold at the thought of someone following me. I turned and looked around to make sure Jack Holden wasn't in the vicinity. Near as I could tell, he wasn't. Recalling my close encounter with Kenny Verrett, I wondered if I should also worry about him coming after me. I shook off my concerns and stepped up to place my order.

Five minutes later, the woman at the counter called out my number. Grabbing the tray with my food, I searched the room for an empty table. Josh, hamburger in one hand, waved to me from his seat near the back of the restaurant, inviting me to join him.

"Hey," he said. "I'm surprised to see you in here."

I grimaced. "Why? Did you expect me to be at home where I should be? Where I should be working on my novel while the kids are in school," I added.

He eyed me with suspicion and carefully placed his hamburger back on the plate. "You've been out getting into mischief, haven't you?"

I stalled with my reply by carefully transferring my food from the tray to the table. I placed the tray a vacant table nearby. "What makes you think I've been up to something?"

"You look upset." Narrowing his eyes, he studied me for a short moment. "And maybe a little scared. Did you run into…um…what's his name…Jack Holden again?"

Good thing I don't play poker. "No, but I went somewhere I shouldn't have gone."

He raised both eyebrows. "That doesn't sound good. Where have you been?"

I toyed with the napkin. "I got to thinking about where some of the undocumented immigrants might have been taken." I watched his face. No reaction except curiosity. "You said probably New Orleans. Considering the number of people who might qualify as such that we see at the food pantry, I suspected there could be safe houses here in Allemand Parish."

He nodded. "Go on."

"There's an area right on the outskirts of Foretville. It's a little two street neighborhood. I believe the homes are mostly rent houses."

"So you've been over checking out the area." He took a bite of his burger.

I nibbled on a French fry. "Yes, and I feel like I'm correct. I saw Lucie Celestine walking to one of the houses carrying a large shopping bag. She went around the back of this house and went inside."

Josh perked up. "She's the woman who works for Claire Gallagher, right?"

"I hoped to be able to speak to her when she came out, but things didn't work out." I told him about Kenny Verrett driving down the road. "He saw me and I'm certain he recognized me from the reception at the Baums'."

He stared at me for a while. "We need to talk to Megan and Carole about this."

I started to get out of the chair, but he stopped me with a wave of his hand.

"Relax, finish eating," he said. "Before I contact them, maybe we could take a ride out there. She might still be out there."

"You mean you and me?" I couldn't believe he would want me to tag along.

"Yeah, why not? Unless you have other plans. You know her, so she might open up to you before she'd talk to me."

"That sounds like a winner."

As ridiculous as it sounds, the prospect of investigating with a partner excited me. Or maybe simply the idea of having a partner was what energized me. The fact that Josh was an attractive man didn't hurt matters at all.

I suddenly didn't feel those hunger pangs, but I forced a few bites of hamburger down.

"You need to eat more than that," he said with a grin. "I wouldn't want you passing out on me."

"Don't worry. I'm stronger than that."

"I believe you are."

I took a few more bites of hamburger, and then pushing the Styrofoam plate away, I collected my purse from beneath the table. "I'm ready to go. Lucie may be getting away if she hasn't already."

"Yeah, I thought about that, but…"

"You didn't want to rush me," I interrupted. "I might do something rash."

He shook his head. "Stop being so paranoid about my motives. I could've left and gone by myself. I figured even if she was gone, the place would still be there. You never can tell what important info might be picked up there.

"I know you're familiar with law enforcement telling you to not to get involved," he continued. "A lot of them around here, even some of the younger guys, are good ole boys who still don't believe a woman should be a cop much less a civilian investigating a murder on her own."

I heaved a deep sigh. "Sorry. My last statement about doing or saying something rash has become my trademark. And your opinion of most of the men trying to prevent me from looking into a crime is right on. Can you blame me for being paranoid?" I eyed him cautiously, hoping he would forgive my outburst. "Besides, I don't like to follow orders, especially if I believe I'm right about a person's innocence or guilt. I couldn't be a cop. Too many of them have tunnel vision..." I considered my accusation. "Maybe that was the pot calling the kettle black, as my Grandma Kelly used to say."

"No, I understand all too well. You have good instincts. You ought to get a PI license...get your own business. Then you wouldn't have to worry about following so many orders."

I smiled. "Actually I considered the idea for a while after Jim's death." My voice cracked. "But the idea got lost in the realization I'd lost the love of my life and I had two children to support."

He shifted uncomfortably in his chair. "Okay, let's go see what we can discover."

I walked out of the restaurant with him, wondering when I was going to learn to keep my most intimate thoughts to myself. I'm sure Josh felt awkward about my expression of grief. Most people don't know what to say to console you.

Thirty-nine

A few people could be seen walking about in the area. The sight of a vehicle driving down the road caused most of them to make a hasty retreat behind several houses.

I pointed to a wood frame house. "That's the place I saw Lucie go into. She walked around the right side and disappeared into the back yard."

Josh appeared to study the area as he drove slowly by. "It would have been nice if that one would have been on a corner."

"Yeah, we can't very well go up to the front door and knock." I thought a moment. "I could slip around the side and see what's in back."

He frowned. "There's no way in hell I'm letting you go by yourself."

"But if anyone inside sees you, they're not going to answer the door."

"We need to check the area a little more for another access." He made a left turn at the corner and slowed the truck to a crawl.

A small drainage ditch ran between the two streets. Wooden fences lined either side of the ditch. There didn't appear to be a way to slip into any back yard. Josh drove to the next corner to turn around.

"Look, that's her." Lucie walked down the road leading from the houses.

This paved road, cracked and potholed, extended about an eighth of a mile through empty lots once intended for development.

Josh sped up. The truck bounced and jolted us as it ran over the rough surface. Regardless of the seatbelt strapped over me, I had to grab hold of the hand grip at the top of the window to keep from bouncing around.

Lucie froze at the sound of the advancing vehicle. When we got closer, she turned and ran toward Liberty Road.

I opened the window and called out to her as loudly as I could. "Lucie, please stop. It's me...Susan Foret. I only want to talk."

She slowed her pace and looked in my direction.

"Stop the truck and let me out so she can see me," I said to Josh.

He obliged. "Yes, ma'am."

I glanced at him, noting to myself that I'd apologize later for being bossy. Opening the door, I stepped out. Walking slowly toward her, I ordered myself to be calm. My heart didn't get the message. It beat soundly against my chest.

"Lucie, I need to ask you something."

She stopped and allowed me to approach, but she appeared ready to flee at any moment. Her dark eyes darted back and forth as if searching for an escape route.

"I don't mean you any harm. I'm trying to find evidence to prove Alex Narcisse didn't murder Celina Baum."

Her eyes widened.

"Do you know Alex?"

"No..." She squeezed her eyes shut and heaved a sigh. "Yes, he is my brother. I overhear on the television about his arrest. But I cannot do anything to help him. I was not there at that place."

"But you might know someone who was there. Who is in the house I saw you go into about an hour ago?"

"All the people who were let off the boat that night. The ones who managed to get on the other boat. Those people who could not climb on board are whose bodies that were found later."

"Were you aware Alex was coming here?"

Lucie nodded. "I did not know when." She glanced over her shoulders. "I must return to Miz Claire's house. I have been gone too long already. She will wonder where I am."

I wanted to ask her more questions, but I didn't know how much longer I could hold her here. "Can you name some of the people in the house? People who might know what happened?"

"Celeste Joseph is one. Another is her husband Andre. He is a cousin of Octave." She started to walk away.

"Wait, one more question," I said. "Why are they all staying in that house?"

"They are waiting for the people to take them into New Orleans."

"Do you know who?"

"There's one man I know…Verrett. There are others." She turned and ran toward the highway.

I jogged back to Josh's truck digesting the information she had given me. He looked at me expectantly when I climbed in.

"She supplied me with some information but I'm not sure what we can do with it."

"Like what," he asked.

I relayed what Lucie had told me. "At least the name Verrett might be helpful."

"Those other names she furnished could be too, but I think Carole might have to deal with ICE to have access to them, providing Verrett and company don't move them out before Immigration gets to them." He put the truck in reverse and backed up to the cross street to turn around. "Let's go to the law office. Buckle up."

"By the way," I said. "I'm sorry if I got a little bossy when I ordered you to stop the truck."

"Never crossed my mind."

As we neared the corner, a black pick-up sailed past us headed toward Liberty Road. I didn't get a good look at the vehicle, but I'm pretty sure it was a GMC. Maybe I'm beginning to believe every black pick-up is the one that tried to run over me.

Josh turned his truck onto the road and slowly drove after the other pick-up, which by this time had reached the intersection. The truck turned left.

"If he had driven a little slower, maybe we could've gotten a plate number," I said, mentally urging Josh to speed up.

"We couldn't have."

"Why not?"

"When he passed us I noticed that the plate was covered in mud."

"How could you have seen his license when he flew past us so fast?" I asked, astonished.

He kept his eyes on the road ahead. "In the military and in this business you can't miss anything. Even a small thing you fail to notice can mean the difference between life and death."

I was impressed, but I wondered if he'd had experience with such a situation. Maybe in the military. Being in a war zone, I imagined one has to always be alert.

"Is it a GMC?"

He nodded and stopped at the corner. "Is the Gallagher place to the left? I believe the truck turned in there.

"Yes, you and your super vison," I said. "I can see part of the house through the trees."

Josh moved his truck a short distance toward the Gallagher property and stopped. "I don't want to get too close. ICE could be watching."

He kept an eye out while he reached into the back seat and pulled out a case holding a pair of binoculars. Handing them to me he said, "Check out the area by the house and tell me if you see anything of interest."

I searched the vicinity, coming up empty on the first pass. A second look brought a black vehicle into view parked near the house. A figure emerged from the driver's side. A woman—a blonde dressed all in turquoise. I immediately knew her identity. I handed the glasses back to Josh. "Quick, take a look. A blonde woman got out of a black vehicle. I'm pretty sure it's the same truck."

He held the binoculars up to his eyes. "Do you know her?"

"I certainly do. She's Marcie, Rick's wife."

I recalled Cypress Lake police chief Ken Wallace's question to me about why I was so sure the driver of the truck who tried to hit me was male. Could Marcie have been the one who attempted to run me down in front of the law office? And why?

Forty

Josh placed a call to Megan and told her he had important information that could help Alex. We headed to the law office.

"I noticed you didn't mention I was with you."

He kept his eyes on the road. "That's because she would've been mad because I *put you in danger*. I didn't want to hear it now. She's probably going to give me hell anyway."

"I should be pleased that so many friends and relatives keep trying to shield me from harm, but I wish they would quit."

Once inside, he explained to Megan and Carole how he had run into me at Burger House and about my visit to the safe house neighborhood. "She and I went back over there. I'll let her tell you the rest."

Carole looked interested. Megan looked slightly upset.

"Josh, what on earth were you thinking? Why couldn't you return to check things out by yourself?"

"Would you rather I went back alone?" I interrupted.

Megan shook her head and sighed. "No, but if anything happened to you I'd never forgive myself and Steven wouldn't forgive me either."

"That's one reason I declined to officially work for you." I hugged her. "I love you and Steven, but y'all aren't responsible for me. If I worked for you I would be."

She appeared resigned. "Tell us what happened."

"Okay, first I'll explain why Josh asked me to go with him. I had seen Lucie Celestine walking toward one of the houses carrying a large shopping bag. She went around the back of that house. I thought if I waited around I could catch her when she left.

"Kenny Verrett showed up driving down the road. He saw me, so I decided to get out of there. Since I knew Lucie, Josh thought she would speak to me a lot quicker than to him."

Josh spoke up. "I wasn't sure if Lucie would still be there, but as it happens it was worth the chance." He nodded to me.

I repeated the information she had given me and surveyed both attorneys to see their reactions. Neither woman responded for what seemed like forever. I could almost see wheels turning behind Carole's eyes. Megan looked hopeful.

Finally Carole spoke. "If we can get access to those people, we might have our case. If ICE is aware of the house, they may be planning a raid soon. I'll have to beg ICE to get permission to speak to them. Let me see what I can do." She left the room, keying in a number on her cell phone as she walked.

She was out of the room for quite some time. I kept glancing at my watch. The kids would be getting off the bus soon.

Finally Carole returned. Looking at Megan, she said, "Tim…uh, Agent Gorman wants to meet with you and me in about an hour." She turned to me and Josh. "He asked to meet with both of you later this evening."

"It'll have to be at my house," I said. "I've left the twins with babysitters too much lately."

Carole nodded. "I'm sure he'll be agreeable to that arrangement."

"If we're done here, I need to get back to my car and go home. The school bus should be arriving about a half an hour from now."

"I'll give you a ride back to the burger joint," Josh said.

"I'll phone each of you when we have an exact time he can meet with y'all," Carole said.

"Steven and I will come by your house to be there when he interviews you." She smiled. "After all, I am your attorney and Steven can entertain the twins during that time."

"I will feel more comfortable with you there, even though I can't imagine why I would need an attorney."

"Hey," Josh said. "Does he intend to talk to us together or separately?"

Carole thought a moment. "He didn't say. But I can't think of a reason why he would talk to you separately. I'll let you know when I call."

Interviewing us separately seemed more like interrogating suspects. Hopefully that's not what the ICE agent had in mind.

Forty-one

Agent Tim Gorman turned out to be a fortyish blond with a few strands of gray around his temples. He wore dark jeans with a blue pullover shirt unbuttoned at the neck. His black-framed eyeglasses made him look owlish. It was hard to tell whether his casual clothes were any indication of how he would react to what local law enforcement referred to as meddling in their investigation.

Since this was my first experience being interviewed with a federal agent, I felt slightly intimidated. I was glad Megan could be in the room with us.

Josh arrived a few minutes after Agent Gorman. We all settled in the family room after introductions were made. Naturally I chose my security blanket chair.

"First of all," Gorman said. "Thank you for agreeing to speak to me."

I didn't think we had a choice. "I hope the information we give you helps prove Alex Narcisse is innocent of murder."

"Even if he's proven innocent of murder, he'll most likely still be deported," he said curtly. "Now as I understand, you and Mr. Broussard located a so-called stash house where illegals are being housed prior to being moved elsewhere."

"Correct," Josh said. "Susan had discovered the place earlier and when she informed me, she and I drove back to the location with the idea of speaking to Lucie Celestine."

"You're a private investigator, Mr. Broussard?"

"Yes, I'm currently working exclusively for Megan Whitehall."

It seemed strange to hear Megan's last name as Whitehall, but she used her maiden name for business purposes.

"Mrs. Foret, do you work outside the home?"

I was getting annoyed with these personal questions which I'm sure he already knew. "I believe you already know I'm a published mystery writer and I volunteer at the food pantry here in the parish while taking care of eight year old twins."

Megan's look said 'cool it.'

Gorman cleared his throat. "Tell me about how you met Lucie Celestine."

I told him how I originally met Lucie and her husband Octave and about my visit to the Gallagher place to check on how they were doing.

He cocked his head to one side. "In your opinion, the conversation you overheard suggested the couple might be from Haiti and not Martinique as their papers indicate."

"Yes, as far as I know the *Tonton Macoute* was a Haitian organization."

Gorman questioned me and Josh for another half hour. Finally he rose to leave. "Thanks so much for answering my questions. I appreciate your cooperation. If you think of anything else, please give me a call." He handed both me and Josh one of his business cards.

Megan and I walked with Gorman to the door with Josh following us.

He turned to me. "One last question, Mrs. Foret, are you acquainted with a man by the name of Keith Parker?"

"No, I don't think so. The name doesn't sound familiar." How odd was that? His question seemed out of the blue.

The agent nodded. "Thank you again for the information."

I watched him get into his car and drive away. "What was all that Keith Parker business all about?"

Megan shook her head. "I never heard the name before. What about you, Josh?"

He clamped his jaw. "I know him. Keith Parker was an MP who served with me in Iraq."

I looked at him with surprise. "Why didn't you say something?"

Josh narrowed his eyes. "Until I know why Gorman asked you about Parker, I don't intend to say anything. And you don't either."

He jerked open the door and practically ran to his truck, leaving Megan and me both stunned.

Forty-two

Saturday, August 8

Josh ended his phone call with a friend who served with him in Iraq as a fellow MP. He sat silently for a long moment, contemplating the disturbing information he'd received. He didn't feel comfortable calling Brad or anyone else for that matter, but he needed to do something.

Susan needed to be told. But he decided to first talk to someone in law enforcement with whom he felt a little more comfortable. As much as he hated to make this call, he keyed in Danny Marchand's cell number.

"Hey, Josh Broussard here. Can you talk a minute?"

"Sure, I'm at home now. What's up?" Danny sounded cautious yet curious.

"I have some information about a guy who served in the Army with me. His name is Keith Parker, aka Jack Holden. Are you interested?"

"I might be. What kind of info?"

"I believe he's passing himself off to the sheriff as being undercover for ICE."

"What do you mean by passing himself off?" Suspicion laced his voice.

"An Army buddy of mine currently works for ICE and he tells me that Parker was employed by the department for a few months and was dismissed for a number of infractions."

"When was Parker employed by ICE?"

"A little over ten years ago."

After a short but uncomfortable silence, Danny said, "I'd appreciate it if you wouldn't mention any of this to Susan, at least not yet." He hesitated a short moment. "I assume you know the name Jack Holden from her."

"Yeah, she told me he was coming on to her and seemed to be following her. He told her he worked offshore. I saw him on the street a while back and he pretended not to recognize me. Then a few days ago I happened to drive past that park and spotted him talking with Sheriff Theriot.

"I suspected then he might be working undercover or maybe as an informant. After Susan told me where he was from, I knew Holden and Parker were one and the same."

"So what made you decide to check him out?"

"Last night Agent Gorman from ICE met with me and Susan." He explained the circumstances. "As he was leaving, Gorman asked her if she knew Keith Parker. Of course she said no because she knows him as Jack Holden."

"Thanks for the heads up."

"Listen, Susan needs to be told ASAP. Sounds like ICE might have seen her talking to him and they most likely believe she's involved with whatever they're looking at him for."

"You're right. First let me make a few calls and I'll get back to you. We can tell her together if you like."

"Fine."

"I'll call you later." The line went dead.

Josh suspected Parker might have some past connection to Danny. He neglected to say he'd also seen Danny in conversation with Parker. Or maybe Susan told him about the guy and the former sheriff had already figured out something wasn't right.

~ * ~

Danny's stomach tightened. *I must be getting senile. I sure as hell wasn't thinking straight.* If what Broussard told him proved to be true, he had made a terrible error in judgment by not vetting Keith Parker when he first showed up at his back door.

I should have known something was off when Keith told me how much he trusted me. He even provided me a phone number if case I needed to reach him. Burner phone, no doubt. I bet the little bastard has gotten rid of that phone after our latest face to face conversation.

Brad didn't admit he'd been in contact with the fake ICE agent, but Danny had no doubt Keith charmed his way into Brad's confidence. In fact, Keith said right out Brad had talked to him. He likely was privy to a lot of things about Celina's murder and other topics to which he shouldn't have access. But why? Was he involved in some way with Gallagher Salvage?

He sat at his desk, searched through the drawer, and retrieved a tattered book labeled Phone Numbers. When he found the name he wanted, he punched in the Mississippi phone number.

"Hello," a woman answered with a drawl.

"Rose? This is Danny Marchand."

"Oh, my goodness. It's been a long time."

"Yes, it has. I should have kept in touch with you. I'm sorry."

"Well I'm sure you've been pretty busy with being the sheriff and all. Anything related to law enforcement always kept you and Buddy on the go."

"True, but I'm retired now. I didn't run for reelection last time."

"Oh, but I'd be willing to bet you're still involved with the department."

Anxious to get to the real reason for the call, Danny laughed, hoping it didn't sound forced. "You know me too well. So how've you been?"

"Oh, I have the usual aches and pains for someone my age," she said with a chuckle.

"How are the kids?" He inched his way into bringing up the subject of Keith.

"Great. Janie is still teaching school over in Poplarville. She's got a son and daughter who are both married."

"What about Keith? Where is he now?"

She heaved an audible sigh. "I haven't heard from Keith in years."

"Years? Did y'all have a falling out?"

"He served three years in the Army, one of which was in Iraq. He wasn't the same after he came back. He went to work for the government—the Immigration Department. He was only with them for a few months. He didn't say so, but I believe they fired him. The last time anybody heard about him he was on some island in the West Indies working for a scuba diving company."

Scuba diving…that's interesting. "How'd you find out he was in the West Indies?"

"A boy he went to school with had gone on vacation there…I think it might have been Jamaica, and he ran into Keith."

"But you don't hear from him at all?"

"No." She sniffed. "I'm very hurt by his decision to cut himself off from his family and go live in a foreign country. We raised him to respect our values."

"That's a shame. I'm sorry to hear he's hurt y'all like that."

Danny made small talk for a while and finally ended the conversation. He keyed in Brad's number and waited for him to answer.

"Has a guy named Jack Holden made contact with you?"

A long silence ensued. Finally Brad answered, "Yeah, he's working undercover with ICE."

"Well, he's not who he says he is."

"What the hell do you mean?"

"His name is Keith Parker." Danny relayed the call he had from Josh Broussard and his phone conversation with his late partner's widow.

Brad was silent for several moments. "You knew he was here in town? Why didn't you let me know?" Anger evident in his voice.

"He came to me on the sly. I knew him as Keith Parker, my old partner's son. He wanted to touch base with me. Said he was undercover with ICE and asked me not to mention his presence in town. I had no reason to doubt his identity."

"Man, that sucks. Thanks a lot for keeping me in the frickin' loop," Brad snapped, abruptly ending the call.

Brad's reaction to the news was all Danny needed to be convinced of this young man's inability to handle the job he'd been elected to do. His gut told him Brad had revealed a lot of information to Parker *aka* Holden. At thirty-two, Brad really didn't have enough experience to be sheriff. He should have known better than to support him for office. But then, there wasn't much choice in the selection of candidates.

He felt guilty for not informing Brad about Keith's presence in town, but he didn't have any idea Keith would get in touch with the sheriff. Not the usual actions of a federal undercover agent. At least not the ones he dealt with during the investigation into Jim's death. Danny shook his head. *Hell, I can't hold Brad's hand forever.*

Leaning back in his chair, his thoughts went back in time to when he was a detective with the sheriff's office.

His old partner, Buddy Parker and his family were living in Allemand Parish at the time. Parker used to bring his son Keith, then seven or eight years old, up to the office on occasion. Keith had been so enthralled with law enforcement back then. Buddy knew for sure, the boy would follow in his footsteps.

Poor Buddy must be rolling over in his grave now.

He reached for the phone and called Josh. "How soon can you get over here?"

Forty-three

A strange feeling hit me in the pit of my stomach when I saw Danny and Josh standing at my door. "What's wrong?"

"There's something we need to discuss," Danny said. "We have some information about Jack Holden."

My heartbeat went crazy. I motioned them inside without speaking. This has got to be serious stuff for both men to come talk to me. We all took seats in the family room.

Danny rubbed his chin with his hand. He seemed pensive or worried.

"What about him?"

He cleared his throat. "Holden's real name is Keith Parker."

"Keith Parker? That's the name Agent Gorman asked me about. Who is he?"

"He's the son of my old partner from my days as a detective with the sheriff's office. He's been posing as an ICE undercover agent named Jack Holden."

I looked at Josh. "What does he have to do with you?"

"As I told you and Megan last night, he served in Iraq with me. I spotted him on the street here in town one day, but he pretended not to know me. I figured I either was mistaken or he could be doing undercover work.

"Then you told me about this guy Jack Holden," Josh continued. "Your description fit Parker. I tried to get in touch with some of my old Army buddies. I finally heard back this morning from one who actually works for ICE."

"Danny, you said Keith or Jack, whatever his name, is *posing* as an ICE agent?"

"He sneaked over to the house a while back to talk to me privately. He confided to me he was working undercover for ICE and asked me to keep quiet about him."

"Then apparently he got cozy with Brad and told him he worked undercover and said his name was Jack Holden."

My mouth gaped open. "Brad must have leaked all kinds of information to him about Celina's murder. That can't be good."

"No, it isn't," Danny said, a serious look crossing his face. "I don't know if Gorman is aware of Brad's contact with Keith. I suspect he is. However I'm pretty sure he knows you have been meeting with him."

"That's why Agent Gorman asked me if I knew Keith. He thinks I'm involved in some illegal activity..." My voice trailed off. "But what did Keith Parker want from me?"

"I contacted him after you told me and Rachel about your meetings with him," Danny said. "At the time I still thought he was undercover and using Holden as a cover name. He told me he suspected you were involved with the Gallaghers, mainly because you appeared to have easy access to the Gallagher Place."

I frowned. "I went there once. Why—?"

Danny cut me off. "He wanted to find out what you knew about Gallagher Salvage operations. He was especially interested in why you were researching the attack on Claire's boat."

"That's his reason for stalking me?"

"He must have some connection to the attack on Claire's boat and thinks you're getting too close. Maybe he believes you have those emeralds. Today, after I discovered Keith wasn't with ICE, I suspected he could be the guy in the GMC pick-up who tried to run you down."

"No," Josh and I both said at the same time. Josh motioned for me to talk.

I told him about Marcie.

"Well, that's interesting. The Gallaghers are more involved here than anyone thought."

"Did Brad know his real identity?" I asked, still thinking about the possibility Brad divulged some confidential information.

"He knows now," Danny said, brusquely. "He'd been meeting with him on the sly, so more than likely he bought Keith's act."

"You'd think Brad would be smarter than that," Josh said. "Could he be dirty?"

Danny shook his head. "I doubt he's in with Keith. At least I hope not."

"If he's not, he's pretty dumb." Josh glanced at Danny. "Sorry, but that's the way I see it."

Danny nodded, but didn't comment further.

"Has ICE been in contact with the Gallaghers?" Josh asked. "Or do they simply have them staked out?"

"Both," he said. "They believe they have been smuggling artifacts and immigrants into the country. That I know. I'm not certain why they're after Keith, but apparently they suspect he has a connection to the Gallaghers.

"It would be advisable for all three of us to schedule another meeting with Gorman." Danny's shoulders sank. "If Keith's father were alive he would be devastated to think his son had such a dark side."

I patted Danny's arm. "Knowing someone you love or even a trusted friend has turned into a criminal can destroy you. I can imagine Jim's last thoughts when his good friend Bill Kaufman turned out to be his killer. If he had survived his wounds, I know he would be shattered."

Forty-four

Before we left to meet Agent Gorman, I called Renee Hart and asked if she could watch the twins while I was gone. That was one item off my worry list taken care of when she agreed.

The second meeting with Agent Gorman made me even more nervous than the first one. I felt apprehensive that he wouldn't believe my story about Keith Parker *aka* Jack Holden. Both Danny and Josh tried to calm my fears, but my heart pounded against my chest the entire drive downtown to City Hall where the two ICE agents had set up a temporary office.

We were greeted by a smiling Agent Jackson, a burly African-American man with a shaved head. He seemed pleasant and more relaxed than his partner. Gorman was on the phone when we arrived.

Gorman ended his call and invited us to be seated in front of the only desk in the room. "I understand you have more information concerning Keith Parker." His gaze narrowed in on me. "You told me earlier you didn't know him. Is that correct?"

"Yes, that's what I told you. It was the truth at the time as I knew it."

"Would you care to explain?" He eyed me with suspicion.

I cleared my throat. "I knew him as Jack Holden. I had never seen this man before in my life until the day he literally ran into me in front of Coffee Heaven." I went on to explain that and the two other occasions when he turned up at the same location I happened to be.

He leaned back in his chair and steepled his hands. "So what did the two of you discuss?"

"Idle chatter, mostly," I said. "He was charming and he flirted with me. I told him a little bit about myself. He did the same. Of course as I learned this morning almost everything he told me was a lie."

"You said almost everything he told you was a lie," Agent Jackson spoke up. "What did he tell you about himself that was the truth?"

"His home town in Mississippi." I glanced at Danny.

"I knew him as Keith Parker, the son of my old partner when I was a detective with the sheriff's office," Danny explained. "A few weeks ago, he came to my home and told me privately that he was working undercover with ICE and asked me not to mention to anyone of his presence in town."

Gorman frowned. "And you believed him?"

Danny shrugged. "I had no reason not to."

He went on to explain why he met with Keith at the park. "I still thought he was undercover and Jack Holden was a cover name."

"What about you, Mr. Broussard? How do you know Keith Parker?" Gorman asked.

"He served with me in Iraq in a military police unit," Josh answered. "I spotted him here in town recently, but he avoided me. I thought maybe I mistook this guy for Keith until Susan mentioned Jack Holden. Her description of him fit Keith to a tee. That town in Mississippi was a giveaway." He went on to explain his investigation into Keith which indicated he wasn't working for ICE. "That's when I spoke to Danny about him."

"Is there a reason why you didn't contact Brad Theriot about this matter?" Agent Jackson asked. "He is the current sheriff."

"I had seen him in conversation several times at the park with Keith. Frankly I didn't know whether to trust him or not."

Jackson and Gorman nodded in unison like two bobble-head dolls. Under other circumstances, I would have found their action comical.

Gorman turned to Danny. "Do you have any idea where Brad Theriot is? We have been unable to locate him today. No one at the sheriff's office seems to know his whereabouts."

A frown wrinkled Danny's brow. "I spoke to him briefly this morning. I'll see if I can locate him and have him get in touch with you." He rose from his seat.

"Thanks, I'd appreciate it," Gorman said, rising. He shook hands with each of us over the desk. "And thanks for your cooperation." He looked at me and Josh. "Your information about the stash house was extremely helpful."

I was so happy to get out of there. I couldn't help wondering why no one knew Brad's location. Did he leave town? No, why would he? Unless those meetings with Keith Parker were something other than related to this case.

Outside City Hall, I followed Danny to his truck. Josh walked alongside me. As we turned into the police parking lot next door, several units belonging to the sheriff's office pulled out of the lot with lights flashing and sirens blaring.

We hurriedly got inside the truck where the police scanner crackled with voices. Then Danny's phone rang.

"What's going on?" he asked the caller. A long pause followed. "I'm on my way.

"They got an officer down call. Ronnie said the officer is Brad."

Forty-five

"Are they sure it's Brad?" I felt guilty for thinking he'd left town.

Danny stared at the road ahead. "He managed to call in and tell dispatch he'd been shot. After that they lost communication with him."

"Maybe he passed out," I said.

"We can hope," he said softly.

"Was he able to say who shot him?" Josh asked.

Danny shook his head. "Listen, I don't have time to drop you two off, so I'm taking you along for the ride. But you won't be allowed to go past the tape."

We rode along in silence for what seemed like a long time. Thoughts of the day Danny informed me Jim had been shot flooded my mind. As if sensing my distress, Josh took my hand and squeezed it gently.

Up ahead, the road teemed with emergency vehicles and deputies guarding the perimeter to prevent unauthorized access. Danny pulled up and parked behind a marked sheriff's unit.

He exited the truck and spoke to a young deputy I recognized as Victor Tran. His Vietnamese parents ran a small market that catered to the local Asian community.

"For once I'm glad we can't go up to the crime scene."

"It's probably for the best. You don't need to see any more bodies."

"You think he's dead, don't you?" I felt my eyes tearing up.

"Just a feeling. I hope I'm wrong."

"Brad and I didn't get along and I've been really angry with him. But I sure didn't wish this upon him."

He squeezed my hand again. "What say we get out of the truck and get some air?"

"Good idea. It's getting stuffy in here."

He helped me down the high step from the cab to the ground. We walked as far as allowed.

I stood on tiptoes and tried to get a look at the location. My view was obstructed by trees and shrubbery. "Can you see anything?"

"Not much," he said, craning his neck. "I see a bunch of officers moving around."

The sound of a vehicle approaching the scene caught my attention. I turned to see the white van of the Coroner's Office pull up behind Danny's truck. My heart sank.

A few minutes after the coroner walked under the crime scene tape, another deputy made his way toward me and Josh.

"Mrs. Foret, Danny asked me to give you folks a ride back to your house," he said. His boyish face reminded me of Toby Hahn. I glanced at his name tag. No wonder I saw a resemblance...his last name was Hahn.

I needed a distraction. "Are you related to Toby?"

He nodded. "Yes ma'am. He's my brother. I'm Logan." He pointed to his left. "My unit is over here."

Obviously he didn't want to do small talk. I didn't know whether he would answer or not but I had to ask.

"Is it true? The victim is Brad?"

"Yes, Sheriff Theriot is deceased."

~ * ~

Alex Narcisse eyed Agent Gorman nervously. He worried his story wouldn't be believed. He glanced at his two attorneys. Megan nodded, indicating he should answer the man's question.

"The man in Jamaica who gave me the package of emeralds is a scuba diving shop operator. He provided me with directions about the location I was to meet the person to give the emeralds to. At the time I didn't know what the package contained."

"Did he give you a name of the man you were to meet?" Gorman's expression was all business.

"Verrett," Alex said. "He was to meet me at the first drop-off place. But the woman was shot and everyone ran toward the other boat."

"Why didn't you run with everyone else?"

"I thought I might be able to help her. But she was dead. I heard a noise and felt someone watching me. I grabbed her backpack and ran into the swamp." He rubbed his bandaged arm lightly.

Agent Gorman noted the bandage with what seemed like a hint of sympathy. "That's where you got cut in the jail?"

"The other man said he didn't like people who came here illegally."

"So what did you do with the emeralds?" Gorman was back to business.

"I buried them at a spot along the bayou."

Gorman frowned. "That covers a lot of area. Can you be more specific?"

Alex thought for a moment. "There was an old shack nearby. It was almost falling apart. That's all I can tell you. I'd been out there for many days. I didn't know where I was."

The ICE agent blew out a long breath. "Tell me about Lucie and Octave Celestine."

Alex looked at the attorneys for permission.

"Go ahead," Carole said. "Tell him everything you told me about your family."

"My sister and I, as well as her husband, hold legal citizenship in Martinique. We were all born in Cap Haitian, but our family left during the time Baby Doc Duvalier took over from his father. I was a small child, but I remember many good times and also bad times in Haiti. Our father was being threatened by Baby Doc's hoodlums worse than he had been during Papa Doc's reign because he was educated and the family had money. My father paid for passage out of the country.

We could have come to the U.S., but Mama insisted we go to a French country."

"So how did you end up back in Haiti?" Gorman asked.

"When the earthquake happened, Lucie, Octave, and I went back to check on family members and friends still in Haiti and to help where we could. Then we were kidnapped by a group of men who sold us to another group. I escaped them before Lucie and Octave were smuggled out here.

"I ended up being recaptured by the same men. That's when I was brought to the dive shop owner in Jamaica and given the package of emeralds to bring to Verrett."

"Was the name Gallagher ever mentioned to you?"

"Not to me directly," Alex said. "I overheard some of the men speaking of them. Someone named Gallagher was the one who was paid to bring immigrants here. I was not the only one ordered to smuggle in artifacts and jewels." He took a quick look at the attorneys. "You see, I pretended not to speak or understand English."

Gorman looked impressed. "What happened to your papers showing you as a citizen of Martinique?"

Alex shook his head. "They were lost when I escaped from the first group."

"I appreciate your information." Gorman turned to Megan and Carole. "I'll inform you about those individuals we spoke about when they are in custody. Everything will be decided at that time after we get their testimony about the shooting.

"Meanwhile, I've made arrangements with the hospital to keep Alex here," Gorman continued. "It's safer than in jail. Deputies will be on guard outside the room. No one except you two attorneys are allowed to visit."

Alex wondered whether any decision would be in favor of him and his family members or if the bias of illegal immigrants would prevail.

Forty-six

I had a strange feeling in the pit of my stomach when Logan Hahn pulled into my driveway. Something wasn't right. I tried to dismiss my apprehension. I told myself the anxiety stemmed from the news about Brad's murder.

Josh and I exited the unit and walked up to the door under the carport. My heart jumped. The door wasn't completely closed.

"Wait," Josh said. "Don't go inside." He turned and waved at Logan who was by then backing out the driveway.

Logan pulled back in and got out of his unit. "Something wrong?"

"There may be," Josh told him. "The door is ajar."

"Stay here both of you," he said, removing his gun from its holster. Pushing the door open with the toe of his shoe, he slowly stepped inside. "Alarm's not set."

"I know I set it before we left," I said, confused. "Josh, you saw me, didn't you?"

"Yeah, I did. You definitely set the alarm."

I held my breath as Logan walked in and out of each room down the hall. From what I could see, the house had been ransacked. What in the world happened? Why was the alarm off?

"Oh no, where's my cat? Katy must have been terrified." I surveyed the area to see if maybe she'd escaped and was hiding outside.

"She was inside when we left?" Josh asked.

"Katy is inside all the time."

Minutes later, Logan returned. "The place is clear now, but it's a mess."

"Did you see my cat?"

"Yeah, she was hiding under the bed in the master."

I felt relief, but my reprieve from anxiety didn't last long.

"Looks like your power is out," Logan said.

"What? Someone cut the power?" This suddenly got even crazier.

He examined the lock and then surveyed the area for a moment. "Where's your breaker box?"

I pointed to the rear of the house. "It's on the back wall close to the a/c unit."

He strode around the corner. Josh and I followed him. A muted metal clank sounded as Logan carefully lifted the cover of the breaker box with a pen he had taken from his pocket.

"Breakers are tripped," he said.

My cell phone buzzed in my pocket. I frowned as I looked at the display. "It's my alarm company."

The woman on the phone announced, "We received a signal your power was out. Tri-Parish Electric reported no power outages in your area."

"Why didn't you notify me earlier?" I asked. She probably noticed how annoyed I was by the tone of my voice.

"We did," she huffed. "Our calls kept going to voice mail. Do you want us to notify the police?"

"You should have called the police when you couldn't get in touch with me. No thanks to you, they're already here." I disconnected the call and checked my phone. Several missed calls were listed. "I guess I didn't hear or feel the phone vibrating. I must be losing it."

"With everything going on, that's easy to understand," Logan said. "Since this is their jurisdiction, I'll put in a call to CLPD and tell them what I found. They'll want to do a walk through and dust for fingerprints. Then you need to see if anything is missing. Whoever broke in was obviously looking for something."

He walked down the driveway back to his unit.

I felt sick. "Who could have done this?" Then I remembered the earlier conversation about Keith Parker's interest in me. "Danny suggested Keith Parker might think I have the emeralds, although I can't imagine why he would have such an outrageous idea."

"In my opinion, Parker is a likely suspect for this break-in," Josh said. "As to why he would think you had the emeralds, your guess is as good as mine. Maybe he was grasping at straws. He probably knows by now the feds are on his tail."

"I should know better than to say this, but…This day couldn't get any worse."

Josh frowned. "You're right. You shouldn't have said that."

Logan rejoined us under the carport. "CLPD is sending a unit over to examine the scene. I know it's hot out here, but I suggest you don't disturb anything inside until after they do a once over, including the breaker box." He started back to his unit.

"Thanks, Logan," I called to him.

"Sure thing." Before he even approached his vehicle, two CLPD units turned onto my street, lights flashing.

I gave a mirthless chuckle. "Boy that was fast."

Logan greeted the other officers with a handshake. They conversed for a few minutes, and then the two CLPD officers walked up to us.

I recognized Ike Pierre, a corporal with the city police, but not the other officer, an Asian woman.

"Mrs. Foret," Ike greeted me. "This is not the best of circumstances, but it's good to see you again." Dozens of brown freckles dotted his mocha-colored skin.

"Good to see you too, Ike." I nodded toward Josh. "This is Josh Broussard."

"Ike Pierre." The two men shook hands.

The other officer introduced herself as Amy Nguyen. "Please wait outside while we go through the house," she said, business-like.

Ike raised his eyebrows, but didn't comment.

The pair entered the house to begin their search. A few minutes later a couple of crime scene techs arrived.

"The neighbors must be having a field day." I glanced at the Marchands' house. "I wonder where Rachel is."

As if on cue, Rachel drove up in her driveway and practically sprinted over to us. "What happened?"

"Someone broke in and trashed the place," I explained.

"It appears he was looking for something in particular," Josh said. "He flipped the breakers to disable the alarm.

"My goodness," Rachel said. "Sounds like a professional burglar."

A few minutes later, Renee joined us, a concerned look on her face. "Did you have a break-in?"

I nodded. "Unfortunately."

She peered inside the open door. "Oh, wow. What a mess." She paused for a short moment. "This is going to take hours to straighten out. Why don't you let the twins stay over at our house for the night?"

"Renee, that's such an imposition. You've got three kids of your own."

She shrugged and laughed. "What's two more?"

"But what about Ronnie?" I argued. "He may want peace and quiet after the...earlier event."

"It's doubtful he'll be home at all," she said, her expression solemn. "He is Brad's second in command so he's in charge now."

"Okay, I'll bring some pj's and another set of clothes for them over to your house once I can get back inside."

"That'll be fine." She turned and started across the yard toward her house.

"Thank you," I called to her. "I owe you."

"I'll be sure to collect," she said with a wave.

"Why don't you two come next door to my house?" Rachel asked. "It's a lot better than standing outside in the heat. I'll fix something cold to drink."

I gratefully agreed. My clothes felt damp. I could tell Josh was feeling the heat as much as I was. Sweat beaded up on his forehead.

I poked my head inside the door and got the attention of the crime scene tech snapping photos. "I'll be next door at the Marchands' house if anybody needs me."

Could this day get any worse? Yikes, I said it again. Now I had the feeling the worst was yet to come.

Forty-seven

An hour later, Ike came over to Rachel's to tell me I could enter the house as their examination of the scene was complete.

"There were a lot of prints," he said. "Most of them were children's by the size. We'll have to put the rest through AFIS and see if we come up with a match."

"Thanks, Ike," I said. "I'll let you know if I discover something missing. I hate to think about trying to straighten all that mess."

"Yes, I can imagine. Let us know as soon as you can about any items that might have been stolen so we can start searching the pawn shops."

Ike joined Amy Nguyen and the pair walked back to their respective units.

"If you need help sorting things out, I can help you," Rachel offered.

"No, I can probably get the majority of it back together by myself."

"You're not going to be by yourself," Josh said, his expression serious. "It's not a good idea, considering everything that's already occurred."

Rachel nodded in agreement. "What if the person who broke in comes back?"

"Exactly," he said. "Deputy Hahn may not have known or suspected who shot Brad, but my guess is Keith Parker and he's probably the one who broke in your house. He might decide to come back."

"That's a scary thought." I felt a shiver run up my spine.

"How about if I stay with you and help?" Josh said. "For a while, at least. I'm not sure if Megan has a job for me later. I'll check in with her in a little bit." He turned to Rachel. "If I have to leave, we'll let you know."

"Sounds like a good idea," she said. A faint smile moved her lips.

I knew what she was thinking. Here's a ready-made match for Susan. She didn't even have to plan. That's okay. I didn't mind this time.

Glancing at Josh, I said, "Well, I guess we'd better get to work."

By nine p.m. my house was pretty much back to normal except for Matthew's bedroom. I wondered if the fact Matthew had hidden the murder weapon in his room several weeks ago had anything to do with his room being in worst shape than any other place in the house. But even that idea didn't make sense.

Josh and I sat in the kitchen taking a break and drinking iced tea. I stared into space, trying to come up with a reason Keith Parker would be searching for something in my house.

"What are you thinking about so intently?" Josh asked.

"I want to know why this happened." I waved my arm in a silent indication of the previous chaos in the house.

"You mean why did Parker target you from the beginning?"

"Yes. How did I even get on his radar?"

Josh looked thoughtful. "Maybe he was told you and Rachel discovered Celina's body and you liked to investigate on your own. He wanted to make certain you didn't find any clues leading to his true identity."

The realization hit me. "Of course. Brad told him because he believed him to be an ICE agent." I leaned back in my chair. "And I'm sure he filled Keith in about my reputation for getting involved."

"Keith must have played a part in the attack on the Gallaghers' boat. Danny found out from his mother that he was in Jamaica at that time working as a diver."

"Really? But if he and other men boarded the boat, killed Walt and Gary and wounded Claire, who ordered the hit?"

"Who has the most to gain from the deaths of family members?"

I shook my head in disgust. "The remaining family member."

Josh agreed. "However, in this case there are two."

"Originally I suspected Mike Doucet of betraying his family on that boat. He did come out of the ordeal without a scratch. But after the attack on him, I considered the possibility he might be cooperating with Immigration and Customs. I doubt my first instincts were correct about him."

"He is cooperating with ICE."

"How do you know that?

He shrugged. "I have a few contacts who know these things. I called in some favors when I was checking out Parker.

"There's a great deal of money involved with the Gallaghers," he continued. "And in a case like this, family members tend to turn on each other."

I couldn't imagine Steven arranging to kill me or our parents or me committing such a terrible act. But murder has become all too common everywhere, family or not.

"To me, murder, especially killing members of one's own family, is the most grievous of sins."

The scene in the cemetery and the look of disdain on Rick Gallagher's face came to mind. Could he be the person Lucie compared to a member of the *Tonton Macoute*?

Forty-eight

The house was dark and quiet except for the sound of Rick's voice. Claire sat listening to him for a while before she flipped on the light switch in the living room.

Through the arched doorway she saw him standing in the dining room talking on the phone. From his tone of voice, the person he spoke to had made him angry. Nothing unusual. Lately he became enraged for any little slight or what he considered to be a slight.

"Can't anyone around here do anything right?" he yelled into the phone. "Well, you're on your own now. If you can't do the job, I'll do it myself." He disconnected the call with a flourish.

Claire glared at her son. "What job is that?"

His angry scowl frightened her, but she tried not to show her fear.

"We have more important business to discuss," he said.

"I don't know of any business we need to discuss," she huffed. "Right now, I need to go to the hospital to check on Mike. It's time someone brought me up there."

"Visiting hours are over, so you're not going anywhere," he said. "Besides, I'm the only one here who can drive you, and I don't plan on catering to you any longer."

"What is wrong with you?" She felt her face burn as anger coursed through her.

Every muscle in Rick's body seemed to tense. His cheeks came close to matching his red hair. "I'm tired of you indulging your bastard son Mike exactly like you did for Gary." He narrowed his eyes and shook his fist at her. "At least Gary was legitimate. Or was he?"

"How dare you?" Like her son's, her face reddened with fury. "Gary is quite legitimate. Walt is his father. You know the story about Mike's conception and birth. My father made me give him up for adoption because I was fifteen years old."

Rick moved closer to her, his every muscle tensed.

She flinched, thinking he planned on striking her. He was famous for losing his temper, mostly about her alleged favoritism toward Gary. Then after the attack, he turned his anger on Mike. She'd never felt threatened by his outbursts...until now.

He took a few steps back, his hands still fisted at his side. The scowl on his face remained ominous. "Both of them got what they deserved for getting involved with your obsession with that frickin' shipwreck."

She straightened her back. "How dare you speak ill of your brother! Gary didn't deserve being shot down. Neither did your father. Do you think he got what he deserved?"

"Dad was an unfortunate casualty."

She narrowed her gaze. "Are you responsible for what happened on the boat?"

"I didn't pull the trigger if that's what you mean."

A wave of nausea swept over her. "Are you saying you ordered the attack? You hired those men to kill us all?" Her son...her own son did this.

"Too bad they didn't complete the job."

"What kind of person murders his own family and feels no guilt? What about Mike? Are you also responsible for his present condition?"

His answer was a smirk.

She retrieved her cell phone from a pocket on the side of her wheelchair. "I'm calling the sheriff."

In a single stride he reached her and grabbed the phone away. "Do you want all your precious treasures taken away when the authorities discover they were illegally brought into the country?"

Claire met his gaze. "I get the impression you plan to take them from me anyway. I'd rather lose the pieces than to see you go unpunished."

"Don't worry, you may get a chance to tell your story. ICE is probably on their way with a special response team to take us into custody." A smug expression showed on his face. "Your precious Mike was willing to give you up to the cops. He made an agreement with ICE to tell everything about the artifacts."

"You always blamed Mike for the attack on our boat. You're lying."

"I'm not lying." Rick pulled a small pistol from his pocket and pointed it at her. "And I don't plan to be here when ICE arrives."

Her eyes widened. "Are you going to kill me too?"

He held the pistol against her neck. "If you don't do what I tell you."

Claire took a deep breath. "What do you want?"

"First you're going to open your collection room. Then you're going to give me those emeralds you have in your possession."

"Not my emerald cross," she gasped.

"What are going to do to stop me?" At this moment he looked evil. "If you don't open the door, I'll shoot the lock off."

"Then that's what you'll have to do." She motioned with her hand toward the collection room.

He fired shot after shot into the lock. Kicking the door in, he raced inside.

She squeezed her eyes shut. The sound of breaking glass continued for what seemed like hours. *He's destroying everything*!

Suddenly the room was quiet. She saw Rick leave with her most prized possession.

~ * ~

"I need to go out to my truck for a minute," Josh said.

I started to ask for what, but changed my mind. He walked quickly out the door. A few minutes later I heard the truck door slam.

He returned, looking nonchalant, and sat down in the same chair as before.

"I hate to move from here," I said. "But the mess still awaits me. If you don't want to stay I can handle Matthew's room by myself."

"Are you trying to get rid of me," he asked playfully.

"No, I don't want to impose on you."

"You're not, so let's get to it."

His phone rang as we got up from the table to begin tackling Matthew's room.

"It's Megan." He quickly answered. After a short pause he asked her, "Can I put you on speaker phone?"

She obviously asked his location.

"At Susan's. Her house was broken into while we were talking to Agent Gorman. After what happened to Brad, I thought I ought to keep an eye on her." He laid the phone on the table, then he pressed the button to put the call on speaker. "Okay, go ahead."

"Alex told us where he buried the emeralds…sort of," Megan said.

"What do you mean?" I asked.

"He was unfamiliar with the area so he wasn't sure of the exact spot. He did mention an old shack nearby. Susan, do you have any idea where that might be?"

"Let me think a moment." I really didn't want to remember about the night I ran for my life through a part of that swamp with Jason Bordelon, the Mardi Gras killer, chasing me. "I believe that shack is an old fishing camp that was close to your family's camp. It used to belong to Tank Hebert."

"Who?"

"You know, he was the chief of police before Jim and the man who…"

"Oh," she said. "How could I forget him? Thank goodness he's in jail now for his attempt on my life."

Josh glanced at me, raising his eyebrows. I mouthed 'I'll explain later.'

"I'll pass the information on to Agent Gorman," Megan said. "ICE has two special response teams ready to pounce on the Gallaghers' compound and the stash house you discovered. Don't know the exact timing, but it'll be soon." Megan went on to explain Alex's complicated immigration status. "Agent Gorman told me a decision would be made as soon as all the individuals were in custody."

"So he and Lucie are brother and sister and legal residents of Martinique. I wasn't far off in my scenario to Carole."

"Don't let that go to your head," Megan advised me.

"I won't," I said.

"Right. I'll believe it when I see it." She paused a short moment. "I spoke to Ronnie Hart earlier. He told me about Brad's death. He suspects Keith Parker to be his killer. There's a big manhunt going on for him. You and Josh be careful."

"Count on it," Josh said. He ended the call and picked up his phone. As he was about to tuck the phone back into his pocket, it slipped out of his hand and fell to the floor.

"Hope the screen didn't crack. I'd hate to be forced to buy another one." He appeared embarrassed at his clumsy action.

I noticed he had placed his left hand over the area where I had seen the scar, but quickly removed his hand. I guess he hoped I wouldn't notice.

He stooped down and reached under the table to retrieve the phone. "Damn."

"What? Is the screen broken?"

He looked up at me with a frown. "No, but whoever broke in today left something." Reaching around the edge of the table he pulled out a tiny object. "He heard every word that we said."

I blew out a deep breath. "Including our conversation with Megan."

"There's got to be more bugs. There's no way he could know we would sit there." Josh started searching the furniture in the family room. He pulled out another microphone beneath one of the end tables. "Bet you there's one in your bedroom."

Sure enough. Tucked behind the headboard he found a third listening device. Discovering those made me feel even more violated than the break-in. "If Keith Parker is the one who did this, he must really have believed I knew where the emeralds were buried." I shook my head in disgust. "Well, I do now and so does he."

Suddenly the house went dark. My heart raced. The power had gone out again. Or rather shut off on purpose again.

I heard the muffled sound of my cell phone ringing in the family room. With the cordless phone inoperative without electricity and both our phones out of reach, I prayed my alarm company would automatically call the police this time if they couldn't reach me.

Forty-nine

"Do you have a flashlight handy?" Josh asked me in a low voice.

"Yes, it's in this bedside table."

He opened the drawer and felt around inside, finally coming up with the flashlight.

Hopefully the batteries are good, I thought. I felt relief when the light came on. "What are we going to do?"

"*You* are going to stay put right now. I'm going to check out things up front." He reached behind him and pulled a pistol from the waist of his jeans. Placing the flashlight on top of the gun, he edged toward the bedroom door.

I don't know why having a weapon on him surprised me. Josh is a private investigator and probably has a concealed carry permit. He must have retrieved his gun when he went out to his truck.

A loud crash sounded from the front of the house. My breath caught in my throat. Someone had broken the door in.

"Get down on the other side of the bed on the floor and don't move," Josh whispered an order to me. He continued walking slowly with the flashlight pointed down. As he reached the bedroom door, a male voice called out.

"I know y'all are in there, so you might as well come out."

His Mississippi drawl sent a chill running through me. Keith Parker, no doubt.

"I don't want to come back there to drag you two out. I have a gun."

"So do I," Josh called back. "You won't use it because we have info you need."

"I have the same info, but I do need you to take me there. I won't shoot you now."

"Oh, but you will shoot us later?"

"Yeah, exactly like I did that stupid sheriff. He thought he could arrest me. The only thing he could prove me guilty of was making a fool out of him."

I hated to hear his demeaning remarks about Brad. Guilt about my own comments haunted me. But feeling ashamed of myself didn't count for much in this situation. Josh and I might be killed. I didn't know where Katy was hiding. Poor baby, she must be traumatized. But my kids were safe and nothing else mattered right now.

"Parker, you know the neighbors probably heard all the racket," Josh said calmly. "The cops ought to be here soon."

"That's why we're going to get out fast before they have a chance to get here." His voice sounded louder as if he were coming closer to us.

The next words Keith spoke made my heart bang against my chest. He must be in the doorway. "Drop the gun, Cowboy." Obviously he was speaking to Josh.

The blast of a gunshot echoed through the room. A whiff of gunpowder hung in the air. All I could hear were moans of pain and a few curses. Oh my God. Is Josh hit? Am I going to be next? I was afraid to look.

Moments later, what sounded like a dozen police sirens blared in the distance. Then their wail grew closer. I summoned up the courage to rise up to a kneeling position. I almost cried for joy when I saw Josh standing over Keith, pointing his gun at the man's figure on the floor.

"Don't move, Parker," Josh ordered. "I will shoot you again if I have to."

Footsteps sounded. A male voice I recognized as Ken Wallace ordered Josh, "Put your gun down. We've got the situation now."

More voices filled the hallway. I heard Ken ask for EMS. After that everything was in a blur.

Rachel stood on her front porch, hugging herself as if she were cold. I waved to her and she rushed over to us.

"We're okay," I said. "We're not hurt."

Josh nodded in agreement.

Ken Wallace interrupted our reunion with Rachel. "You and Josh have to come down to the station to make a formal statement. I'll have one of my men drive you there, and I'll join you shortly."

I turned back to Rachel. "When they say it's okay to go in, can you see about Katy?"

"Of course," she said. "If I can coax her out from hiding, I'll bring her to my house."

Hours later, Josh and I were seated in separate rooms at the police station. I felt like I was about to be interrogated for a crime. Time passed in discomfort. I was tired and hungry. I needed to relax.

Finally the door opened. I was surprised to see Danny step inside. He looked tired, which wasn't surprising. In a few hours it would be Sunday. Nobody had gotten any sleep. I went on another guilt trip for complaining about being tired and hungry.

"Hey," he said. "You okay?"

"Yes, I'm alright," I said. "But I don't understand why Ken separated me and Josh. It makes me feel like I'm about to be interrogated for a crime."

Danny pulled up a chair and sat next to me. "Ken's more interested in Josh's statement."

I raised my eyebrows. "Why? I was there, too."

"Oh, he'll talk you, but Josh is the one who shot Keith. They'll verify his account with yours."

"He's not in trouble, is he?"

"It's routine. Don't worry. If there ever was a good shooting, this was it."

"There is no such thing as a good shooting," I said, frowning.

"I meant a justifiable shooting. I'm sure Josh has a concealed carry permit and his weapon is registered. Keith broke into your house with a gun and threatened to use it on you and Josh. So Josh shot him. Isn't that what happened?"

"Pretty much," I said. "How is Keith? Will he live?"

"His wound is serious, but not life threatening." Danny looked down at the floor for a short moment.

I placed my hand on his arm. "You must feel bad about all this, considering your close friendship with his father. Keith admitted or rather bragged to us about shooting Brad."

"I heard through the cop grapevine. Since the sheriff's headquarters is in the same building with CLPD, the word is guaranteed to spread. Some officers listening in on Josh's statement told another one who told a deputy and so on." He brushed his hand over his silver hair. "I hate seeing the downfall of Buddy's son."

Fifty

It was after midnight when Josh and I stepped outside City Hall with Danny who offered to give us a ride back to my house. He planned to check on Rachel again and maybe get a few hours of sleep. I could use more than a few hours myself.

"By the way," Danny said to me. "When I spoke to Rachel earlier she told me she rescued your cat from your house and brought her over to ours."

I closed my eyes for a brief moment. "That's great. I didn't know whether she was still under my bed or not after everything that went on."

He smiled. "So now you don't have to worry about your four-legged child."

"I noticed extra officers and deputies hanging around City Hall," I said. "Is something else going on besides our encounter with Keith Parker?"

"ICE has special response teams ready to raid the stash house and the Gallagher compound," Danny said.

"Oh yes, Megan mentioned that." I glanced at Danny. "Don't you want to stick around for the results? I assume they'll be housing some prisoners in Parish Prison."

"I did want to stay, but Ronnie decided that I and several other reserve deputies might be better utilized tomorrow." He looked disappointed, despite his obvious fatigue. "But it's for the best. I am tired."

"I know what you mean," I said. "Right now I feel drained."

"You'd think the Gallaghers, Verrett, and any others involved in this smuggling operation would be long gone by now," Josh commented.

"Not from what I've heard," Danny said. "The lure of those jewels and the money for the illegals has a strong pull. Look at Keith. He risked everything to get y'all to lead him to the emeralds."

I didn't have a response to his words. Neither did Josh. He placed his hand in the center of my back as we walked to Danny's truck.

I didn't object to his intimate gesture. A twinge of guilt tugged at me. Was I being disloyal to Jim? I dismissed my concerns for the moment.

No one spoke for a while on the drive home. Then a thought suddenly occurred to me. "We still don't know who killed Celina."

"Yeah, and her murder was what started this whole case," Josh said. "We were all so fixated on Keith. He admitted killing Brad, but I don't believe he shot Celina."

"Me neither," Danny agreed. "Her killer most likely is the person who was supposed to meet Narcisse to pick up the emeralds."

My first thought was Kenny Verrett. *If he's not caught soon, Willow might be in danger.*

"Danny, has anyone questioned Willow Baum about her and/or Celina's connection to Kenny Verrett?"

He frowned. "Not that I know of. Why do you think there's a connection?"

"I told you about the reaction Willow had when he showed up at the post funeral reception."

"Yes, but that doesn't mean it's related to Celina's death."

"There's more," I said. "I ran into Willow one day on the lakefront walkway." I repeated my conversation with her and her speedy departure when I asked her to explain her reaction.

Danny pursed his lips and appeared to consider my theory. "It might be worth looking into. I'll get in touch with Ronnie, but I may not be able to reach him until later. He's waiting on a call from Agent Gorman about their raids. He and some other deputies are going to be on the two scenes with the special response teams. Don't forget. ICE took over Celina's murder case from Brad, so don't get your hopes up about the info getting through to them."

I glanced at my house when Danny pulled his truck into the driveway. Would I be able to live there again after this is over? There's blood on the floor right in front of my bedroom door where Josh shot Keith. I wasn't sure I could deal with the image even after the scene had been cleaned up.

Rachel met us at the door when we walked up to her house. She hugged me for a long moment. "I'm glad you weren't hurt." She turned to Josh and hugged him. "That goes for you too."

"How about me," Danny said jokingly. "Don't I get a hug?"

She smiled. "Of course you do, plus a big kiss."

He leaned down and embraced her, planting a kiss on her lips.

"Would you like some coffee or something to eat?" Rachel asked him.

"All I want right now is a shower and a few hours of sleep." He glanced at me and Josh. "We'll all talk in the morning, depending on what's in store for me tomorrow. By the way, Susan, you shouldn't stay in your house tonight. At least not by yourself."

"She's not staying at her house period," Rachel said, nodding to me. "You can sleep in the guest room."

"You don't have to convince me. Trying to sleep there would be impossible."

"Josh," Rachel said. "We have another bedroom. You're welcome to stay."

"Thanks, but I need to get back to my place and check on things there," he said. "Susan, I know you'll be safe here, so I'll call you tomorrow." He retrieved his keys from his pocket and started for the door.

"I'll walk you out." I followed him outside and we stopped next to his truck.

His face looked drawn. I could tell he was tired, but I suspected shooting Keith had more effect on him than his fatigue.

He placed both hands on my shoulders, standing so close I thought he might kiss me. "I'm glad you didn't get hurt tonight."

"I would have if you hadn't been there." I really wanted him to kiss me and I could tell he wanted to but apparently he decided against the idea.

"I'll call you in the morning." He opened the truck door and slipped inside.

I watched him drive away. Undeniably, I was disappointed, but my woman's intuition told me a kiss and more would come later. On another subject my instinct also told me, I might still be in danger until Kenny Verrett and the Gallaghers were all in jail. Who knew how many other people heard our conversation with Megan?

Fifty-one

Sunday, August 9

The smell of coffee brewing greeted me when I awoke. After a few hours of sleep, I certainly could use a cup or two. I heard low voices coming from down the hall.

Reaching for my watch on the bedside table, I checked the time. Six-thirty. No chance of me going back to sleep. I swung my legs over the side of the bed and sat for a while, urging myself to move.

Katy finally crawled out from under this bed. She seemed confused about her surroundings. Not that I blame her. Her food and water bowls were on this side of the room; her litter box on the other. I was here, too. But this wasn't her house.

I patted a spot next to me and she jumped up on the bed. "My sweet Katy," I murmured, rubbing her head. "We've all had a rough twenty-four hours."

She purred loudly.

A phone rang somewhere, then stopped. Most likely Danny was being called back into work. There were several questions on my mind. Had the ICE raids taken place? Were the Gallaghers and Kenny

Verrett in custody? What would happen to Alex and the other illegals in the safe house? I guess stash house is a more appropriate name for that place. They were being stashed there until someone moved them to another location.

I got up and quickly put my clothes on…the same ones I had on yesterday. I'd retrieve clean ones from my house later. Closing the door behind me, I left Katy in the room and headed for the kitchen, inhaling the aroma of bacon.

Rachel was seated at the table drinking coffee while Danny finished off what appeared to be a couple of eggs over easy.

"I expected you to sleep a lot later," she said.

"So did I," Danny said.

I stifled a yawn. "Maybe tonight. I was too wound up to sleep. It was after midnight when we got back so I slept about two hours. To be sure, I'll pay for it later."

I knew my way around Rachel's kitchen so I retrieved a mug from the cabinet and poured myself a cup of coffee.

"If you want something to eat I can fix more bacon and eggs," she offered.

"I'll eat in a little while." I turned to Danny. "Did the ICE raids go down?"

He took a swallow of coffee before he answered. "Yes they did. When they arrived at the Gallaghers' place, Claire was by herself."

I widened my eyes. "Her family took off and left her there?"

"She claims Rick held her at gunpoint and ordered her to open her collection room. When she refused, he shot the lock and broke into the room where she keeps all the artifacts, most of which she smuggled into the country. The pieces are almost all from Spanish shipwrecks."

"That must be why she didn't allow many people into her home. She was afraid someone might see something she didn't want them to see." I thought a moment. "I don't remember seeing anything suspicious. Of course, I was in the house for a very short time."

"You probably wouldn't have seen anything anyway. Her collection room has a combination lock on the door," he said.

"Did Rick take any of the artifacts?"

"He destroyed everything in there. According to Claire, he took an emerald cross and a few loose emeralds."

"There were other emeralds?"

"It seems the cross she had is a mate to the one Alex buried."

I wondered what sort of arrangements had been made all these years to have these items smuggled into the country. If Rick destroyed everything except the emeralds, a lot of history had been lost. "Have Rick and Kenny been apprehended?" My anxiety must have shown in my face.

"No, both are still on the run as of a half hour ago." He glanced at Rachel and then back to me. "You two need to be very careful until they are taken into custody."

"I will."

He raised an eyebrow. "You better. You might not be rescued the next time."

"I promise. What about the other raid at the stash house?"

"That I don't know about. Ronnie told me about the Gallagher raid when I spoke to him earlier." Danny pushed his chair away from the table. "I need to get to the station so I can find out what's in store for me today." He kissed Rachel on the lips. "Ladies, I'll check in with y'all later. Stay out of trouble."

"Don't worry," I said. "We'll be fine. I promise." The look on his face didn't indicate confidence in my pledge. "Will you remember to mention to Ronnie about Willow and Kenny Verrett?"

"I can't promise the opportunity will come up," he said. "City Hall could be a mad house by now."

After Danny left, Rachel and I sat for a while as I nursed a second cup of coffee in silence. I needed to go over to my house to pick up clean clothes. Then I should check on the kids. They couldn't stay at the Harts' house forever. The day had only begun, but I wasn't anxious to proceed.

"Rachel, did you hear the noise when Keith broke the door in?"

"I thought I heard something so I came in the kitchen to look out," she said. "Your house was dark, which made seeing anything difficult. Then came the shot. That's when I called nine-one-one."

"I wonder if my alarm company called CLPD when the power went off this time."

"According to Danny, they did, along with me and several neighbors," she said, her voice shaking. "I was absolutely terrified that either you or Josh had been hurt...or worse."

"Well, we're okay now, except for being shaken up. I'm sure Josh is worse off emotionally than I am. Even though I've never shot anyone, I imagine it would be a terrible experience."

She nodded in acknowledgement. "Years ago, Danny shot a man in the line of duty. He felt bad for a long time afterward about having to shoot him."

I didn't want to think about shooting another human being.

"Would you believe Keith had installed listening devices in several places in the house? Megan phoned Josh to tell us Alex had informed Agent Gorman of the location where he buried the emeralds. Josh put her on speaker."

Rachel looked horrified. "And he heard everything she said."

"Shortly after we discovered the rest of the bugs, Keith cut the power off."

"Can the average person buy those things in a store?"

"I believe so," I said. "If not in a store I'm certain any electronic item such as those can be purchased online." I rose from my chair and carried my coffee cup to the sink. "I have things to do. Time to get moving."

Rachel frowned. "Don't you want something to eat?"

"No, I'll grab something from my candy bar stash at the house."

"What is so important that you have to rush back to your crime scene of a house?" She eyed me with suspicion. "I hope you're not thinking about finding Willow to warn her about those men on the loose. I'm sure she's aware of the situation by now."

"I need to at least get some clean clothes from my house," I said, slightly annoyed. "Then I have to go to Renee's and get the twins. She doesn't need two more kids to deal with."

I really had considered doing something on the order of going to the Baums' house. Rachel knew me too well. But that would be a stupid and dangerous move.

After fifteen more minutes of talking Rachel out of accompanying me next door, I stepped cautiously inside a house that had been two different crime scenes within twenty-four hours. I hoped there wouldn't be a third.

Fifty-two

An eerie quiet greeted me inside the house. Maybe it was my imagination, but I could still smell a hint of gunpowder in the air. I edged my way down the hall and stopped in front of my bedroom door. I didn't want to look at the floor because I knew there was blood on the carpet. Thank God it wasn't Josh's blood, but I still couldn't bear to see it.

The intense fear I had felt last night huddled on the side of the bed came rushing back to me. My legs shook. I plopped down on the side of the bed and took several deep breaths. How was I ever going to be able to live in this house again?

I needed to take a good look at myself and reassess my priorities. Was getting involved in a murder investigation worth my life or the lives of Matthew and Caroline? They haven't even recovered from their father's death. All this disruption might be more than they can deal with.

Our house would require a professional cleaning service to get rid of the blood stain and the black fingerprint dust marking the doorways and other surfaces that were checked by CLPD. Tomorrow I would call and make an appointment to have that done.

I glanced at my watch. The morning was half over. Staying here brooding didn't help matters at all. It might be a good idea to get my clothes and go back next door.

I opened the dresser drawer and pulled out a pair of shorts. A blue tee-shirt and clean underwear were retrieved from the other drawers.

After one last look around, I walked down the hall and out of the house. I stood for a long moment staring unseeing out into space. I jumped when I heard Rachel call my name.

"Is everything okay?" she asked.

"No, and I wonder if things will ever be okay." Tears welled in my eyes.

She put her arm around my shoulder. "Don't say that. You have to think positively. Come back inside and let me fix you something to eat. You'll feel better after you've eaten."

An hour later I had eaten and taken a quick shower, which did help my mood a great deal. I had spoken to Renee earlier and told her I was coming to get the kids. Naturally she wanted to know what had happened last night, but I told her we could talk about it later when the kids weren't around.

Rachel stood at the kitchen sink cleaning up the breakfast dishes. "Are you going to get the kids now?"

"I think Renee has put up with them long enough," I said. "We're not going to be able to stay in our house until I can get a cleaning service over there."

"You know y'all are more than welcome to stay here. The kids can sleep in the other guest bedroom. There's also the sleeper sofa in the den if they don't want to sleep together in the same room."

I smiled appreciatively. "Thanks for everything."

"No thanks are necessary."

I decided to walk to Renee's so I cut across my back yard toward the street. The sound of a vehicle squealing out cut through the air and startled me. My view of the road had been blocked by that patch of woods behind our house.

My heart pounded as a familiar black GMC pickup barreled toward me. The truck braked with a loud screech. Although I couldn't see her face due to the tinted windshield, I knew Marcie Gallagher sat in the driver's seat.

A man jumped out of the passenger door. *Kenny Verrett*! I turned to run but he grabbed me from behind. I screamed and tried to wrestle my way out of his grip. He was too strong. He struck me in the face, then covered my mouth with his hand and dragged me to the truck.

He threw me into the rear seat of the double cab pick-up and got in beside me, keeping me restrained by waving a gun in my face. Marcie floored the accelerator and the truck roared off down the street.

Even without the threat of being shot, I couldn't have resisted anyway. My jaw ached from the blow from Kenny's fist. I was still seeing stars.

~ * ~

"Oh, no," Rachel cried. "They took Susan!" She grabbed her cell phone and punched in nine-one-one. "Susan Foret has been kidnapped."

After speaking to the operator, she sent a text to Danny. *SOS. Susan kidnapped. Black GMC pick-up.*

Fifty-three

The truck traveled at a high rate of speed, turning several corners and swerving around curves on Richard Road. I had whiplash from being jerked around. I hoped any law enforcement officers who were out searching for these people would come after us if for no other reason than this driver was a danger to society with her erratic driving.

After what seemed like hours, Marcie whipped onto a gravel road and then made another sharp turn. She drove slightly slower because of the ruts in this dirt road. I had no idea where we were, except out in the woods.

"Dammit, Marcie," Kenny yelled. "Take it easy on the ruts."

"You want to get back quick or in one piece?" she shouted back.

He uttered an expletive. "I'd like to do both. You can slow down now. There are no frickin' cops after us yet."

"No but they will be soon," I said in an amazingly calm voice.

He grabbed my face with one hand and squeezed my cheeks. "Shut your frickin' mouth."

Maybe my hope for a quick rescue was wishful thinking. Who knew if Renee or Rachel had seen what happened.

A wood frame house elevated on ten foot pilings came into view. The building looked to be in good shape. A small porch complete with two wooden rocking chairs crossed the front. Under ordinary circumstances, this place would be a cozy weekend retreat. Today it might end up being a death trap.

Marcie turned into a gravel driveway next to the house and pulled the truck around the back.

I couldn't help but wonder if this house belonged to the Gallaghers. Surely these people couldn't be that stupid. This would be one of the places authorities would look for Rick and Kenny. Or at the very least they would search here for Rick and Marcie.

The first person I saw inside the house was Willow Baum. What was she doing here? I couldn't imagine why. Huddled in a chair, she appeared frightened. Had they kidnapped her too? None of this made sense. Maybe we were to be hostages.

Rick Gallagher rose from a wingback chair nearby and walked over to where Willow was seated. He held a small pistol in his hand.

He studied me for a short moment, and then turned his gaze to Marcie. "I see you finally did something right."

Marcie clamped her lips tight as if to keep from responding to his belittling declaration. She averted her eyes and tugged at the hem of her sage green halter top.

When I overheard her argument with Jill at the Gallaghers' home, Marcie had seemed a more forceful woman. Maybe she was only compliant with her husband.

Lucie Celestine may have been correct in her comparison of Rick to the likes of a *Macoute*. Although his comment to Marcie might be characterized as emotional abuse, I wouldn't be surprised if he was also guilty of physical abuse.

I stepped closer to Rick. "Why are Willow and I here?"

His smarmy smile grated on my nerves. "Two reasons," he said. "First of all, you and Willow make excellent hostages. Secondly, one of you knows where Narcisse buried the emeralds."

"What makes you think either one of us knows where the jewels are buried?" I hoped my voice didn't betray my quaking insides.

He narrowed his eyes. "Of the two of you, I'd have to guess it's more likely you know the location."

"Keith Parker thought the same when he broke into my house, but he was wrong. How would I know?"

Rick grabbed Willow by her arm, yanking her out of the chair. He pointed his gun at her head. Her body tensed. "You're always going to bat for people you believe are innocent. I'm sure you don't want to see Willow get hurt."

His piercing gaze seemed to see inside my head. Did he know about the listening devices Keith placed in my house?

"You talked to Narcisse several times. Your sister-in-law is his attorney. She must have given you the scoop."

"She couldn't. Attorney-client privilege," I said.

He squeezed Willow's arm tighter until she cried out.

My first instinct was to rush to her aid. I could feel Kenny's presence right behind me, waiting to prevent me from making such a move. The conversation from Megan's phone call raced through my mind. I sure hoped she had passed along the information to Agent Gorman.

"Okay, I'll tell you what I know about the location. He told her he buried the emeralds near an old shack out in the swamp. I believe I know how to find the place."

"You had best not be leading us on a wild goose chase," Rick said. "Both of you ladies will regret doing so." He moved his gaze to Willow. "Is there a shovel in that shed behind here?"

She nodded. I realized then that this cabin belonged to the Baums.

Rick ordered Kenny to retrieve a shovel and any other item that might be of use to them. "And hurry up. We don't have time to waste."

Kenny didn't appear anxious to go back out into the heat. Or perhaps he resented being ordered around by Rick. His walk to the door was slow and deliberate.

Out of the corner of my eye, I saw movement through a small gap in the curtains. "I have to assume Keith Parker worked with you."

"He worked *for* me on one occasion about ten years ago," he said proudly. His expression suddenly clouded. "Then he decided to go out on his own. We all know how that ended up."

"I'll bet he's telling ICE and local law enforcement about his arrangement with you to attack your family's boat." My heart raced. I was really going out on a limb with my accusation.

Rick frowned, but didn't deny the charge.

Kenny came charging back from his spot by the door to confront Rick, uttering one obscenity after another. "What the hell? You sent Parker to murder your whole family? That's sick."

"I can't believe you actually believed the attack was random." His voice dripped with sarcasm. "You consider yourself a much better person because you shot and killed Celina and put our half-brother in the hospital?"

"At least I had a good reason. Both of them were going to blow our smuggling operation."

"You were partially at fault in Celina's case. Like an idiot, you allowed her to seduce you and fed her with confidential information about our operation. If you had left well enough alone, she might not have been at the drop-off spot." He glanced at Willow. "Even her little sister knew how Celina played you."

"You sanctimonious bastard," Kenny yelled, advancing toward Rick.

My heart banged against my chest. Both men had guns. Willow and I might get caught in the cross fire, especially if the movement I saw outside was a bird flying past the window. Nothing like me causing havoc among the bad guys to make them turn on each other.

The back door crashed open. A male voice shouted, "Federal agents, drop your weapons! Get on the floor." A team of armed men in SWAT gear swarmed into the room.

Not wanting to get shot, I followed orders for once. I dropped to the floor and folded my arms under my face. I held my breath waiting to hear gunfire, but all I heard was complete chaos, crashing noises and men shouting obscenities and the loud tromping of footsteps. I curled up into a fetal position.

I felt the presence of someone near me. He called my name. Recognizing the voice, I dared to lift my head up. Ronnie Hart, dressed in SWAT gear, knelt beside me.

"Come on, I'll get you out of here." He helped me up off the floor and ushered me toward the door.

My mind was a blur as though my brain wasn't registering what my eyes saw. I couldn't tell whether our three kidnappers were in custody or not. The hot August air outside felt like an oven, but at least my head started to clear.

"What about Willow? Where is she?"

"Don't worry, we'll get her out," he said, holding on to my arm as we walked down the stairs.

Good thing he held on to me. My legs felt like rubber bands.

Fifty-four

A line of police vehicles and an EMS truck all with bar lights flashing came streaming onto the dirt road toward the cabin. I looked at Ronnie with surprise.

Apparently anticipating my question, he explained, "The team came in on foot. A bunch of cars going over gravel roads would have given away our presence." He alerted my attention back to the house. "There's Willow coming out now."

An officer escorted her down the stairs and over to our location. We met half way and hugged.

"I'm so glad to be out of there alive," she said. Tears rolled down her cheeks.

"You and me too," I said, trying to keep from crying.

She and I walked back to the where Ronnie stood with several other deputies. We spoke to them for a few minutes.

"How were you able to find us," I asked.

"Yes, I'd like to know. I couldn't imagine y'all would even consider our cabin as the place they would take us," Willow said.

Speaking to her, he explained, "Your mother reported your kidnapping a short time before we heard about Susan's. We first asked

Claire if the Gallaghers owned a camp or cabin by the river. She said they did have a fishing camp out on Bayou Shadow." He turned to me. "Then Miriam told us about this place that was built by her late husband. Even though criminals aren't always the brightest color in the box, we figured Rick wouldn't be stupid enough to hold up out at their camp."

A number of the officers in the crowd became alert and looked toward the house. "Here they come," one of them said. Three officers escorted the handcuffed Rick, Marcie, and Kenny down the stairs and into awaiting police vehicles.

Willow and I exchanged a look of relief.

"Agent Gorman and I will want to speak to you ladies about the incident," Ronnie said.

"Hopefully not today," I said. "All I want is to go home, even if it's still a mess from the break-in."

"I understand. Tomorrow will be fine." He looked around. "I'll get one of the deputies to take y'all home."

The sound of a vehicle driving up the road drew everyone's attention in that direction. A pick-up that looked like Danny's pulled up behind the last police unit. Both the driver's side and passenger doors opened. Josh emerged from the truck. He and Danny strode down the road toward me. I ran to meet the two men.

"Hey, you," Josh greeted me.

I fell into his arms. He held me tight for a few minutes. I didn't want to leave his embrace.

Finally he pulled back slightly and shook his head. "What am I going to do with you? I leave you for a few hours and you go and get yourself in trouble."

"In the nine years I've known her, I still haven't figured out what to do with this woman," Danny said.

At first I thought he was angry, but I noticed a twinkle in his blue eyes. I playfully slapped him on the arm. "I'm not that bad, am I?"

He opened his mouth to answer, but three vehicles turned onto the road. "Hell, now the fun starts."

Press vehicles, their station call letters and channel numbers emblazoned on the side, pulled up behind the police units.

"I don't want to speak to reporters," I said. "Maybe later I'll agree to talk to Remi. Right now I don't know what information I can or can't talk about until Agent Gorman interviews me tomorrow."

"Good idea," Josh said. "I say we need to leave."

"Let's see if we can maneuver our way out of here," Danny agreed.

His excellent driving skills managed to get us past the reporters and the live truck.

I spotted Remi getting out of her car with a photographer. She tried to flag Danny down, but he waved to her and kept driving. She didn't look happy.

"I'll have to pay for that later," Danny said jokingly.

"I doubt she'll stay mad at her grandfather for very long," I said.

The drive back home seemed long. I was anxious to see the kids... and the cat. I'd been away from them too long.

Rachel, Matthew, and Caroline came out to meet us upon arrival. I held the twins, giving them a lot of kisses. Even Matthew didn't object to being kissed. Renee walked over to check out the situation.

"I can't tell you how relieved I am to see you unhurt," she said. "When I saw that man grab you, my heart stopped."

I put my hand on her arm. "Everything is okay now. I can't thank you enough for taking care of the twins."

She smiled. "They were not a problem. Whenever you've recovered from your ordeal, we'll get together for coffee. Now I'll let you go get some rest."

"Thanks again." I watched her walk back to her house. Then I looked around at the others...my kids, my wonderful friends, Danny and Rachel...and of course, Josh. I felt grateful for all of them. Physically I was exhausted. Rest was what I needed. Tomorrow might be an equally tiring day being interviewed by Agent Gorman.

Fifty-five

Monday, August 10

Cries of "don't go, Mom" came from the twins, their voices and faces full of anxiety.

"I promise you, I'm coming back." I had agreed to allow them to stay home from school today so we could spend some time together. But here I was leaving again. "I have to meet with Agent Gorman of the Immigration office to give him a report on what happened to me yesterday."

"When will you be back?" Caroline asked.

"I'm not sure, but this meeting shouldn't take longer than an hour." Hopefully it'll be less than an hour, but I knew better than to count on a short meeting. "Mr. Josh is coming to pick me up in a little while, so promise me you'll both be good for Ms. Rachel."

"We will," Caroline said, nodding at Matthew. "Won't we?"

"Okay," he said. "Mom, is Mr. Josh your boyfriend now?"

I should have expected that question coming eventually. "Right now, he's a very, very good friend. In fact he saved my life Saturday night when that man broke into our house."

He appeared satisfied with my answer, maybe even impressed.

The brief dream of Jim I had last night came to mind. He spoke one sentence, "You're going to be fine." Then he smiled and disappeared. I'd ponder the meaning later.

Fifteen minutes later, Josh and I were on our way to City Hall. Happily the interview went smoothly and I was out of the agent's office in forty-five minutes.

I admit to being nervous about this meeting, which was crazy after such a chaotic weekend. However, my life seems to be full of chaos, so I can never be certain how anything will turn out.

Josh drove into the Marchands' driveway, but left the engine running.

"While you were in Gorman's office, Megan called. She's got a job for me checking out info regarding Alex's case. I'll have to go into New Orleans to do this. If it's okay with you, I'll come back by here later this evening."

"Of course, it's okay," I said.

"Good. I'll give you a call when I get back." He leaned over and planted a kiss on my cheek.

I got out of the truck and watched him drive away.

I spent the better part of the day at Rachel's house talking to the twins or simply being in the same room with them. Rachel joined us for a game of Monopoly at her kitchen table.

About three that afternoon I heard the school bus rumble to a stop near the house. The chatter of children's voices as they got off the bus sounded cheerful. Shortly after the bus departed, Rachel's front doorbell rang.

She exchanged a curious glance with me. I shrugged. She left to answer the door. I heard a woman's voice and a few words from several children.

"Sure, come on in," Rachel said. "Y'all can sit in here. I'll get her."

She returned to the kitchen with a strange look on her face. "Susan, I hope you won't be upset, but..."

"Who was at the door?"

"Mary Hernandez and her kids," she said. "She wants to speak to you and the twins to apologize for something."

"I think I know what this is about."

Mary Hernandez rose when I entered the living room. The children followed their mother's example.

Mary looked quite thin, much leaner than the last time I saw her a year ago. Gray strands salted her dark curly hair. With a long prison term hanging over her husband Joe's head, she'd probably been having a hard time.

"Mary, please sit down."

She shook her head and remained standing. "This won't take long, but I want your twins to hear this. I understand my kids have been giving them a hard time."

All three children looked down at the floor.

"Okay, I'll get them." I went into the hall and called to Matthew and Caroline.

Both looked wide-eyed at the sight of the Hernandez family.

"What's going on, Mom?" Matthew asked.

"Mrs. Hernandez has something she wants to tell you." I was a little wary of what she would say.

"Caroline, Matthew, I discovered accidently that my children have been saying things that are untrue about your father's death. Is that right?"

"Yes ma'am," the twins answered in unison.

"It's mostly my fault because I hadn't explained to them clearly about why their father was arrested. They understand the situation a lot better now after I told them the whole story. They have something they want to say to you both." She turned to the children.

Mark, the oldest boy, looked at the twins. "I understand why my dad was arrested now," he said in a low voice. "I'm sorry I came down on you so hard, Matthew."

"Thanks." Matthew's expression was surprisingly neutral.

The two younger kids both expressed sorrow at their behavior. Caroline echoed her brother's short acceptance of their apology.

I wondered if it was really necessary to put all the kids through this. What I had in mind at the time Matthew got into the confrontation with Mark was to speak to Mary and have her talk to her children and to hope the kids would all work it out among themselves. Back then I didn't think speaking to her would be advisable legally since I have to testify against her husband.

I thanked her for coming and the kids for their apologies. I sat on the sofa for a while by myself after they left. At least seven children's lives had been messed up by the senseless murder of my husband. The Hernandez' three, my twins, and Bill Kaufman's two kids might be damaged forever. Not to mention me and Mary and Tracy, Bill's wife.

Every time I think about Bill Kaufman, I get angry all over again. He had been a childhood friend of Jim and the mayor of Cypress Lake and one of the main reasons Jim accepted the job as chief of police. Bill's drug problem led him to do the unthinkable.

My cell phone rang. Josh's name showed on the display. I shook off my ill feelings about those people from the past and answered the call.

~ * ~

I received two bits of news from Megan while I waited for Josh to arrive. For me the first item was great news. All the defendants involved with Jim's murder had agreed to plead guilty in order to avoid lengthy trials. I wouldn't have to testify against them in court. Her second news was possibly good for Alex and his relatives. Nothing was definite yet, but Agent Gorman had told her everything looked positive for them to be allowed to remain in this country because their testimony had aided law enforcement in the arrests of the Gallaghers, Kenny Verrett, and Keith Parker.

Josh came over later as he had promised. After I got the kids settled in bed at Rachel's for the evening, he and I walked over to my house and sat together on a wooden bench on the patio.

"How was your trip to NOLA?"

"I was able to finish up with Megan's job pretty quickly, so I took care of some personal business while I was in town."

"Oh? May I ask what kind of personal business?" I winced. "Sorry, that's probably none of my business."

"It wasn't anything secret," he said. "I had leased an office in New Orleans several years ago for my PI business, but for quite a while I've been working exclusively for Megan as her investigator. I got out of my lease on that office and signed a lease on another one in Cypress Lake. By the way, I have it on good authority that Megan and Steven are considering buying a house here in town."

"Really? Nobody told me," I said with mock indignation. "Of course I've been too busy getting into trouble by sticking my nose into dangerous places."

Josh laughed. "That's true."

"Steven didn't even tell me he planned to leave town for an IT convention in New York until a few hours before he left for the airport Saturday." In reality nothing would make me happier than to have my brother and sister-in-law close by. My parents would never dream of moving out of New Orleans, especially Mother.

"Steven worries about you." His voice softened. "A few times in the last few days I did too."

I didn't know what to say, so I steered the conversation away from the subject of people worrying about my actions.

"Back to your change of office location, will you still be working exclusively for Megan?"

"She'll be my main client, but I've been able to pick up a number of possible future clients in Allemande Parish while working here."

"That sounds promising." I hesitated to bring up Saturday night, but I was curious about a few things. I really didn't know much about Josh. "Can I ask you something personal?"

"Sure," he said. "Ask away."

"When Keith made his way to the door of my bedroom, he called you 'Cowboy.' Did he pull that name out of thin air or is there a story behind it?"

"Since I wear western boots a lot and my folks raised cattle on a big place just north of Jennings, my Army buddies dubbed me 'Cowboy'."

"Jennings is between Lafayette and Lake Charles, right?"

"That's right."

"I won't ask how you ended up in New Orleans," I teased.

"That's a story for another time." He tilted his head to one side. "I know how you love getting involved in an investigation, but after experiencing the weekend from hell you might want to slow down for a while. I admit it scared me when you were kidnapped."

"It'll definitely be a good while before I go the investigation route again. At least I hope so. However, I always seem to get pulled into these cases, especially if I'm the one who discovers the body of a murder victim. Then my curiosity draws me right in."

"Remember when we met up in your office at the food pantry? I told you how much I admired your tenacity in solving Jim's murder. I feel the same about your involvement in this case. I've gotten to know you a lot better."

He seemed to have turned the conversation in a new direction. I couldn't tell where this was headed. "What are you getting at?"

He didn't answer for a long moment. "I don't want you to think I'm trying to push you into anything…"

"If I think you're being pushy, I'll tell you so in no uncertain terms." I meant those words, but I kept my tone light."

"What I'm trying to say is this: I'd be happy if you would consider working with me in my new office."

That wasn't exactly what I expected to hear. "With you? Why would you want an amateur like me working with you?"

"You have a talent for the work. Your investigation skills need a little restraint, but you have good instincts about elements in the case."

"By needing restraint, you mean my 'leap before I look' technique?"

He chuckled. "Something like that. Besides, I enjoy being with you. Think about it."

"Okay, I'll agree to consider your offer later…much later."

"There's no hurry." He pulled me close and kissed me on the lips instead of on the cheek. "In the meantime, I'd love to see you again under more pleasant circumstances than the most recent ones… maybe dinner and a movie."

My heart did a little flip. "I'd like that very much."

Meet A. C. Mason

A.C. Mason is a Louisiana native and resident. A very spoiled cat named Wiley shares her home. Her two daughters and their families live in nearby communities. The love of a great mystery led her to write her own. She's a member of Sisters-in-Crime and Sisters-in-Crime New Orleans.

Other Works from the Pen of
C. Mason

April Fools - Susan Foret, an aspiring mystery writer, takes on a real life mystery when she tries to prove her brother didn't murder his wife.

Mardi Gras Gris Gris - Susan Foret is again thrust into a murder scene when one of the town's wealthiest citizens dies near her as the local Krewe's parade ends.

Deadly Bayou - Cypress Lake Police Chief Jim Foret's death is ruled a suicide. Susan Foret believes her husband was murdered and sets out to prove his death is a homicide.

The Mistletoe Murders - Oak Point, Louisiana homicide detective Caleb Bourque is tasked with finding a serial killer who leaves a sprig of mistletoe on each victim.

Letter to Our Readers

Enjoy this book?

You can make a difference.

As an independent publisher, Wings ePress, Inc. does not have the financial clout of the large New York publishers. We can't afford large magazine spreads or subway posters to tell people about our quality books.

But we do have something much more effective and powerful than ads. We have a large base of loyal readers.

Honest reviews help bring the attention of new readers to our books.

If you enjoyed this book, we would appreciate it if you would spend a few minutes posting a review on the site where you purchased this book or on the Wings ePress, Inc. webpages at: https://wingsepress.com/

Thank You

Visit Our Website

For The Full Inventory
Of Quality Books:

Wings ePress.Inc
https://wingsepress.com/

Quality trade paperbacks and downloads
in multiple formats,
in genres ranging from light romantic comedy
to general fiction and horror.
Wings has something for every reader's taste.
Visit the website, then bookmark it.
We add new titles each month!

Wings ePress Inc.

3000 N. Rock Road

Newton, KS   67114

www.ingramcontent.com/pod-product-compliance
Lightning Source LLC
Chambersburg PA
CBHW061028120726
47910CB00006B/2142